Praise for #1 *New York Times* bestselling author Linda Lael Miller

LINDA LAEL MILLER

BIG SKY
Secrets

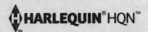

HARLEQUIN® HQN™

Recycling programs
for this product may
not exist in your area.

ISBN-13: 978-0-373-77831-7

BIG SKY SECRETS

Copyright © 2014 by Linda Lael Miller

Printed in U.S.A.

Dear Reader,

I'm so happy to welcome you back to Three Trees and Parable, Montana, and to bring you the story of Landry and Ria.

Big Sky Secrets has been one of my favorite stories to write. Early on, we meet Ria Manning, who's bought a defunct flower farm that borders Hangman's Bend Ranch, property of Zane and Landry Sutton. Ria's had problems with the Sutton herd before, but when she's trapped in her home, held hostage by an unruly buffalo that's made its way over to her land, she's had enough. It's time to confront the cocky financial-whiz-turned-cowboy, Landry Sutton.

Having almost decided to sell his part of the ranch to his brother Zane and return to city life, Landry is taken by surprise when he falls in love with the land—and with the feisty, dark-haired beauty next door. Sticking around will mean coming to terms with his past, but each meeting with Ria convinces him that staying in Parable may not be such a bad idea after all.

I'll be teaming up with the talented folks at Montana Silversmiths to produce another wonderful piece of jewelry. For now, I'm keeping it a secret, but you'll read all about it in this book, and might even find yourself wanting one of your own. Just go to www.montanasilversmiths.com. My share of any profit goes straight to my scholarship fund.

Meanwhile, stop on by www.lindalaelmiller.com for my (almost) daily blog, excerpts from my books, videos of some very sexy cowboys, scholarship news and fun contests, along with a few surprises now and then.

Happy trails!

With love,

Linda Lael Miller

CHAPTER ONE

SCOWLING AND WARM behind the ears, Landry Sutton picked himself up off the hoof-hardened ground of Walker Parrish's main corral. Stubbornly setting his jaw and squaring his shoulders, he laid silent claim to his dignity and finally bent to retrieve what remained of his hat. The bronc, a gelding aptly named Pure Misery, had stomped it flat in the brief but hectic process of throwing him that third and—for today—final time.

Landry reckoned he should be glad his skull hadn't met the same fate as his headgear, but he couldn't quite make the philosophical shift from adrenaline-fused annoyance to gratitude. He was frustrated, embarrassed and pissed off—and those were just the emotions he had *names* for.

Arrogance on four legs, the sweat-lathered horse took a few prancing turns around the corral, moving outward in ever-widening circles. He snorted once or twice, nostrils flared, neck bowed into a curve, head held high and proud, ears laid so far back they were almost flat against his hide.

Finally, the gelding came to a purposeful halt

about a dozen yards away from Landry, hind legs planted firmly in the dirt, flanks quivering with a barely contained strength that seemed about to bust loose in a whole new way, like a primeval thunderstorm.

Go on, cowboy—try it again. That was the message.

Slowly, Landry became aware of their immediate surroundings, his and the horse's—that son of Satan—though most of what lay beyond their battleground was still a dust-roiled haze, a void with its own heartbeat. Landry did register the presence of his brother Zane perched on the top rail of the corral fence. He knew his sibling was looking on with charitable, even benign, interest, waiting to see what would happen next.

Was Landry fool enough to get back on that crazy cayuse, he might have been wondering, or would he finally see reason and call it a day?

"Anything broken?" Zane called, in a jocular drawl. He was only thirteen and a half months older than Landry, but the gap might have been wider by a decade, considering the dynamics between the two of them. Zane tended to come from the place of older-and-wiser, like a father, or a venerable uncle—or a justice of the Supreme Court.

Stung anew, Landry merely glared in Zane's general direction for a few moments, then slapped his ruined hat against one thigh to vent some of the steam still building inside him. A handful of ranch workers—all employed by Walker Parrish, local rodeo-stock contractor and older brother to Zane's wife, Brylee—ducked their heads briefly, in half-assed attempts to hide their grins of enjoyment.

It was no big stretch to figure out what the other men were thinking, of course. After nearly a year in Montana, Landry was still an outsider, still that dandified greenhorn from Chicago, still the perennial dude. Still and always the great Zane Sutton's kid brother.

And not much more.

Six feet tall, smart as hell and a self-made man, an independently wealthy one no less, and a ranch owner in his own right, Landry normally didn't sweat the small stuff. The fact was, he'd never failed at anything he set out to do, in all his thirty-plus years of life, unless you counted his efforts to stay married to Susan Ingersoll without committing murder, that was. To him, the ill-fated marriage had been a disaster, yes, but he wouldn't have described it as an actual defeat. He and Susan never should have tied the knot in the first place, if only because they hadn't wanted the same things, even in the beginning.

Now, aching in every muscle, bones seeming as brittle as if he'd aged by twenty years since breakfast, his pride chafed raw as a sore with the scab ripped off too soon, Landry watched glumly as one of the ranch hands roped the bronc, led him out of the corral and turned him loose in the adjoining pasture.

Zane stood next to Landry now, there in the

slowly settling dust. "Buy you a beer?" he said quietly. He started to raise one hand, as if to slap Landry on the back, perhaps in brotherly reassurance, but he must have thought better of the gesture in the end, because he refrained.

It was just a beer, and Landry wanted one badly, but his first impulse was to refuse the offer, all the same. He and Zane had been close as kids, and right up through their late twenties, but then, around the time their mom died...

Well, things had just gone to hell. Some kind of chasm had opened between the brothers, and there didn't seem to be a way across. For the most part, they'd gone their separate ways, Zane taking to the rodeo circuit and eventually winding up in the movies, of all things, while Landry headed for Chicago, a place that had always intrigued him. By going to night school and working days and weekends as a barista at one of the coffee franchises, he'd gotten his degree, taken a job with Ingersoll Investments, originally landing in the mail room. He'd climbed the corporate ladder and eventually met and married the boss's daughter, Susan.

Certain he'd found his niche at long last, Landry had pushed up his figurative sleeves and proceeded to make money—a shitload of it—for the company and, through bonuses and finally a partnership, for himself, as well.

"I wouldn't mind a beer right about now," Landry heard himself say, instead of the "No, thanks" instinct dictated. The more sensible thing would have been to take his sorry self straight home, of course, back to his half of Hangman's Bend. There, he could have tossed back a Scotch or two, gulped down some aspirin and maybe stood in a hot shower until his muscles stopped screaming.

So it was that they walked out of the corral together, Zane and Landry, passing through the gate, shutting it behind them. Zane waved a farewell to the others as he and Landry headed for his rig, a silver extended-cab truck so covered in dried mud that it might have been any color in the spectrum. Zane's adopted mutt, Slim, waited patiently in the bed of the pickup, panting in the bright June sunshine, perfectly content to be just what and where he was.

A person could learn a lot from a dog, Landry reflected silently. Stepping up onto the passenger-side running board, he paused long enough to pat the critter on the head and ruffle his floppy ears. "Hey, dog," he said, with gruff affection. "How ya doin'?"

Talk about your rhetorical question.

Slim wagged his tail, appreciative but, at the same time, taking the greeting as his just due, and then settled down for the short ride over to neighboring Hangman's Bend.

Without pausing, Zane climbed behind the wheel, pushed the ignition button and looked back over one shoulder, acknowledging the dog with a grin. He loved that goofball canine, no question about it, would have let him ride in the cab if the critter had shown any inclination to do so. Slim had recently developed a preference for the back, though, seemed to like riding with a pile of feed sacks and whatever else Zane happened to be hauling at the time, and he showed no signs of changing his mind anytime soon.

"You ought to get yourself a dog," Zane remarked, maneuvering the truck into a slow, wide turn. "They're real good company, you know."

His brother, the authority on loneliness, Landry thought, with an ironic inward sigh. As if Zane had ever suffered any lack of "company," even before he'd settled on the run-down, abandoned ranch outside Three Trees, Montana, the one he and Landry had bought together, sight unseen, a few years before. These days, Zane had his beautiful bride, Brylee, first and foremost. And then there was the formidable but ever-faithful Cleo, their housekeeper— and Nash, Zane and Landry's half brother, a rowdy thirteen-year-old with a childhood behind him that made their hardscrabble upbringing look downright pampered.

"I'll get around to it," Landry allowed, still distracted by other thoughts. "Getting a dog, I mean." A pause, followed by an irritated "There's no hurry, is there?"

Zane didn't answer, and that was all right, because sometimes—and this was one of them—they didn't feel a need to talk. The rig bounced down the long, rutted driveway, dog and gear rattling in the back.

Walker's place, called Timber Creek, was a pros-

perous spread, to put it mildly, but the dirt trail leading to the main gate was in little better shape than
a cow path after a month of pounding rain followed
by a ten-year drought. Out here in the wilds of Montana, Landry had observed, folks weren't overly
concerned with either convenience *or* appearances,
whether they had two nickels to rub together or not.
It probably wouldn't have occurred to most of them
to smooth the way with a layer of asphalt. Sure, one
or two showy types might have sprung for a load
of gravel, if the bills were current and the price of
beef was decent, he supposed, but nobody paved a
driveway.

Nope, even ranchers as successful as Walker Parrish seemed content to cope with whatever conditions
presented themselves—waist-high snow in the winter, the sticky mud of spring, which the locals called
"gumbo," or the deep, dry dirt furrows of summer
and fall.

There were times, usually short-lived, when the
lure of the place eluded Landry completely—like
now.

Still cheerfully pensive, Zane drove on. The living
quarters on his share of Hangman's Bend Ranch were
relatively modest, considering the size of his bank account. He'd been what amounted to a modern-day John
Wayne before he suddenly decided to leave movie star-
dom behind for good, go back to the land and subsequently reinvent himself. Now he and Brylee shared a
nicely renovated stone house, large and comfortable,

but certainly nothing fancy, by Hollywood standards at least. The barn was sturdy and the old-fashioned garage was detached, with a dented aluminum door that had to be raised and lowered by hand. Neither a tennis court nor a swimming pool marred the landscape.

Brylee was weeding the vegetable garden when Zane and Landry drove in, her ever-present German shepherd, Snidely, supervising from the sidelines.

Zane's bride wore a floppy straw hat, her rich brown hair stuffed fetchingly up inside, a sleeveless blouse and denim jeans, frayed where she'd cut them off above the knees to make shorts. Brylee's long legs were sun-browned, like her arms, and her feet were probably muddy and probably bare.

Seeing the truck, she beamed like a war bride at the approach of an overdue troop train and came toward them, hurrying but graceful, moving between rows of corn and green beans and Bibb lettuce.

Watching Brylee, Landry felt a pang of something sharp and forlorn, bleaker than loneliness, but not quite qualifying as envy, while Zane jumped out of the rig, strode to meet his wife and, with a laugh, swept her right off her feet, swinging her around in a broad circle of celebration and then kissing her soundly.

Slim, like any good country dog, bounded down from the back of the truck and rushed toward his master and mistress, barking, delighted by the ruckus, making himself part of it.

Brylee had lost her hat by then, and her hair

spilled down over her shoulders in glorious, coffee-colored spirals, threaded with gold. Belatedly noting Landry's presence, his sister-in-law blushed apricot-pink, a modern-day Eve just now coming to the re-alization that she and her Adam weren't blissfully alone in the Garden of Eden after all.

So much for a bout of lovemaking right there in the tall grass, Landry thought. He wouldn't have put it past them, if the circumstances were right. Wouldn't have blamed them for it, either.

He smiled a "hello" at Brylee, reached for his hat and remembered that he'd tossed it into the back of Zane's pickup, but the words in his head, surpris-ingly affable, were meant for his brother. *You lucky bastard.*

"I promised this yahoo a beer," Zane announced, still grinning, cocking a thumb toward Landry to identify him as the yahoo in question. The taut air around the couple almost snapped, like a rubber band stretched beyond its limits, and then let go. "As you can see, the man's a little the worse for wear."

Although he was sure Zane hadn't meant anything by it, the remark reminded Landry with a wallop that he'd been thrown three times, that his clothes were stiff with dust and dried sweat and a combination of the two and that his boots were caked with manure. Plenty of good old-fashioned dirt had ground itself right into his hide, filling every pore, coating every hair on his head.

Again, it swamped him, that sense of self-consciousness mingled with some indefinable loss, a factor he'd never had to cope with before the move to Montana.

"I'll be fine out here on the porch," he suggested, and instantly wished he'd kept his mouth shut, if only because the offer sounded so lame.

Brylee smiled warmly. Although she hadn't liked Landry when he first arrived in Parable County, she'd mellowed noticeably since last Christmas, when she and Zane had gotten married. "Don't worry about it," she responded, with a rueful glance at her own grimy feet. "This is a ranch, and dirt comes with the territory."

The screen door creaked just then, and Cleo— Zane and Brylee's housekeeper—trundled through the gap and out onto the porch, her skin a glistening ebony, her dark eyes flashing, her gray hair partially tamed by a bandanna scarf. She looked stern, but that was a pose, Landry suspected, the ruse of a tenderhearted person trying to hold on to a little personal space.

"Say what, Mrs. Sutton?" Cleo challenged, making it clear that she'd overheard Brylee's statement about ranches and the inevitability of dirt. "I just now finished mopping the kitchen floor—it isn't even dry yet—and I don't care *how* much dirt it takes to make up this ranch. You're *not* setting foot in my clean house until you hose those feet off good." In the next instant, Cleo's gaze moved over both Zane and Landry, sweeping them up into her good-natured consternation. "Same goes for the two of you. I don't work my fingers to the bone around this place for my health, you know. And a person's got to have standards!"

Zane, apparently used to being lectured, simply grinned and gave the woman an affable salute of acquiescence. The discourse sounded familiar to Landry, too—he could easily imagine that warning coming from Highbridge, not quite so colorful, but with better enunciation and grammar.

Ah, Highbridge. Yet another reason Landry fit in around here about as well as an extra toe in a narrow-soled boot. He employed a butler. What self-respecting cowboy did that?

"You tell me what you want and I'll bring it out here," Cleo prattled on, hands on her hips, elbows jutting. By then, the hint of a grin had appeared in her eyes, and the corners of her mouth twitched slightly. Like Highbridge, she clearly relished stating her opinion, asked for or not.

"Beer," Zane replied lightly. "And make sure it's cold, if you don't mind."

Cleo narrowed her eyes, then fixed Brylee with a look. "Iced tea or lemonade for you," she informed her crisply. "If you're not pregnant, it's not for lack of effort, now, is it, and we both know alcohol is no good for babies."

Brylee shook her head, but her color was high again. *"Cleo,"* she scolded, laughing a little.

Cleo remained undaunted. "Iced tea or lemonade?" she repeated, folding her plump arms now.

Brylee sighed, put up both palms in a gesture of surrender and sat down at the small wicker table in a shady corner of the porch. Zane and Landry joined her.

"Tea, please," Brylee said, almost primly.

Cleo gave a stiff nod and ducked back into the house to fetch the refreshments.

"Cleo can be a tyrant sometimes," Brylee confided, smiling, but still pink in the cheeks. Every time she glanced in Zane's direction, the air sizzled.

"But only between the hours of midnight and twelve a.m.," Zane said. He'd taken Brylee's hand by then, and their fingers were interlaced, the gesture easy, ordinary and yet somehow profoundly intimate.

Landry did a quick mental scan of the few tempestuous years he'd spent with Susan and was saddened by the swift, searing realization that they'd never been close in the way Zane and Brylee were, not even in the best of times. The sex had been good, he thought, but then, in his experience, which was relatively broad, *bad* sex was a rarity.

He shoved a hand through his filthy hair, wondering what had prompted all this introspection.

The two dogs meandered up onto the porch then and curled up in separate shady spots for an afternoon snooze. Bees buzzed in the flower beds nearby, and way off in the distance, one of the cattle bawled, probably calling her calf.

Cleo bustled and banged out of the house again, lugging a tray this time. On it were one glass of iced tea, a plateful of cookies and two long-necked brown bottles with thin sleeves of ice melting off their sides.

She served Brylee first, then plunked a beer down in front of each of the men.

"You seen Nash lately?" she asked, evidently addressing the whole group. Before anybody could reply, she continued. "I'm fixing to wring that boy's neck if he doesn't pick up his dirty laundry, like I told him. A person can't walk across the floor of his room for all the empty pizza boxes and soda cans. This keeps up, well, the next thing we know, this whole place will be crawling with bugs!"

Zane, who had just taken a swig of beer, made a choking sound, part chuckle, and lowered the bottle from his mouth. "Nash went to that bull sale up in Missoula, with Walker and Shane," he reminded the disgruntled woman. "When he gets back, though, I'll be sure to have him slapped in irons."

Cleo didn't smile at the joke. "I'd like to know who told that child he could go off gallivanting that way, and not a one of his chores done," Cleo fussed. She lifted three snow-white, crisply pressed cloth napkins from the otherwise empty tray and slapped them down on the tabletop in a fan shape, like a winning hand of cards.

"That would have been me," Zane responded mildly.

"Spoiled, that's what Nash Sutton is," Cleo harrumphed, before turning on the heel of one lime-green high-top sneaker and storming back inside the house.

Brylee swatted at Zane with the hand he wasn't holding, but she was smiling and the flush was still in her cheeks, as fetching as ever. Landry predicted, silently of course, that the two of them would be in the shower together within five minutes of his departure, and twisting the sheets five minutes after *that*.

Cleo might have surmised that, too, because she came right back out of the house, still in her cotton scrubs but wearing a red sun hat now, along with a pair of knockoff designer shades. She carried her big purse close against her side, as though she expected to find herself wrestling with a mugger at any moment.

"*Some* of us," she tossed off in passing, waddling down the porch steps and marching toward an old station wagon parked near Zane's truck, "have better things to do with our time than sit around in the shade. I'm going to town for some groceries, and I'll be gone awhile."

Brylee shook her head again, amused.

Zane laughed.

Landry, feeling downright superfluous—in this case, three was definitely a crowd—immediately pushed back his chair and got to his feet, ready to hit the trail.

Startled, both dogs lifted their muzzles from their forelegs to look at him.

"What's your hurry, little brother?" Zane asked, frowning slightly. "You haven't even finished your beer."

Did the man have a clue? This was his chance to be alone with his breathtakingly beautiful wife and he was worried about leftover beer?

Landry sighed and bent to kiss Brylee's cheek in brotherly farewell. "I've got things to do at home," he said. Then he reconsidered his beer, decided he'd rather have Scotch from his own bar and, leaving the bottle where it was, headed for his truck, left behind earlier in the day when he'd ridden over to Timber Creek with Zane.

Though Cleo's vehicle was long out of sight when Landry drove away from his brother's house, the dust her tanklike station wagon had churned up was still billowing in the air as he took a left onto the county road.

Briefly, he wished that he had somewhere else to go besides home, where no one was waiting for him but Highbridge and a two-animal herd of buffalo.

TWILIGHT TURNED THE famous big Montana sky lavender at the edges, spilling the first thin shadows over the rim of the valley, softly draping fields of colorful zinnias and gerbera daisies in the cool, gentle promise of a summer evening. Ria Manning felt mildly unsettled as she gazed out over her small patch of land. Something vaguely like homesickness stirred within her, which was ridiculous since she *was* home, wasn't she? She bit her lower lip, deftly winding the garden hose into a thick coil of green rubber and hanging it from the sturdy hook on the wall of the toolshed.

She'd mowed her lawn earlier, and the sprinkler system was just coming on. The sweet scent of cut grass soothed Ria as she skirted little geysers of water, making her way toward the back porch. The structure sagged slightly, weathered and rickety, and Ria added yet another chore to the daunting to-do list she carried in her head—*replace porches.*

Behind the cottage—it was actually just a small house, so calling the place a "cottage" was on the creative side, to Ria's mind—the weeds were thick and tall enough to hide a variety of outmoded farm equipment and other relics of previous productivity. The fields on that side were empty, plowed under and left to recover from repeated overplanting.

In another year or so, with proper fertilization and maybe a burn-off, carefully controlled, of course, the soil would be fertile again—or so the county extension agent maintained anyway. Some people might have been impatient, but Ria understood the basic concept of long-term investment, that good things really *did* come to those who waited.

Once a bean counter, she thought, with a slight, rueful smile, *always a bean counter.* As Frank, her late husband, used to say, she was so left-brained it was a wonder she didn't tip over every time she tried to stand up.

Sighing, because memories of Frank always made her sigh, Ria kicked off her muddy sneakers just inside the back door, leaving them on the newspaper she'd laid out for the purpose. The kitchen floor gleamed with cleanliness, and she took a moment's satisfaction in that before flipping on the overhead lights.

Ria had discovered long ago, possibly even in childhood, that if she stood still too long, the loneliness would overtake her, so she got busy right away, washing her hands at the sink, filling the old-fashioned copper teakettle, setting it on a burner, turning the appropriate stove knob to "high."

She took a pretty cup and saucer from one of the cupboard shelves, dropped in a tea bag and then crossed to her desktop computer, wriggling the mouse to wake the machine from its slumber. While the thing booted up, she took her cell phone from its charger to check her voice mail.

Heat surged rhythmically through the kettle on the stove.

There was a single message awaiting her—that was one more than she usually received—and it was from her half sister, Meredith. Ten years Ria's senior, Meredith didn't contact her often, since they had little in common besides a father, now long dead. When she *did* initiate a phone call or an email, Ria usually wound up wishing she hadn't. Meredith wasn't actively hostile—not all the time anyway—but she was one of those people who didn't suffer fools gladly,

and, though she never said so outright, it was understood that she thought Ria slotted right into that
category.

Against her better judgment, Ria pressed the
speaker button on her cell and plunked the device
down on a counter before zipping over to the refrigerator, in search of supper prospects.

Meredith's recorded voice filled the small kitchen,
educated and shrill, and Ria's back molars automati-
cally locked together.

"Are you there, darling?" Meredith chirped. "I
was hoping you'd pick up." *For once.*

Ria sighed again, decided on a grilled cheese
sandwich and canned soup for her evening meal,
set the makings out on the counter in an orderly row.

"Listen, sweetie, this is important," Meredith went
on brightly. "I've had to fire another manager—at
our Seattle branch, this time—and the result is complete and utter *chaos.* I'm talking possible *embezzle-
ment* here. The *feds* might even be a factor. If you
don't get over there and straighten out the situation—
well, we'll have to close that office, and there will
be government audits and all sorts of bad publicity,
and you *know* how Daddy would feel about *that.*"
Meredith paused to drag in an audible breath, then
launched into the big finale. "*Call* me when you get
this message, *pretty please.* No matter what time it is.
You have my numbers." A beat passed. "Love you!"

And Meredith hung up.

Love you!

Right, Ria thought, wishing she could ignore her sister's request to call her back and already fully aware that she couldn't. She was just too damn *responsible,* that was her problem.

Still, she intended to eat first. She'd been working hard all day, weeding and watering, making preparations for Saturday's farmers' market over in Parable, and she was hungry. Not to mention tired.

Ria grilled her sandwich, heated her soup. Her tea was brewed by then, and cool enough to drink. She served her food up in pretty dishes, using the good silverware she and Frank had received as a wedding present, trying to invoke some semblance of a family meal.

Frank. He'd been her mainstay, the only man she'd ever truly loved—or could even *imagine* loving. Now, when he'd been gone for just two and a half years, she occasionally forgot what he'd looked like and had to study their wedding pictures to reacquaint herself with his features. She'd memorize his angular jaw, his strong mouth, his thick, dark hair, his brown eyes and his quick smile.

And then forget again.

Although Ria knew the phenomenon of not being able to recall a departed loved one's face wasn't unusual among the bereaved, she always panicked a little when it happened, and the guilt could last for hours, if not longer.

Why was she so bereft now, though?

It was the time of day, Ria reminded herself silently, sitting down to her lonely supper, spreading a napkin over her blue-jeaned lap and taking a deep breath in an effort to restore her equanimity.

She'd been hungry before, but now, suddenly, her appetite was iffy. She nibbled at one half of the sandwich and spooned up some of the soup, then gave up and cleared the table. Methodically—because Ria Manning was nothing if not methodical—she tossed the leftovers into the trash and rinsed off her plate and bowl in the sink before wandering into the front room, taking her cup of lukewarm tea with her.

The face, dark brown, hairy and horned, and roughly the size of an armchair, loomed suddenly in the center of the picture window. And even though Ria knew, on one level, exactly what she was looking at, she was startled enough that she gave a little squeal of alarm, leaped backward and nearly dropped her china cup and saucer.

The creature at the window made an awful, plaintive sound, a sort of forlorn bellow. The drapes, still open, of course, gave the impression of stage curtains, as though Ria made up the entire audience at a horror show.

Recovering slightly, Ria set her tea aside on an end table, her hand shaking all the while, and pressed splayed fingers to her pounding heart.

Bessie. As the shock subsided, Ria's temper kicked in.

"Not again," she said, coming to a simmer. "*Damn it, not again!*"

By contrast, the cow buffalo standing in Ria's flower bed seemed to have calmed down considerably. After that one harrowing cry, Bessie ducked her massive head out of sight, and when she raised it again, she was chewing on a big clump of freshly planted petunias. In the near distance, Ria spotted Bessie's yearling calf, now nearly as big as its mama, making a meal of the bright orange poppies growing in an old wheelbarrow.

For a moment or so longer, Ria was frozen where she stood. Bessie looked quite content now, but that didn't mean she wouldn't get riled again. Since she probably weighed as much as a farm truck, the prospect was terrifying. With one swing of that gigantic head, she could shatter the picture window to smithereens. Why, she might even scramble through the opening and run amok in the living room.

Get a grip, Ria admonished herself. *This is not an emergency.*

It didn't help much.

Walking backward, she fled to the kitchen, dived for the landline receiver on the wall above her computer desk and speed-dialed.

"Sutton residence," Highbridge intoned formally. "May I help you?"

"They're out again," Ria announced. "Those—*creatures*—"

"Oh, dear," Highbridge commiserated. "I do apologize. Have they done any damage?"

"Besides scaring me half to death and eating my

flowers, you mean?" Ria knew the situation wasn't Highbridge's fault—he was a butler, not a ranch hand—but since he was directly in the line of fire, he got the worst of it. "Do you realize, Mr. Highbridge, that Oriental poppies don't bloom until the second year after they're planted?"

"Just Highbridge, if you don't mind," he interjected mildly. British to the core, he managed to convey both concern and carefully controlled amusement.

"And one of these animals just pulled them all up?" Ria went on.

"Mr. Sutton will be right over to collect the beasts," Highbridge replied. "And I'm sure he'll be happy to compensate you for any damage, as usual."

Mr. Sutton will be right over.

Well, that was something, Ria thought, simmering down slightly. When Landry arrived, she'd simply pretend she wasn't home.

CHAPTER TWO

RIA DID NOT like Landry Sutton, did not like him one bit—never had, never would—which was why she intended to make herself scarce when he came to round up his smelly, flea-bitten, *poppy-scarfing* buffalo.

Landry had arrived in Parable County at about the same time as Ria, a little over a year before, and, from the very beginning, he'd struck her as bullheaded, full of himself and, for the most part, insufferably stubborn. Only his impossibly good looks—the classic square jaw, those perfectly sculpted features and blue eyes that changed, according to his mood, from periwinkle to cornflower, that shock of shaggy, wheat-blond hair, a lean but powerful build, not to mention innate masculinity—kept him from being *entirely* unendurable.

Physical qualities were genetic, after all, accidents of birth; it wasn't as if the man could take credit for having good DNA, for Pete's sake.

But, being Landry, he probably did anyway. He had the air of a man who had never failed at anything he attempted, and since that was humanly impossible, Ria had long since dubbed him a poser.

Now, stepping up to the darkened picture window—an act that set her barely calmed heart to pounding all over again, because she knew she'd jump right out of her skin if she found herself face-to-face with Buffalo Bessie for a second time in one night—she squinted through the glass.

The lumbering creatures were nowhere in sight—not surprising considering the density of the gloom—but Ria had no illusions that the animals had wandered conveniently homeward, never to trouble her again. That would have been too easy, and while her life hadn't been any more difficult than anyone else's, she was accustomed to dealing with obstacles.

She checked her watch, frowned. The great Landry Sutton was certainly taking his sweet time getting over here and tending to business, that was for sure. At least an hour had passed since she'd called his place to demand action.

Following a surge of renewed frustration, Ria stretched out her arms, grabbed hold of the drapes and yanked them shut. She might have been in a more forgiving state of mind if this same disaster hadn't befallen her, and her struggling crops of zinnias and gerbera daisies, half a dozen times in the past few months.

Then she heard the noise. It was an alarmingly loud and wholly horrific combination of furious thumping and repeated scraping, and it was coming from the front, right-hand corner of the cottage, just a few feet from where she stood, in the questionable safety of her own living room. Holding her breath, Ria crooked an index finger to pull one of the drapes aside by a couple of inches and then looked out again, but she still couldn't see what was going on.

Which was not to say she hadn't guessed.

Incredibly, the nerve-shattering racket intensified. Once or twice, she would have sworn that the whole house trembled on its ancient and probably cracked foundation.

Her sense of caution exceeded only by a need to confirm her suspicions, Ria tiptoed over to the door, flipped on the porch light, turned the dead bolt from its locked position with a decisive twist of one wrist and stepped outside, poised to run back over the threshold in a heartbeat if the situation warranted.

Inside its bug-speckled cover, the single bulb glowed a sickly yellow, throwing a small spill of light onto the welcome mat, no threat to the thick darkness of a near-moonless night in the Montana countryside.

All around her, crickets croaked in the balmy gloom, and although the sky was spangled with stars, they certainly didn't illuminate the landscape.

A sudden, roaring bellow froze her blood in an instant.

But this was her house, her property. And, damn it, enough was enough.

Steeling herself, Ria ventured a few steps closer

to the corner of the porch, where shadows loomed, knowing, on some level, what she'd find there, but, at the same time, not quite believing it.

Sure enough, there was Bessie, scratching her mangy hide against the corner of the house.

"Shoo!" Ria whispered hoarsely, making a flapping motion with both hands but otherwise standing still. "Go *away!*"

The response was another earsplitting, window-rattling bellow. Was the animal warning her? Issuing some kind of primitive protest?

Ria neither knew nor cared. She wasn't fool enough to move any closer, but she wasn't about to retreat, either. Damn it, she had rights.

Being a buffalo, Bessie couldn't be expected to know that, but her *owner* sure as hell should have. Especially since this certainly wasn't the first time her farm had been invaded by his livestock.

And what was keeping him anyhow? He lived on the next place over, and he'd had plenty of time to saddle up a horse or whatever.

After pushing up her mental sleeves in preparation to do battle, Ria drew a deep breath and tried once more to scare the creature away, this time raising her voice to a near shout. "Shoo!"

Again, nothing happened, except that the floor of the ancient porch seemed to ripple slightly under her feet as Bessie heaved her gritty brown bulk against the corner of the house.

As if in answer to her exasperated wonderment

of moments before, headlights swung in at the top of Ria's long dirt driveway, and she heard wheels bumping over hard, rocky ruts as a large vehicle barreled toward the house.

Mercifully distracted, Bessie stopped the awful bawling and the assault on the cottage, and Ria put her fingers to both temples and gave a sigh of angry relief as the tension-tight muscles between her shoulder blades relaxed slightly.

As the rig drew nearer, she could make out the outlines of the trailer being hauled behind it.

Bessie's calf, invisible before, trotted out of the darkness and stood still in the cone-shaped gleam of the truck's headlights. The animal didn't seem frightened, as a deer or other wild creature would have been; instead, the calf remained where it was, giving a single, low grunt. A moment later, Bessie ambled over to stand beside her baby boy.

Ria was astounded by this behavior, and annoyed, too. She'd been sure both animals would charge her if she dared step off the porch, but now they were acting like well-trained pets.

Were they *tame?* Hard to believe, after the way they'd carried on like banshees with bellyaches, trampling her flower beds, trying to knock down her house.

As casually as if the incident were no big deal, though admittedly an inconvenience on his part, Landry opened the truck door, activating the interior lights and thus becoming deliciously visible. He raised one hand to Ria in a desultory wave, got out of the vehicle and started toward the back of the trailer. He whistled once, low and through his teeth, and, miraculously, both buffalo obeyed the summons as readily as a pair of faithful farm dogs.

Despite her earlier intention to avoid direct contact with her neighbor at all costs, Ria didn't disappear into the house, shut the door and wait for Landry to retrieve his stray critters and leave, as she probably should have. Instead, she remained where she was, stubborn and indignant and, though this was completely unlike her, spoiling for a fight.

She listened through the thrumming of her blood in her ears as Landry opened the rear door of the trailer, soon heard the metallic rasp of a ramp being lowered, the steely, resounding *thump* as one end struck the ground.

Landry muttered some gruff command, and hooves clattered like thunder as two beasts the size of mastodons clattered up the ramp and into the trailer, which seemed too flimsy to contain them.

An instant later, the ramp clanked back into place, and then the doors were closed with a bang and bolted shut.

Go inside, Ria told herself. *Let Landry Sutton take his stupid bison and get out of here.*

It was prudent advice, since no good could come of a confrontation, but Ria still couldn't bring herself to back down. Anyway, it was too late to pretend she wasn't at home, as she'd planned to do, since Landry had obviously seen her.

Finally, the rancher rounded the truck and trailer, idly dusting his hands together as he moved, probably congratulating himself on a job well done. With just the wimpy porch bulb and the truck's headlights to see by, Ria couldn't make out his expression, but she didn't need to, because she caught the brief flash of his grin.

Cocky bastard.

"It took you long enough to get here," she blurted, folding her arms tightly across her chest, as if she were cold. She had a legitimate gripe, and she was still furious, but she regretted giving voice to the complaint, because instead of getting back into his truck, turning it around and heading out of there, he approached her.

His walk was slow and easy, loose-hipped and damnably sexy.

He came to a stop at the base of the porch steps, features awash in the light from the bulb beside the front door, and his grin was affable, generously tolerant and amused.

"If they did any damage," he said mildly, "just send me a bill."

No remorse at all. He thought the incident was *funny.*

People like Landry—*rich* people—always seemed to think money was the solution to every problem. Ria's belly twisted.

She glared at Sutton—they were almost at eye level, since he was standing on the ground and she on the porch—and held her folded arms even more tightly against her chest. "Maybe you've heard the old saying?" she bit out. "'Good fences make for good neighbors'?"

Landry sobered a little, but a glint of mischief lingered in his eyes. "Do they?" he countered, charitably amenable.

Condescending SOB. He was nettling her on purpose and, worse, he was *enjoying* it.

Ria glowered back at him. She was a sensible person, so what was stopping her from just turning around, without another word, and marching straight into her house and slamming the door in his handsome face for good measure?

No answer came to her.

Landry sighed heavily, as though sorely put-upon, his broad shoulders rising and falling slightly as he inhaled and then thrust out a breath. "Look," he said, sounding resigned now. "I'm sorry about what happened, but all I can do is apologize and make restitution—"

"You could also build better fences," Ria suggested tersely. Who *was* this snippy woman inhabiting her body? Her normal self was pleasant and friendly, at least most of the time, but there were things about Landry Sutton—some of them impossible to put into words—that just plain got on her last nerve and stayed there.

Now he folded his arms. Was he doing that rap-
port thing, reflecting her stance? Trying to win her
over with body language?

Fat chance.

"My fences," he replied tautly, "are just fine. Most
likely, somebody left a gate open somewhere, that's
all."

"That's all?" Ria sputtered, still wondering why
she was prolonging this conversation when all she
wanted was to go back inside, take a hot bath, read
for an hour and then fall into the warm oblivion of a
good night's sleep. Once she drifted off, she wouldn't
have to think about her too-sexy neighbor, her demanding half sister, Meredith, or the fact that she'd
bought a flower farm in the heart of Podunk County,
Montana, and was barely making a go of the enterprise, even *without* the perils of free-range buffalo.
"These flowers aren't just for decorating my yard,
Mr. Sutton," she added primly. "I earn a good part of
my living selling them. I won't know for certain until
morning, when I can see clearly enough to assess the
damage, but there's a reasonable chance that some
or all of my crop has been wiped out." She sucked
in a breath, huffed it out. "Surely, you can see why
I'd be concerned?"

Her tone implied that he couldn't, being oblivi-
ous and all.

At this, Landry looked both exasperated and apologetic. He sighed again, shoved a hand through his

hair. "Yes," he answered, in a measured tone. "If I didn't say it before, I'm sorry."

"You didn't," Ria said briskly. She hadn't intended to say what came out of her mouth next; it just happened, and she didn't have the luxury of unsaying the words. "Why can't you raise cattle or chickens or hogs or sheep, like everyone else around here? Why does it have to be *buffalo?*"

A muscle tightened in Landry's fine jaw, relaxed again, as if by force of will. "Well, for one thing, I'm not like 'everyone else around here,'" he retorted. Then he narrowed his eyes, studied her for a long, scrumptiously uncomfortable moment and added, "And unless I miss my guess, *Ms. Manning,* you're not, either."

Heat suffused Ria's entire body, and a rush of— well, *something*—quivered in her belly and hardened her nipples and set her heart to pounding. All her life, she'd wanted to fit in, to belong, though something inside her always rebelled, in the end, causing her to go her own way instead of following the herd.

She'd thought, until this night, until this *instant,* that no one else knew her secret, that she *was* different. Even her late husband, Frank, had never seen through the act, as intimate as they'd been, and now here was *Landry Sutton,* of all people, calling her out, subtly questioning the facade she'd worked so hard to maintain.

Damn him.

"Since this conversation is getting us nowhere,"

she said, quietly reasonable, "it would probably be best if we said good-night."

The evening, balmy before, had grown chilly, and goose bumps rippled across Ria's flesh. Conversely, her insides felt molten, like lava about to blow out the side of an otherwise tranquil mountainside.

Landry chuckled, but it was a rueful sound, a little raw, a little broken. He looked away, looked back, and, inside the trailer, Bessie and her huge "calf" fidgeted impatiently, and it seemed possible, at least to Ria, that they might actually turn the whole thing over, right there in her driveway.

"You're probably right," he conceded, without a trace of generosity. "But I'll be back tomorrow. We can look the—crops—over together, and come to some kind of agreement." A brief pause. "Not that I can really picture you agreeing with me about much of anything."

By then, Ria was fresh out of bluster and ready comebacks—civil ones anyhow.

So she let the gibe pass, nodded stiffly and, at last, went back inside the cottage. Once over the threshold, she shut the door hard behind her and turned the dead bolt with a reverberating click.

Through the door, she heard Landry Sutton laugh.

"THAT IS ONE hardheaded woman," Landry remarked aloud as, back behind the wheel of his truck, he negotiated a wide U-turn and drove slowly back up Ria Manning's driveway to the county road beyond.

Minutes later, at his own place, he backed the trailer he'd borrowed from Zane up to a corral gate, got out of the truck and proceeded to release Bessie and her calf into the pasture at Hangman's Bend.

That done, he parked the truck, still hitched to the trailer, alongside the house.

Thanks to Highbridge, light glowed in the kitchen windows, and Landry felt a shade less lonely—and less bleak—because, for the next little while anyway, he wouldn't be alone.

"Alone," of course, was a relative term.

He tended to a few chores in the barn, checking on the horses, making sure there was hay in every feeder and no debris in the waterers in the stalls and finally headed for his half-finished house.

He'd borrowed the stock trailer from Walker Parrish, but there was no need to return it tonight. Anyhow, his muscles were starting to ache again, from the bronc ride that morning, and his pride wasn't in great shape, either. Bad enough that he'd been thrown three times in front of half of Parable County; the confrontation with Ria Manning had left him feeling scraped raw on the inside.

Okay, yeah, the lady had a right to be pissed off about the damage Bessie and her strapping calf might or might not have done to her property, but, hell, he'd offered to make good for that, hadn't he? What else could he do, at this point?

Damned if he had a single clue.

One thing was abundantly clear, though—nothing

he said or did was going to please Ria. She just flat-
out didn't like him, buffalo-on-the-loose notwithstanding, and while Landry didn't usually give a rat's
ass about other people's opinions, this was different. This time, with this particular woman, he cared.

And that might have been the most troublesome
part of all.

Reaching the house, Landry crossed the flagstone
patio and stepped into the kitchen, which was spacious and ultramodern, with travertine tiles on the
floors, gleaming granite on the counters and the latest in top-of-the-line appliances. He nodded a greeting to his butler, Highbridge, before heading for one
of several steel sinks to wash up a little.

Highbridge, tall, skinny as a zipper turned sideways and exuding English dignity from every pore,
stood with his hands clasped behind his back and his
spine straight. For him, this was relaxed.

"I trust the most recent—buffalo incident—is behind us?" he murmured, obviously stifling a smile.

Landry dried his hands. "For the time being," he
conceded, a mite on the grumpy side now.

Highbridge consulted his heirloom pocket watch,
drawn from a special pocket in his long-tailed butler's
coat. Cleared his throat. "Will there be anything else,
sir?" he asked.

Landry moved to the oven—make that *ovens*—
where his dinner awaited, carefully covered in foil
and still warm. "No," he responded tersely. "You can

change out of that monkey suit and do whatever it is you do, once the workday's over."

Using a potholder, he removed the plate from the oven, lifted a corner of the foil and peered beneath it. Cornish game hen, roasted to crispy perfection, wild rice, exquisitely seasoned, and green beans cooked up just the way Landry liked them best—boiled, with bacon and chopped onion.

His mood might have been on the sour side, but his stomach rumbled with involuntary anticipation.

Highbridge, usually anxious to vanish into his well-appointed quarters to watch some reality show on TV or, conversely, read from one of his vast collection of multivolume tomes, like Churchill's *A History of the English-Speaking Peoples,* lingered. Cleared his throat again, a clear indication that there was more he wanted to say.

With a silent curse, Landry carried his plate to the trestle table in the center of the vast room, where cutlery, a starched linen napkin and a glass of red wine awaited him, and sat down.

"What?" he nearly barked.

"Ms. Manning," Highbridge began carefully. He faltered and made another attempt, but that failed, too, and he just stood there, hands still clasped behind his rigid back, looking reluctant and stubborn, both at once.

"What about her?" Landry demanded, plunging a fork into the succulent game hen on his plate.

"Well," Highbridge ventured, "she *did* have something of a scare this evening, you must admit." *Even you.* "Is she all right?"

Landry reached for the saltshaker and proceeded to oversalt his food, mainly because he knew the act would bug his butler, who made every effort to serve healthy meals. Right or wrong, Landry felt like bugging somebody.

"She's as prickly as a porcupine with PMS," Landry answered flatly. "I don't know if she's 'all right,' but she's definitely her usual ornery self."

A corner of Highbridge's normally unexpressive mouth quivered just slightly, though whether this indicated annoyance or amusement was anybody's guess.

Taking his etiquette cues from Henry VIII, Landry ripped off a drumstick and raised it to his mouth, bit into it, chewed and swallowed with lengthy deliberation, hoping Highbridge would take the hint and retire for the evening.

Landry had, after all, used up his quota of words for the day, and felt no inclination to chat—especially if the subject of the exchange was Ria Manning.

Yet again, Highbridge cleared his throat. "I see," he said.

Landry might have rolled his eyes, if he hadn't been so busy chowing down on all that good food. After the day he'd put in, he was ravenous. "And?" he prompted pointedly. "Obviously, you have more to say. Spill it, okay?"

Highbridge arched both bushy white eyebrows

and stood his ground. "'Spill it'?" he echoed, letting it be known that he considered the freewheeling use of slang one of America's many lesser charms.

"Explain," Landry explained, and none too politely.

"It's just that Ms. Manning is a very nice, hardworking person," Highbridge supplied.

"Hardworking," Landry conceded, somewhat testily now, "yes. 'Nice'? I don't think so."

"She has very good manners," Highbridge insisted, sounding miffed.

Landry paused in the act of devouring his supper and studied the butler solemnly. Highbridge, a man with a mysterious past, had been working for him since before he'd married Susan—a lifetime ago. "Really?" he replied. "I hadn't noticed."

To Highbridge, hard work and good manners were everything. Reasons enough, as far as he was concerned, to overlook proclivities ranging from littering to international terrorism.

"You do understand that Ms. Manning is a widow?" Highbridge went on.

"Yes," Landry admitted, thinking of the wide gold wedding band on Ria's left-hand ring finger. If she was wearing it after all this time, it followed that she was still hung up on her dead husband. An oddly discouraging insight. And where was this conversation headed, exactly? He had no idea. "So I've been told," he finished.

Highbridge sighed, as though balancing the unwieldy weight of the world on his narrow shoulders. "If there's nothing else—"

Landry leveled a look at his only full-time employee, a look that said Highbridge should have gone off duty hours ago.

Some of Zane's ranch hands moonlighted for Landry now and then, and a cleaning lady came in three times a week, but other than that, Highbridge was the whole staff. When a picture of the butler dressed to ride the range popped into Landry's mind, complete with a Stetson, a sun squint and woolly chaps, he had to smile.

"Have a good night," he said.

Highbridge nodded, with his usual formality, and left the kitchen.

Once he was gone, a rush of fresh loneliness passed through Landry, which was crazy, because Highbridge wasn't the type to shoot the breeze, whatever the time of day, but there it was.

He finished his dinner, imagining how things were on his brother's half of the ranch, over beyond the creek. By now, Cleo would have come back from town and made supper, and after the meal, Brylee would have chased the housekeeper off, good-naturedly, of course, so she and Zane could clear the table and load the dishwasher. They'd talk about their day—Zane, no doubt, would offer a comical account of Landry's bronc-riding episode, and Brylee would elbow him and tell him to be nice, and then she'd blush as they both remembered summer-afternoon lovemaking.

Whoa, Landry thought, derailing his previous train of thought by shoving his chair back from the table and getting to his feet. He carried the remains of his supper—gourmet fare by anybody's standards, so he had no business complaining on that score— over to the sink. There, he tossed the bones in the trash bin and scraped and then rinsed his plate and stowed it in the machine, along with his utensils and the wineglass.

Maddie Rose Sutton had raised her boys to clean up after themselves, swearing she wasn't about to unleash a couple of slobs on a world full of women who had enough to do as it was, without kid-gloving some man. By now, it was a habit.

Landry stood still, there at the sink, remembering his mom. She'd had it tough, Maddie Rose had, but she'd never complained, as far as he could recall. Just when he was getting established and Zane was about to sign the contract to make his first movie, and they could have been assets to their mother for once, instead of liabilities, she'd come down with a case of flu that turned out to be some virulent strain of leukemia instead. After a week in a small hospital in the backwater Dakota town where she'd been waiting tables for the past few months, Maddie Rose had breathed her last.

Worse, she'd been alone when the time came, except for a friend or two from the café where she'd worked. He and Zane had both been far away, doing their own thing, blissfully unaware that Maddie Rose's flu wasn't flu at all.

Once they were informed, it was too late to say goodbye, or thank you, or I love you, Mom.

Landry sighed. Maybe one of these days, he'd be able to think of his mother without guilt and regret, but, just now, that day seemed far off.

He should have been there for her—Zane, too. The way she'd always been there for them.

He was just about to shut off the lights and retreat to his bedroom, to read or watch TV or maybe just lie down and stare at the ceiling with his hands cupped behind his head, waiting in vain for sleep, when the wall phone rang.

Landry scowled at the thing for a moment or two, tempted to ignore it. Unlike the phones in his bedroom and home office, this one hadn't come equipped with caller ID, wasn't even cordless. Highbridge's doing, he recalled grimly—the butler didn't entirely approve of too much modern technology, was suspicious of what he considered unwarranted convenience.

So Landry picked up the receiver, in case something was wrong over at Zane and Brylee's, or those damn buffalo had broken through a fence line somewhere and made for Ria's flowers again. He answered with a rather brisk "Hello?"

If the caller turned out to be a telemarketer or a survey taker, he might just take the person's head off, long-distance.

The reply was a low, rumbling laugh, gratingly familiar. "Landry? Is that you, boy?"

Jess Sutton—his father.

"What do you want?" Landry asked. He didn't hear from the old man for years at a time, and when he did, it was because a favor was about to be asked, so there was no point in beating around the proverbial bush.

Jess gave another chuckle. "Is that any way to talk to your old dad?" he chided, with just the slightest edge in his voice.

Landry said nothing. He knew what was coming, and saw no reason to make it easy.

His father sighed, long-suffering, patient as the day was long. *As if.* "I was wondering how Nash is doing," Jess went on quietly, letting it be known that he was hurt but magnanimous enough to generously overlook the injury.

"In that case," Landry replied, frowning, "why didn't you call Zane and Brylee's place? Nash lives with them—but I guess you were aware of that, since you signed him over like a quit-claim deed."

A long silence followed; then Jess cleared his throat. "Hell, Landry," he finally muttered, "I *know* I was a lousy father to all three of you. No need to rub it in."

Landry relented, but only a little. "Lousy" didn't begin to describe the kind of parent Jess Sutton had been—back when he and Zane were growing up, the man had mostly steered clear, and they'd liked it that way. After a while anyhow.

At first, they'd missed him to the point of genuine pain. They'd waited for him to change, come and get them and their mother, bring them home for good. They'd all live happily ever after then, like a real family. Not.

"Okay," Landry said. "But I'd still like to know why you'd call here looking for Nash, when you know he's elsewhere."

"Zane and I don't get along very well," Jess said, aggrieved. He never seemed to relate consequences to anything he'd said or done, but that was nothing new. Most likely, he regarded himself as the innocent victim of betrayal, misunderstanding and just plain bad luck.

"He won't ask you for child support, if that's what you're worried about," Landry supplied ungenerously. Zane had had himself a successful movie career, a kind of lucky fluke, before he'd come to Three Trees to settle down and marry Brylee, and money wasn't a problem.

"Do you ever let up?" Jess asked sadly.

Poor, beleaguered Jess Sutton. Good-looking, smooth-talking and not worth the powder it would take to blow him to hell.

"Look," Landry replied, wishing he hadn't answered the call in the first place, "as far as I know, Nash is fine. He's grown about a foot in the last year, he does all right in school, he likes girls and he's rodeo-crazy. All pretty normal."

If only Jess actually cared about any of those things, or about the boy himself. The truth was, asking about Nash was just a way in, a conversation starter.

"I'm in a little trouble," Jess said, after another silence, this one so long that Landry had been about to hang up, thinking the connection had been broken, when the man finally spoke.

Landry closed his eyes. Waited. *Here it comes.*

"Are you still there?" Jess asked.

"I'm still here," Landry confirmed, opening his eyes again, shoving his free hand through his hair. He'd been expecting this, but that didn't make it any easier to handle.

"I need a small loan," Jess thrust out.

Landry felt a stab of pity then, but he didn't let on—not because he was trying to spare his father's pride, though. Jess was the classic con man, always on the lookout for a soft spot, and if he found one, he'd zero in on it like a suicide bomber.

"How small?" Landry asked. With Jess, the word *loan* was a misnomer. *Handout* was the better word, since he had no intention of paying it back.

"Five thousand dollars," Jess said, and now the edge was back in his voice.

Landry gave a low whistle. Five thousand dollars wasn't a lot of money to him personally, not these days anyway, but it was still a respectable sum, hard to come by for most people. "Go on," he said.

"You want an explanation?" Jess asked, testy all of a sudden. It was an interesting approach, considering he was the one in need of some help.

"Yeah," Landry said. "I guess I do. What happened this time?"

Jess took his time answering; he might be sulking, but he could be making up a story, too.

Finally, he launched into his spiel, and damned if it didn't sound like the truth, for once. "I got into this private poker game down here in Reno—one of those backroom kind that aren't entirely legal—and I was doing real good for a while, before my luck went sour. These guys aren't the kind to wait around for their winnings, son. They'll have their money or a strip of my hide if I don't pay them, pronto."

Landry shook his head, tired, disgusted and sore all over. "Damn it," he muttered, "why did you get into the game in the first place, if you were broke?"

"I anted up a hundred dollars," Jess said defensively. "That's all. Before I knew it, I was up a couple of grand, and it was still early, so I couldn't just cash out and leave everybody high and dry, now, could I?"

Shit, Landry thought. "Of course you couldn't," he rasped.

Jess didn't pick up on the irony. Or maybe he just figured he couldn't afford to remark on it. "I started losing, as the night went on," he said hurriedly, as though talking fast would convince Landry that he ought to ride to the rescue, "but I figured things would start going my way again, so I gave my I.O.U. and—"

"And now you're down five grand?" Landry supplied, when Jess fell silent.

"I'm only down three, actually," Jess admitted. "But I've got some other bills to pay before I can leave town."

"To go where?" Landry asked. He didn't really care what the destination was, as long as it *wasn't* Hangman's Bend.

"Boise, I guess," Jess speculated. "I know some people there."

"Right," Landry answered. Jess "knew some people" just about everywhere. Trouble was, if he hadn't slept with their wives or girlfriends, he probably owed most of them money.

Maybe both.

"I've only got till tomorrow morning, when the banks open, to pay up," Jess went on. "Once these guys find out I can't make good on my marker, they're going to want blood." He sucked in an audible breath. "*My* blood. Are you going to help me out, or not?"

Landry let his forehead rest against the door of the cupboard directly above the wall phone. He knew he'd be enabling the old man if he gave him the five thousand, making bad matters worse. Still, the alternative—the strong likelihood that his dad would wind up sprawled in some back alley, beaten and bloody, or even dead—was no good, either.

"Where do I send it?" Landry asked.

CHAPTER THREE

RIA BARELY SLEPT that night, one moment worrying about her financial future and the next, lusting after Mr. Wrong, that being Landry Sutton, the first man she'd really been attracted to since Frank's death. With widow guilt compounding physical and emotional exhaustion, she was out of the house as soon as the sun rose, taking no time for coffee, let alone breakfast.

Those things could wait. Right now she wanted a good look at whatever havoc the buffalo had—or hadn't—wreaked on her farm, without Landry there to gauge her every reaction. Or to guess somehow that she'd lost sleep wondering what he looked like without a shirt, what it would be like if he kissed her or to feel the weight of that hard, uncompromisingly masculine body of his poised over hers, then settling into her softness and, finally, claiming her...

"Stop it!" Ria ordered her inner love slave, right out loud, as she marched through the still-dewy grass in the front yard, bent on inspecting poppies and daisies and other colorful residents of her flower beds, performing a sort of horticultural triage.

Some plants, she soon discovered, had been squashed, or even uprooted, but to her surprise and relief, most of the blossoms had survived. Ready for a new day, they were already raising their brightly colored faces toward the big sky and the first promise of sunshine.

Hardly daring to hope everything would be all right after all, Ria trudged over to the field of zinnias, a glorious ground quilt of red and magenta, orange and gold, pink and purple and white. There was no evidence of the buffalo invasion here, no tracks in the fertile soil, no broken stems and stripped petals. She was moving on to the field of gerbera daisies, which abutted the carnations, when she saw Landry's truck turn into her driveway, glinting silver in the morning light.

Although her first impulse was to dive between the rows of multicolored daisies and hide there until her visitor gave up and left, Ria planted her sneakered feet firmly and stood her ground, lifting her chin a jot to convince herself, as well as Landry, that she wasn't intimidated, and waited.

Landry parked the truck at the edge of the field, got out and strolled toward her in that easy, rolling-hipped way of men who were used to meeting challenges and coming out on top.

Ria gulped. *Unfortunate choice of words,* she thought, glad she hadn't voiced the observation out loud.

Sunlight danced in Landry's hair and lent him

a full-body aura of glittering gold, and last night's fantasies rushed to the surface of Ria's skin, fiercely visceral now, and pulsed there, dangerous and primitive and absolutely delectable.

She frowned hard, hoping Landry wouldn't pick up on the fact that she was ridiculously attracted to him, physically, at least—a man she didn't even *like*. Maybe her friends back in Portland were right— she'd been too quick to start over in a new place, among strangers, wasn't over the trauma of losing Frank, needed grief therapy, not a change of scene.

Landry's smile was taut, but it still opened a trapdoor in the pit of Ria's stomach and made her heart pound under her lightweight sweatshirt. "Well," he said, coming to a stop one row over from where she stood, and she almost giggled at the contrast between his blatant self-confidence and all those delicate flowers at his feet, "what's the verdict?"

Ria felt a blush climb her neck and throb in her cheeks. Damn it.

"There doesn't seem to be any real harm done," she finally managed, after reminding herself that Landry had *told* her he'd be stopping by, and so what if she hadn't believed him for a second? She'd just have to deal. "No thanks to your marauding buffalo." Even as Ria spoke, she was measuring the shadows under his eyes, the tight lines of his jaw, the hard set of his shoulders. He hadn't shaved, she noticed, and the effect was disturbingly appealing.

You've been alone too long, girl, Ria thought.

For one terrible moment, she thought she'd spoken aloud, because Landry gave a rough bark of laughter, as if he'd heard her. He tilted his magnificent head to one side and studied her as though he couldn't quite get a handle on whatever it was that made her tick. Dressed the way he was, in jeans and a long-sleeved green cotton work shirt and beat-up boots caked with manure, it was hard to picture Landry in his former incarnation, managing a multibillion-dollar international investment fund back in Chicago, where he'd surely have worn three-piece suits, custom-tailored, of course, and paid hundreds of dollars for a haircut.

This morning, he was all cowboy.

All *man*.

"You sound disappointed," he observed, after a few moments, his tone on the dry side. "That your crops aren't lying in ruin, I mean."

Ria's blush went from mild to moderate to off-the-charts, all in the space of a second or so. "Don't be ridiculous," she sputtered. "Of *course* I'm not disappointed—"

Landry laughed again, though this time it was more of a chuckle, and there was a rawness to the sound that pinched her heart—the heart she wished she could harden at will, but couldn't. She didn't need all these crazy feelings, didn't *want* them.

"You're hell-bent on hating me, aren't you?" he asked, very quietly. Almost gently. "Why is that, Ria?"

Nervously, Ria twisted Frank's wedding band on

her finger, trying to ground herself. Landry's gaze followed the gesture unerringly. "I don't hate you," she said lamely. "I just don't happen to like you very much."

Again, he laughed, and the sound stirred things inside Ria that were better left alone. "Why not?" he asked.

The question stumped Ria, at least briefly, and left her slightly embarrassed. "Because—well, because—"

While she faltered, searching for something sensible to offer in reply, Landry stepped over the row of tall orange zinnias between them and stood facing her, so close she could feel the heat and the hard substance of his flesh. "Because—?" he prompted. One side of his mouth crooked up slightly, but the expression in his blue eyes was solemn, even a little bleak.

Ria squared her shoulders and lifted her chin, prepared to brazen her way through to goodbye, see you around, get lost, and finally took a stab at putting her opinion into words. "Because you're—I don't know—too good-looking."

His eyes twinkled. They were the most startling shade of blue. Was he wearing colored contacts? And were those impossibly white teeth genuine, or cosmetically altered?

"Excuse me?" he said.

Ria was mortified, but she forged ahead anyway. "*And* you know it," she added.

He frowned, looking confused. "I do?"

Ria folded her arms, drew a deep breath, huffed

it out again. "You'd have to be blind not to," she retorted.

"That's my big crime?" Landry asked, after a
brief, charged silence had passed. "Being 'too good-
looking' and 'knowing it'?"

She didn't have the first idea what to say to that.
She'd gotten herself into this, and she'd have to get
herself out, but she'd be darned if she could see how
that was going to happen.

That was when Landry cupped one hand, cal-
loused and gentle, under her chin, tipping her face up
slightly, so that their gazes locked and their breaths
mingled. Right there in that field of sunlight and
dazzling color and sweet-scented breezes, he bent
his head, and he kissed her.

At first, Landry's lips merely brushed against
hers, but before Ria could so much as catch her
breath, and certainly before she could recover from
the shock of pleasure jolting through her like a series
of violent earthquakes, Landry deepened the kiss.

Ria moaned, knowing she should resist, pull back,
make a run for it—and completely unable to do any
of those things. Instead, she gave herself up to that
incredible kiss, and to the man administering it,
without reservation. The windswept depths of her
need, a vast and lonely canyon yawning within her,
terrified her, even as thrill after sweet thrill rolled
through her.

She wanted to run away. Conversely, she wanted
more of Landry, more than the kiss. Right here, right

now. *Yikes.* She'd been intimate with one man in her
entire life—her husband—and now here she was,
ready to make love in the open, under the morning sun.

In the end, Landry was the one who withdrew, his
breathing ragged, his gaze fixed on something—or
someone—far off in the distance. When he looked
back at Ria, though, an impish light danced in his
eyes.

"*That's* why you think you don't like me," he said.

Ria blinked, still dazed by the kiss and the inter-
nal ruckus it had caused, trying to firm up her melted
knees by sheer force of will. "What?" she muttered,
when she figured she could speak coherently again.

Landry's crooked grin was mildly insolent, maddening in the extreme, and downright sexy. "You're
afraid of me," he said easily.

Ria opened her mouth to protest, to tell Landry
Sutton that she thought he was a smug, overconfi-
dent son of a bitch and, furthermore, she wasn't *at
all* scared of him, so he shouldn't flatter himself
that she was. But this time, nothing came out. Not a
whisper, not a squeak.

Landry, meanwhile, reached out and tucked a
lock of hair behind Ria's right ear. "Admit it," he
said. "You're afraid of the things I might make you
feel if you ever gave me a chance to get too close to
you. You'd have to let go, and that's a risk you don't
want to take."

The gall of the man.

A fresh surge of fury rushed through Ria then, and she fairly trembled with it. "You *have* to be the vainest, most *obnoxious* person on earth," she burst out, though she wasn't sure exactly who she was more put out with at the moment, Landry or herself. If she hadn't let the man kiss her, or if she'd made even the slightest effort to pretend the sensation of his mouth on hers hadn't shifted the very core of her, if she hadn't been instantly and obviously aroused...

Landry was still grinning, the self-satisfied bastard.

"It just so happens," Ria snapped, reconnoitering, "that you don't 'make me feel' *anything,* Mr. Sutton!"

He arched a skeptical eyebrow, folded his arms and waited without speaking for her to continue.

"*Except,*" she qualified, well aware that the conversation was now careening downhill and unable to put on the brakes, "an overwhelming urge to slap you right into the next county!"

At that, Landry actually threw back his head and gave a raspy shout of laughter.

"You're just lucky I'm not a violent person," Ria said. She was digging herself in deeper with every word, and she knew it. *Why* couldn't she just *shut up?*

Landry had stopped laughing, but mischief sparked like blue fire in his eyes as he looked directly down into her face, and maybe into her soul, where she stashed her deepest secrets.

"Prove it," he said.

"Prove what?" Ria demanded, disgruntled and

overheated, even though it was still too early in the day for the temperature to climb. "That I'm not a violent person? I think I just proved *that* by not striking you or running you through with the nearest pitchfork."

Slowly, Landry shook his head from side to side, as though marveling, albeit sympathetically, at the ravings of a dimwit. "No," he drawled, in a voice so low and so quiet that it felt—well—*intimate,* like a caress. He leaned in toward her, until their noses were almost touching. "Prove that you're immune to me," he breathed. "That shouldn't be difficult, now, should it? Not unless the lady protests too much, that is."

Part of Ria reconsidered finding a pitchfork and using it feloniously. Another part of her, one she barely recognized as belonging to her, wanted to rise to Landry's challenge, prove once and for all that, unlike a lot of other women probably, she could live without him. *Happily.*

"That's crazy," she said, after some mental scrambling. "I don't have to prove anything to you or to anybody else."

"How about to yourself?" Landry asked reasonably—so reasonably that Ria thought about breaking her personal code of behavior and slapping him after all. No, *punching* him.

"I don't know what you're talking about," she lied, heading for the edge of the field now, her stride brisk and purposeful.

And slightly desperate.

"The hell you don't," Landry said, keeping pace easily, since his legs were so much longer than hers. "You know *exactly* what I'm talking about. That kiss was nuclear, at least on my side, and you'll have to go some to convince me you didn't feel some of the same things I did."

"I'm not trying to convince you of anything," Ria argued, afraid to look at Landry, because if she did, she might just hurl herself into his arms, wrestle him to the grass right there where the flower fields and the lawn met and have her way with him. In broad daylight.

Oh, God, she thought. What was wrong with her?

She'd loved Frank passionately—she *had*—but the best climax she'd ever reached making love with her husband hadn't rattled her as much as the one and only kiss she'd shared with Landry Sutton.

In the shade of a venerable maple tree, one with some of the lower branches stripped of leaves, almost certainly a casualty of the most recent buffalo raid, Landry caught hold of Ria's elbow and stopped her. His grasp was gentle, but firm, and it sent fresh waves of wanting roaring through her.

"You're right," he ground out, glowering down at her now. "You don't have to convince me of anything. You don't need to prove a damn thing. But *something's* going on between us, Ria, and maybe you're too cowardly to find out what it is, but I'm not."

Her throat thickened, closed tight. She didn't pull away, didn't speak, didn't move at all.

Landry sighed, loosened his hold on her arm, slid his hand down to close his fingers around hers. "I'm not asking you to sleep with me, Ria."

She met his gaze directly, there in the soft shade of that old tree. "Then what *are* you asking me?" she replied, in a near whisper. Her heart felt winged, like something caged, flailing against the bars, frantic to break free and go soaring into that big sky arching high over their heads.

At last, Landry smiled. It wasn't a mocking grin; it wasn't a smirk. It was a genuine smile.

And Ria realized, much to her chagrin, that she was helpless against it. It rocked her first, then settled over her heart like some invisible balm.

When Landry finally answered her question, she was panicking again, and she could barely hear him over the hum in her ears. "There's a party at the Boot Scoot Tavern, over in Parable, this Saturday night. It's a sort of kickoff before the rodeo starts, and half the county will be there, so nothing drastic will happen. Between us, I mean."

Nothing drastic?

Even as she mentally catalogued the most obvious reasons why she should refuse—she'd be tired and grubby after a long day at the farmers' market, selling flowers, and crowd or no crowd, the proposed evening amounted to a date, and what were the implications of *that?*—Ria was stunned to find herself on the verge of agreeing. Was she losing her mind? She wasn't much of a drinker, after all, and she had no clue what else there was to do in a bar.

Again, Landry seemed to be reading her mind, a disconcerting thing. "If you won't trust yourself," he said, "how about trusting me?"

"I *do* trust myself," Ria insisted.

Not so much, argued a snarky voice in her head.

Landry smiled again, and spread his hands wide in a well-then kind of gesture. "Great," he said. "Then we don't have a problem. I'll pick you up around seven—we'll have some dinner and head for the Boot Scoot."

With that, he nodded a farewell and started off toward his truck.

"Just a minute," Ria called after him.

He paused, perhaps ten feet away from her, the sun in his hair, his eyes lively with amusement and something less easily defined. "What?"

It's not too late to beg off. Make an excuse—do something!

"What do people—women, that is—wear at the Boot-whatever-tavern?"

Had she really and truly just asked him such a 1950s kind of question? Brylee could have clued her in on the dress code, or Casey Parrish, both of whom were good friends. Damn, what was up with her mouth?

Landry's gaze glided over Ria, from head to foot, with a look of appreciation and, strangely, nothing that even vaguely resembled mockery. "I figure you'd look good in just about anything," he told her gruffly, "and even better in nothing at all. But the Boot Scoot isn't fancy, so jeans and something short-sleeved will do. It gets hot in there when there's a crowd."

Ria opened her mouth, closed it again.

There was still time to call off the whole crazy idea—she was no cowgirl: she didn't ride horses or dance to ballads on a jukebox or anything like that—but, for some reason she refused to examine too closely, she *didn't* call it off.

Landry reached his truck, turned long enough to nod an amiable goodbye and got behind the wheel. He was driving away by the time Ria collected her scattered wits, willed some strength into her legs and headed for the house.

The wall phone was ringing as she stepped inside and, in need of an immediate distraction, she answered—in spite of the fact that the caller was Meredith—a robotic voice had already announced that.

"Hello," Ria said tersely.

She could almost see her half sister recoil at the tone of the greeting. "Ria?" Meredith asked, sounding wary. "Is that you?"

Ria thrust out a sigh. *No,* she thought. *The real Ria has been abducted by aliens and replaced by a reckless and wanton woman determined to play with fire.*

If she and Meredith had been close, like other

sisters, they could have talked about Landry Sutton and the way he riled her, hammered out some of the whys and wherefores. Ria might have confided in an older and wiser Meredith that she was scared and confused and horny as hell, all at once. But she and Meredith *weren't* close.

"Yes," Ria finally replied, with another sigh. "It's me."

Meredith's voice brightened. *Enough small talk—time to move in for the kill.* "Have you given my offer any thought?" she trilled sweetly, immediately setting Ria's teeth on edge.

Her *offer?* Last night's voice mail had sounded more like an order than a request—come to Seattle, straighten out the financial mess at the branch office there, or else Daddy will turn over in his grave, heads will roll, all will be lost.

Yada yada yada.

"I can't get away right now," Ria said. "Sorry."

A stricken silence ensued. Meredith had a gift for conveying disappointment and disapproval without saying a word, either in person *or* over the phone.

"I guess I didn't make the situation clear in my message," Meredith ventured, after several moments. "Things are dire, Ria. There could be an audit, a scandal, even indictments—"

Not my problem, Ria thought, without bitterness.

When their father had died, the business, as well as the bulk of his fortune, had gone to Meredith, the daughter of Dad's first and only love, his beloved

Marjory. Ria, being the child of a trophy wife who'd earned her living as a Las Vegas showgirl before hooking up with a wealthy Portland businessman, had gotten a few thousand dollars, the used car one of the maids had driven while running errands and a subtle-but-still-plain "don't let the door hit you on your way out."

And she'd never felt a moment's resentment, not over the inheritance anyway—only profound and lasting relief. Wealth was fine for others, Ria supposed, but she preferred simplicity and the freedom that came with it. For her, enough really *was* enough.

"Meredith," she said calmly, after drawing a deep, preparatory breath, "please tell me you haven't done anything illegal."

She *did* care what happened to her sister; it was just that she didn't feel responsible for smoothing Meredith's way.

Meredith immediately bristled, insulted by the very suggestion. "Of *course* I haven't *done anything illegal!*"

"But you want *me* to break the law?" Ria asked, keeping her voice mild.

"I didn't say that," Meredith protested, snappish now, and unable to hide the fact.

"You didn't *have* to, Meredith," Ria said. "You want me to go to the Seattle office and 'straighten things out'—isn't that the gist of it? In other words, I'm supposed to cover someone's tracks—maybe even doctor the books—wave some fiscal wand and make the whole thing go away."

Meredith was even more affronted than before; Ria didn't have to see her sister's cameo-perfect face to know that. "So you're not going to help?" she asked, after a very long time. *"You're really not going to help?"*

"Meredith," Ria responded, "I *can't* help. What's done is done—from what you've told me, there's nothing to do now but deal with the fallout." She paused, bit her lower lip, then tentatively added, "Besides, I have a life here."

"Oh, absolutely," Meredith sniped, obviously still smarting over Ria's refusal to do what she wanted. People generally did what Meredith wanted—it was easier that way.

Indignation rose into the back of Ria's throat and tightened there, like a tiny ball of rusted barbed wire. Normally, she would have allowed the gibe to pass—after all, it had been implied, rather than stated outright—but something had changed. Ria, always ready to lend a hand before, even when she shouldn't have, wasn't the same person she'd been when she'd woken up that morning, the woman she'd been before—before—

Before Landry Sutton kissed you.

"Look," Ria said firmly, "I'm proud of who I am and what I do for a living. Maybe I'm not setting the financial world on fire, like you, but my flowers are beautiful, and they brighten people's lives."

Meredith waited a beat before replying. "Of course, dear," she said, her tone acidly sweet and, therefore, completely condescending. "You *brighten people's lives.* But does your little business even *begin* to pay the bills? Where would you be without Frank's life-insurance money bringing in quarterly dividends? And what about that big salary Whittingford International paid you, after college? If you hadn't socked away most of *that*—"

Ria sucked in a breath, rubbed at one temple with the fingers of her right hand, trying to forestall a tension headache. Whittingford International, her father's company, and now Meredith's, had indeed paid her well, but she'd worked twelve- and sixteen-hour days to earn that paycheck, too. It was only after she'd married Frank, a firefighter, that she'd cut back on her time at the office. "You know what, Meredith?" she shot back. "None of that is any of your business. I've earned what I have, such as it is. And in approximately one second, I'm going to hang up, so, not to be rude, *goodbye.*"

Meredith started to say something more, but the allotted second had passed by then, so Ria put the phone receiver back on the hook.

The ringing began again as she walked rigidly to the other side of the kitchen, took a water glass from one of the cupboards, filled it and drank every drop. She would have liked to ask about her seventeen-year-old niece, Quinn, the only loving relative, now that her mother was gone, that Ria had left. She was close to Meredith's daughter and they usually stayed in touch, via email and texts, but she hadn't heard from the girl in over a week. Was something wrong?

Unfortunately, Ria and Meredith didn't have that kind of relationship. They didn't talk about family, or anything else that was purely personal. The bristly exchange just past was all too typical.

For a moment, Ria considered calling Quinn directly; she knew her niece's cell number by heart, but she decided to wait awhile, until she'd weeded and watered and fertilized a few rows of zinnias. That way, she could work off some of her irritation and not have it spilling over into her conversation with Quinn.

She headed for the field, worked until she was sweating and her nose was surely peeling from too much direct sunlight—she'd forgotten to put on the blue baseball cap she usually wore when she spent more than a few minutes outside—and was on her way back to the house to clean up and have a light lunch when she heard the jaunty honk of a car horn and looked up to see Brylee Sutton's SUV rolling along the driveway.

Ria smiled, made for the edge of the lawn and waited.

Brylee stopped the rig and got out, smiling that warm, wide smile of hers. As always, her dog, Snidely, was riding shotgun, and he leaped across the seats and down to the ground to stand benignly at his mistress's side.

Brylee, her beautiful brown hair pulled back into a ponytail, held out a cloth-covered basket, the contents exuding a marvelous butter/cinnamon/sugar smell.

"Hope we're not interrupting or anything," she said, meaning herself and Snidely. "It's just that I've been on another of my baking jags."

Ria was genuinely glad to see her friend, though she suspected there was more to this visit than an overabundance of baked goods.

"Come on inside," she said.

LANDRY CAUGHT UP to Zane over at his place, where he was standing just outside the barn, next to Blackjack, his gelding. Bent at the waist, Zane was in the process of checking the animal's right rear hoof for pebbles or burrs, and while he didn't stop what he was doing or straighten his back, his eyes blazed at Landry.

"Say *what?*" he growled, in response to Landry's opening statement.

Landry sighed, rubbed his beard-stubbled chin. The jangly state of his insides had nothing to do with the five thousand he'd sent to their dad, via the internet, or with Zane's clear disapproval—and *everything* to do with the lingering scent of Ria Manning and the crazy effects of just one kiss.

"I'm not here to confess my sins and get your absolution, bro," he said. "I just thought you ought to know the old man is up to something again, that's all. In case he turns up in person with a plan to cause trouble."

Young Nash, their half brother, nowhere to be seen at the moment, was settling in at Hangman's Bend just fine, but, like any kid, he wanted to believe, against all evidence to the contrary, that his father loved him. And that meant the boy was susceptible to Jess's influence, easily manipulated. Vulnerable.

Jess wouldn't hesitate to promise the boy everything there was to promise, use him to achieve some purpose of his own—most likely gouging one or both his older sons for more money—and then abandon the kid all over again.

Slowly, Zane let go of Blackjack's shin, walked away from the horse and set the hoof pick on top of a nearby fence post. "Did Jess say he was headed here?" he asked, his tone as taut as his expression. "To Montana?"

"Not exactly," Landry answered, simultaneously shaking his head no. "But he's been gambling, and I think he's in deep—probably deeper than he admitted to me. Even if he settles up with the badasses he told me about over the phone last night, that doesn't mean the heat is off." He paused, sighed. "I think his life is in danger, Zane."

"And I think you're a world-class sucker," Zane answered, but some of the tension drained from his face and the stiffness in his shoulders eased a little. Lightly, he slapped Landry on the back. "Let's go inside and talk awhile."

CHAPTER FOUR

THE DRIVER OF the semi pulled in at a busy truck stop on the outskirts of Three Trees, Montana, reined in the big machine with a squeal of brakes and smiled over at Quinn Whittingford. His eyes were sad and gentle, in a way that made seventeen-year-old Quinn miss having a dad just that much more. He glanced at the ragtag little dog cuddled in her arms, then looked into her face again.

"You sure you'll be all right?" the man asked quietly. His name was Tim Anderson, and there was a snapshot of a pretty woman and three small girls affixed to the driver's-side visor. His wife and daughters, he'd told Quinn earlier. He'd picked her up back at that last rest stop, somewhere in southern Idaho, late the night before. "That little fella can't offer much protection, much as he might want to."

Quinn held the gray-and-white critter she'd named Bones, after finding him alone and hungry, possibly lost but more likely abandoned, maybe five minutes before Mr. Anderson had stopped at the rest stop to stretch his legs and avail himself of some free coffee. He'd already given Quinn the standard lecture on the

dangers of hitchhiking, offering her his cell phone
so she could call home and let her "folks" know she
was okay, but, obviously, he was still concerned.

She knew he was a good person, and that she'd
been lucky to catch a ride with him, considering
some of the stuff that *could* have happened. Quinn
had endured the speech, but since she planned on becoming a cop after college, or even an FBI agent, and
she'd seen all the shows on the ID network about rap-
ists and serial killers, she wasn't completely clueless.

Not, she silently admitted, that her behavior was
any indication she knew better than to take such a
risk. "I'll be fine," she said. "Thanks."

Tim Anderson nodded. "You be careful, now," he
said as she pushed open the heavy door of the truck,
slung her backpack over one T-shirted shoulder and
climbed down onto the running board and then the
pavement, careful not to drop Bones in the process.
"Sure you don't want to use my cell phone? Call your
mom and dad?" he asked again.

"I'm sure," Quinn said politely. She didn't have
a dad, actually, and her mom was probably relieved
that she was gone—if she'd even noticed yet. She had
a cell of her own tucked into her backpack, but the
battery was stone dead, and she hadn't mentioned
it, for whatever reason. "Thanks again."

She stepped back, and smoke billowed from the
truck's gleaming stacks. The horn blew once, a shrill
salute, Tim Anderson waved goodbye from behind
what seemed like an acre of windshield and Quinn si-

lently asked herself a question she'd kept at bay until then: what she'd do if Ria turned her away. Though she'd always been close to her aunt, it was at least remotely possible that Ria was busy with her new life and didn't have the time or inclination to deal with a teenage runaway.

Still, she couldn't, *wouldn't* go home, not only because she was seriously on the outs with her mother, who preferred to be addressed as "Meredith," claiming that being called "Mom" made her feel ancient, but because Bones would almost certainly wind up in a shelter if she did.

Meredith didn't like dogs—or cats, either, for that matter. They were too messy, she claimed, too much trouble, always needing something. Like a kid, maybe?

Furthermore, all the carpets in the upscale Portland condominium the two of them had been sharing for most of Quinn's life were a pristine white.

And the house rules were strict. No shoes allowed past the tiled entryway. No eating or drinking outside the kitchen, at the table or the breakfast bar. No watching television or listening to music in the living room.

The whole setup reminded Quinn of one big and very weird game of hopscotch—whatever she did, she had to be careful not to step on the lines. Naturally she never invited friends over; she'd have to police their every move, as well as her own, if she did. So, when she wasn't at school, Quinn spent most of her time holed up in her bedroom, and even there, she felt like some kind of hostage.

She'd been over at her friend Rosalie's place, cruising social-media sites on her tablet while Rosalie used the desktop in the family room—*family room, what a concept*—when Meredith had called and turned an ordinary day upside down.

Quinn and Rosalie had been having a great time until Quinn's cell phone rang, and Meredith instructed her, crisply and with no preamble at all, to come home and pack. At the last minute, she'd found a summer camp with an opening—Quinn hadn't even known she was looking for one—and promptly signed her daughter up for nearly three months of arts, crafts and songs around the campfire. She'd be leaving first thing in the morning, from the parking lot at their church, by bus.

Koombah-freakin-yah, Quinn had thought, as an overwhelming sense of hopeless misery settled over her.

She'd reminded Meredith that camp was for kids—that she was seventeen, not seven—and she'd be perfectly all right spending the summer at home. Why, in one more year, she'd pointed out, her temper gathering momentum, she'd be going off to *college,* for Pete's sake.

Meredith, being Meredith, hadn't listened. She'd insisted that Quinn would make new friends at Camp Winna-Whatever and have a *wonderful* time swimming and hiking and breathing in all that fresh air.

In other words, it was a done deal, and there would be no negotiations.

Obviously, Quinn's mom wanted a teenager-free summer, though she hadn't actually *said* that straight out, of course. True, Meredith seemed chronically worried and distracted these days, and she'd been working even longer hours than usual lately, and traveling a lot more than usual, too. If something was seriously wrong in Meredith's life, though, Quinn was the last person she'd have confided in.

Quinn had gone right home from Rosalie's— Meredith was still at the office and Hannah, the housekeeper, had already left for the day—and she'd packed, all right. But not for a stint at camp.

No, she'd stuffed fresh underwear, an extra pair of jeans, a favorite T-shirt and her tablet computer into her backpack, along with her cell phone and charger, and lit out. She'd walked for several miles, not exactly sure what to do next, and then, finding an ATM in the convenience store where she'd stopped to buy a bottle of water, Quinn had taken her last eighty dollars out of her account and made up her mind to head for Three Trees, Montana. And Ria.

Two cowgirls on their way to a rodeo in Idaho had offered her a lift, and she was off. They'd bought her a cheeseburger along the way, asked her a lot of questions, like how old she was and if something was wrong at home, and, finally, reluctantly, dropped her off at the rest stop, where she met up with Bones and took a chance on a long ride with Tim Anderson, a stranger.

Now, standing outside the truck-stop café, hot and tired and grungy, Quinn wondered if the people inside would kick her out if she tried to bring Bones in with her. She could sure use something cold to drink and maybe a sandwich, and she needed to use the restroom, too.

She supposed she could say Bones was a Seeing Eye dog, but since he looked more like a walking dust mop than a service animal, the story probably wouldn't fly.

Still, Quinn couldn't bring herself to leave him outside, alone. She didn't want the poor little thing to think, even for one second, that he'd gotten his hopes up only to be ditched all over again. Her stomach grumbled loudly, and she looked around carefully, spotted a phone booth over by the newspaper boxes and the ice machine.

Juggling Bones, she rummaged through her backpack and came up with enough change—she hoped—to make a local call. Accustomed to cell phones, texts and instant messaging over a computer, Quinn had never actually used a pay phone.

She approached the gizmo, frowning a little as she examined the smudged buttons, their numbers and letters partially rubbed off by years of weather and wear. Good thing she knew Ria's number by heart, she reflected, because the skinny directory dangling from a chain beside the telephone looked as though some wild animal had eaten the pages in a single bite.

Murmuring to Bones, who wanted to be set down on his own four feet, wobbly though they were, Quinn plunked several coins into the slot and started punching digits.

Please be home, she thought as Ria's phone rang once, twice, three times.

"Hello?" Ria said, just as Quinn was about to hang up, ask somebody for directions and hoof it to her aunt's farm. There was puzzlement in Ria's familiar voice. "Who is this?"

Quinn swallowed, and the backs of her eyeballs stung. "It's me, Aunt Ria," she managed.

"Quinn?" A smile came into Ria's tone, and she no longer sounded curious. Most likely the read-out in her caller-ID panel had flashed an unfamiliar number or maybe even read "pay phone." "Are you—? Where—?"

Quinn laughed, forestalling the need to cry even as a certain giddiness rose within her. "I'm in Three Trees," she said. "At the…" She paused, turned her head, read the big sign out by the highway. "At the Whistle-By Truck Stop."

"That explains the readout," Ria murmured, probably thinking aloud rather than addressing her niece. "What on earth—?"

"I'm here for a visit," Quinn said cheerfully. "Can you come and pick us up?"

Ria didn't ask who "us" was, as Meredith would

have done. In fact, she didn't hesitate at all. "I'll be right there. Don't talk to strangers."

Quinn smiled at the admonition. *Too late,* she thought. "Okay, I won't." Since pretty much everybody around this little Montana burg qualified as a stranger, she guessed she'd just zip her lip until Ria showed up.

And that would be soon, Quinn hoped, because she needed something to eat, a hot bath and a few hours of sleep. Nice as Tim Anderson had been to her, she'd been afraid to close her eyes the whole night, despite all the subtle indications that he was a devoted family man.

It could so easily have been an act. Quinn shuddered slightly at the silent admission.

She'd just said goodbye to Ria and hung up the clunky black pay-phone receiver, rubbing her hand down the thigh of her jeans in a hopeless attempt to wipe away any lingering germs, when a man's voice spoke.

"Are you all right?"

Quinn's heart sped up a little as she turned, clutching poor, road-weary Bones protectively to her chest, and saw a tall, dark-haired man in a cop's uniform standing directly behind her. His shirt was so crisply starched that the folds still showed, and his badge gleamed in the sunlight, brightly enough to dazzle a person, but she made out the words embossed in the metal just the same: *Sheriff, Parable County.*

"Um, sure," she said, her bravado wavering slightly now. The sheriff looked kind enough, with his warm brown eyes and that crooked cowboy smile, but she still had to fight down a wild urge to turn and hotfoot it right out of there.

Here she was, already breaking the don't-talk-to-strangers rule. Again.

But he *was* a cop, and under other circumstances, Quinn would have pelted him with questions about the job, the life, given her own aspirations to serve in law enforcement someday. And surely it was safe to talk to a policeman.

Plus, making a break for it would have been a bad idea, she decided, since he would surely catch her easily, long before she reached the woods behind the truck stop and found a place to hide—he looked young and fit. While Quinn was pretty sure she hadn't broken any laws—was running away from home illegal?—the affable intensity of this man's focus unnerved her. He clearly wasn't going anywhere until he got the information he was after.

"Boone Taylor," he said, putting out a hand.

Quinn had to jostle Bones a little, but she managed to return the sheriff's handshake. Her throat closed up tight, her nearly empty stomach tightened like a fist, and she felt her upper lip and the space between her shoulder blades go clammy with perspiration.

Sheriff Boone Taylor waited a beat or two, but when nothing came out of Quinn's mouth, he arched one eyebrow and asked, with a glint of humor in his eyes, "Do you have a name?"

It wouldn't do her any good to lie, she sensed that, and anyway, she was rotten at bending the truth. If she tried to shine this guy on, he'd know it by her expression or her body language—or both. In an instant, too.

"Quinn Whittingford," she managed to croak out. "I'm here to visit my aunt, Ria Manning. Maybe you know her?"

Get here, Aunt Ria. Please, get here quick.

"She's a good friend of my wife's," he said, and Quinn relaxed a bit, only to tense up again when he added, "I saw you get out of the cab of that truck a little while ago. Was the driver somebody you know, Quinn, or did you hitch your way here?"

Quinn swallowed. Exactly how far away was her aunt's flower farm? What if Ria lived at the far end of some long dirt road, on the other side of town, a rutted stretch of gravel winding for miles and miles before it finally reached the truck stop? In that case, it might be an hour before she arrived, or even longer.

"I hitched," she admitted.

The sheriff rested his hands on his hips, and his black leather belt—with its gun and holster and various other fascinating cop gear—creaked as he shifted his weight slightly and studied her with a pensive frown on his tanned and handsome face. "That's not good," he said.

Quinn blinked hard, fearing that tears would

spring to her eyes if she didn't, giving away how scared she was. "I know," she said, very quietly. "But my aunt's on her way here right now. Everything's fine, Officer—really."

He absorbed her words, giving no indication whether he believed her or not, smiled at Bones and gently touched the little dog's head, scratched him behind the ears. "Who's this?" he asked.

"His name is Bones," Quinn said, hoping the hurried way she spouted out the answer hadn't made her sound guilty of some crime, like dognapping. "I found him wandering around at a rest stop last night. Maybe he just got lost, but it was pretty far from any towns or farms or anything, so I think somebody must have dumped him."

Boone shook his head, and a muscle bunched briefly in his square jaw. "There's a special place in hell for people who do things like that," he said, frowning again. "Looks like he could use a few good meals and a bath."

Quinn smiled then. She didn't know why she did that, because she was still scared shitless of being arrested or sent straight back to Portland without even getting a chance to make her case with Ria. There would be hell to pay with her mom, and then she'd be packed off to summer camp anyway, and all of this would be for nothing. "Yeah," she agreed.

At that moment, she spotted Ria's car, the same unprepossessing compact she'd driven back in Portland, before Uncle Frank died, swing into the lot out by the big Whistle-By Truck Stop sign.

Saved.

"There's my aunt now," Quinn chimed, pointing. She hoped Sheriff Taylor would get back into his cruiser and drive away, satisfied that the runaway was about to be collected by a responsible adult and, therefore, all was well. No point in hanging around; he must have crimes to solve, even way out here.

"I guess I'll stay and have a word with her," Boone Taylor said, making it plain that he wasn't planning to budge until he had a real handle on what was going on. "Why don't you leave the dog with me, go inside and rustle up a bowl of water for him?"

"He doesn't have a leash or anything," Quinn reasoned, though she wanted, and badly, to ask for water for Bones *and* use the restroom.

"I'll keep an eye on him while you're gone" was the sheriff's quietly pragmatic reply. "Go on inside."

Ria, instead of having a straight shot, had to wait while a huge 18-wheeler made a three-acre turn and wound out onto the highway.

Reluctantly, but desperate for the bathroom and worried that Bones might be seriously dehydrated by now, Quinn set the dog down carefully at the sheriff's feet, told the animal she'd be right back, honest to God, no fooling, cross her heart and hope to die, and entered the truck stop.

First stop, the ladies' room. She peed, washed her hands and face at one of three sinks and slowly straightened to take in her reflection in the long mirror affixed to the wall. No wonder the sheriff was hanging around, she thought.

Her brown hair was tangled, her clothes were rumpled and she looked like a fugitive on the run, straight out of an episode of *Dates from Hell* or *Deadly Women* or some other true-crime show.

Okay, Ria was outside, waiting for her. Probably chatting with the sheriff by now.

But she, Quinn, definitely wasn't out of the proverbial woods.

Resigned, she bent over again, cupped her hands under the faucet and splashed more cool water onto her face until she began to feel remotely human.

RIA, BACK BEHIND the wheel of her car, with Quinn in the passenger seat and the scruffy little dog perched on the girl's lap, couldn't stop thinking of all the terrible things that could have happened to her niece between Portland and Three Trees.

"I can't believe you *hitchhiked,*" she said, well aware that she was repeating herself and quite unable to help it.

Quinn leaned her head back and sighed. Her eyes were closed and her lashes, golden-brown like her hair, fluttered slightly. "I was desperate," she said, very softly, very simply. "Meredith was going to send me away to camp, for the whole summer. I would have been older than most of the *counselors,* never

mind the actual campers, all of whom were probably under twelve."

Ria felt a pang of sympathy then, and the sudden,
wild fear inspired by the knowledge that Quinn had
come all this way, mostly in the company of strangers, began to subside. Yes, the child could have been
abducted, raped, murdered, out there on the highway—hitchhikers disappeared all the time, all over
the country. Especially young women.

Still, none of those things had actually *happened,*
thank heaven. Quinn was right here beside her, safe
and sound, if a little the worse for wear.

"Your mother must be beside herself," Ria fretted.
They were passing through the town of Three Trees
by now, and she considered stopping at the big discount chain store for kibble and a collar and leash for
the dog, along with whatever else Quinn happened
to need, of course, but she decided that the errand
could wait awhile.

Quinn lifted one shoulder slightly, as if to shrug,
opened her eyes and turned to face Ria. "Are you
going to send me back?"

"I don't know," Ria said, in all honesty, her hands
tightening on the steering wheel, her palms suddenly
damp. Whatever her own feelings about Meredith
might be, Quinn *was* the woman's daughter. By now,
her half sister had probably called the police, put up
a reward for the girl's safe return, even hired private detectives to aid in the search. In Meredith's
shoes, Ria knew she would have done some or all of

those things herself. "You have to call your mother the minute we get home, though. She'll be frantic."

Quinn sighed. "Annoyed," she conceded. "Definitely inconvenienced. But 'frantic'? No way. After all, the whole point of sending me to camp was to get rid of me."

Troubled, Ria let the remark pass unchallenged. They were passing a string of fast-food franchises just then, so she picked one at random, slowed the car and signaled to turn into the parking lot. "You must be hungry," she said, in belated explanation.

"A little," Quinn said, very softly. "Can we get Bones a burger, too? I have some money in my backpack—" She indicated the seat behind them, where she'd stashed her one piece of luggage, with a small motion of her head. "I can pay you back later."

"That," Ria said, "is the *least* of my worries right now."

They pulled into the drive-through line, and when their turn at the speaker came, a brief consultation was held and then Ria placed the order—a fish fillet sandwich, fries and a diet cola for Quinn, a cheeseburger off the children's menu for the dog.

"Don't you want anything?" Quinn asked, when the person inside had confirmed their requests and specified the amount they'd be expected to pay at the second window.

She sounded so concerned. And so young.

Ria's heart ached. What was going on at home that had caused Quinn to take to the road the way she had? Surely it wasn't just the prospect of summer camp—much as she apparently disliked the idea, her niece had indeed been "desperate" to get away.

Questions, questions, questions.

And the time wasn't right to ask any of them.

"No," Ria replied, finally, with a shake of her head. "Not just now. I'll have something when we get back to the house."

There was a pause, fragile and quivery, nearly tangible.

Then Quinn asked, "Are you mad at me?"

The subtext was *Because if you are, I'm not going to know how to handle it. I need you to be on my side.*

"No," Ria said, for the second time in two minutes.

There were three cars ahead of them, each one stopping at the designated window to hand cash or an ATM card through, in exchange for paper bags with blotches of grease on the sides and cups the size of oil barrels, and Ria considered the rest of her answer carefully.

"I'm not angry," she said, finally. "Not completely anyhow, and not permanently."

Quinn gave a nervous little giggle. "That was ambiguous," she remarked.

"Hitchhiking is a stupid thing to do, Quinn," Ria pointed out, irritated with herself because that was certainly stating the obvious, wasn't it, and she'd sounded so pedantic, too.

"I know that," Quinn answered, and her beautiful green eyes brimmed with tears.

They reached the window then, and Ria paid for the food, accepted the fragrant bag and Quinn's soda, passed them over, not wanting to say more until they were out of the cheerful clerk's earshot.

The dog—Bones, wasn't it?—had been curled up in Quinn's lap until the transaction was made, but as soon as the food was inside the car, he perked right up, putting his grubby little paws on his mistress's chest and sniffing wildly.

Quinn chuckled softly as they drove away, ferreted out the dog's cheeseburger and tore off a tiny piece for him.

He gobbled it right down and, once again, Ria felt a stab of emotion, a poignant, heart-hollowing awareness that that big world out there could be so terribly hard on the helpless, whether they had four legs or two.

While Quinn and the dog consumed their food, taking turns, Ria drove toward home, thoughtful and silent.

There were still a million questions she wanted to ask her niece, yes, but the girl was obviously worn out, half-starved and God only knew what else. Quinn needed time to catch her breath, get her bearings.

When the farm came into view, with its rows and rows of zinnias and gerbera daisies and other brightly colored flowers, Quinn sat up straighter and gave a little gasp. Bones, having devoured his cheeseburger, had settled back onto her lap again and drifted off into a snooze.

"Wow," Quinn said, in a murmur. "It's beautiful!"

Ria's spirits rose by a smidgen, though she was dreading the necessary call to Meredith, had been all along. But she'd worked hard to keep her small operation afloat, weeding and watering, digging and hoeing, planting and replanting, slogging out to the greenhouse through knee-deep snow the previous winter to tend seedlings and sprouts, and the genuine admiration in Quinn's voice meant a lot. Especially since Meredith and most of Ria's friends back in Portland thought the whole enterprise was a hokey waste of time and financial resources.

"Thanks," she said, after clearing her throat, parking the car in the driveway instead of inside the detached garage because she knew she'd have to make a run into town for various supplies before the day was over. "It's lots of work, for not much money, but I love it anyway." She flashed on last night's buffalo visit and added, "Mostly."

A blush threatened, because remembering the bison incident meant remembering Landry Sutton—and the kiss.

And the date for Saturday night. What had she been thinking, saying yes to that? Now, at least, she'd have an excuse to beg off—unexpected company.

Though that particular thought should have been

a comfort, it left Ria feeling strangely disappointed instead.

Quinn, naturally unaware of the whole quandary, opened the car door and got out, setting the dog on the ground with a tenderness that pinched a tender place in Ria's carefully guarded heart. The girl looked around, taking in the famous big sky, the trees, the mountains and foothills that surrounded both Three Trees and its neighbor, Parable, thirty miles away.

"I can see why you love this place," she said, her voice almost reverent as she took it all in. "It's so quiet—so *peaceful.*"

The dog, meanwhile, trotted to the middle of the lawn, nose lowered to the ground, spent a few moments sizing the place up and finally raised one hind leg to christen the resin garden gnome. After that, Bones wagged his stubby tail and turned a perky gaze on Quinn and Ria, patient even though they were lagging behind when there was some serious exploring to do.

"Sorry," Quinn said, very quietly. "About the gnome, I mean."

Ria grinned. "No problem," she said. "Look— he's still smiling."

With a soft laugh, Quinn retrieved her backpack from the rear seat, but her expression turned solemn again as she started toward Ria, who waited for her on the flagstone walkway leading to the front porch.

"Meredith won't let me keep him, you know," she

said. "Bones, I mean. If I have to go back to Portland—"

While Bones continued to check out the yard, Ria
slipped an arm around her niece's shoulders, gave
her a brief squeeze. "Let's not get ahead of ourselves,
okay?" she advised, though she knew Quinn was
right about the dog. Meredith definitely wasn't an
animal person. Heck, most of the time, she wasn't
even a *people* person. For her, everything had to be
at a distinct remove, and preferably sterile—right
down to conceiving a child.

Quinn didn't respond, except to sigh again and
lean on Ria a little as they walked.

"One thing at a time, sweetheart," Ria told the
woman-child beside her. "Our first order of business is to call your mother and let her know you're
all right. After that, we'll play this by ear."

Quinn tried to smile in response, but her mouth
wobbled, and the attempt fell away. Tears filled her
eyes again.

Ria wanted to cry right along with her niece as
she unlocked the front door and opened it, and Quinn
turned to summon the dog. He darted toward them,
still grungy but full of pep now that he'd eaten and
been invited into the house.

Before she'd even set down her purse and dropped
her car keys into the blue bowl on the small table
beside the entrance, Ria made up her mind on one
thing, at least. If Meredith forced Quinn to come
home—as she well might—Bones wasn't going to

any shelter; he was staying right here on the farm, with her.

After she'd shown Quinn around the cottage—there wasn't much to see, since it was so small—the girl ducked into the bathroom to take a quick shower, and Bones went with her.

Ria didn't have a guest room, since she used the second bedroom as an office, but there was a fold-out couch in there, and of course Quinn was welcome to it.

The shower went on, and on, the sound of the running water a distant hum.

Surely the child was clean by now. The dog, too, probably.

Eventually, it occurred to Ria, sitting at her kitchen table making a shopping list, that the task of calling Meredith was going to fall to her. Quinn was obviously in avoidance mode and, besides, the girl's emotions were at a very low ebb.

Nobody knew better than Ria did that dealing with Meredith was an ordeal, even when a person was at her best. So, with a sigh, she got out her address book, looked up Meredith's numbers and dialed, starting with the one for the office.

It wasn't a huge surprise when Meredith's secretary said she was in and put Ria right through.

Meredith's "hello?" was strained, and a little breathless, but the fact that she was at work, with her daughter missing, was telling.

"She's here," Ria said. "Quinn, I mean."

From there, the conversation went straight downhill.

Meredith didn't weep with joy and relief, and she didn't yell, either. "That little brat is going to drive me crazy," she said.

Ria closed her eyes and counted to ten. She'd best fasten her mental seat belt—with Meredith it was always going to be a bumpy ride.

CHAPTER FIVE

HIGHBRIDGE REMOVED THE steaming pie carefully from the oversized wall oven in Landry's kitchen and sniffed the rising steam with prim appreciation.

Landry, who was just passing through on his way to the shower, having been out in the barn doing chores, paused. "That smells good," he said. "Better than good, actually."

Highbridge looked down his nose at his employer, which was quite a trick, since Landry was taller. "It isn't for you," he stated imperiously. "I baked this pie for Ms. Manning, as a peace offering."

Landry frowned, irritated. He loved pie, and this one was fresh from the oven and redolent of his favorite filling, a combination of cherries and rhubarb. Frustrated, knowing at the same time that he'd already lost the battle, if not the entire war, he shoved a hand through his dusty hair and snapped, "You had a run-in with the lady, too?"

"No," Highbridge answered, his tone and manner lofty, his back straight as a fireplace poker. "I intend to take it over to her myself, as soon as it's cooled down a little, as a token of apology—on your behalf."

Landry felt a slight rush of adrenaline—the unpleasant kind. "It just so happens," he said, almost growling the words, "that I've *already* apologized. Furthermore, Ria—*Ms.* Manning—is going to the shindig at the Boot Scoot Tavern this Saturday night." A pause, well savored. "With me."

Highbridge set the pie down on a nearby counter, returned the potholder-mitts neatly to their drawer. His expression was an annoying mixture of intrigued interest and pure skepticism. "You're taking her to the *Boot Scoot Tavern?*" he inquired presently.

Landry's hackles went up, and his pride smarted a little, too. Something about the exchange reminded him, on a nebulously instinctive level, of the unfortunate soiree with Walker Parrish's horse, Misery. "I'd have opted for someplace fancier," he told the butler acidly, "but, lo and behold, it turns out there *isn't* one. Not in Parable County anyway."

"She actually agreed to go out with you?" Highbridge said, as though such a thing were beyond the reach of his imagination. Not that he had much of one in the first place. To the Englishman, dour reality was the only game in town.

Landry might have mentioned the electric kiss he and Ria had shared, if he'd been the type to carry tales. "Don't tell me you have your eye on the lady," he said, with a grin. "She's about half your age, in case you missed that."

For the one and only time since Landry had

known him—he'd sort of inherited Highbridge after the last divorce from Susan—the butler colored up.

Well, two patches of red appeared on his gaunt cheeks anyway.

"I've noticed that," Highbridge said, at some length and with a swell of dignity that raised his chest and bent his shoulders back a little. "I'd like to point out, if I may, that two people can become friends without—" he stopped, pursed his thin lips "—*sex* being a factor."

Landry chuckled, shook his head. "Why, Highbridge," he said, amused rather than angry, "I think you just insulted me."

Which wasn't to say sex wasn't about to become an issue between him and Ria, because he knew it was. The lightning-rod kiss was all the proof he needed; just the memory of it tended to make him go hard if he failed to dismiss it as soon as it surfaced. Or if he *couldn't* dismiss it, which happened a lot, too.

Not that he intended to confide any of this in Highbridge—or anybody else. Some things, damn it, were private.

In addition, as attracted to Ria as Landry was, a part of him did begrudge her the homemade pie. Highbridge was a master cook, but he didn't bake often.

Maybe, Landry reasoned silently, if he offered to deliver the thing personally, she'd be willing to share it. The chances were just as good, of course, that she'd smash it in his face.

A little zip of anticipation coursed through Landry at the thought.

Highbridge, by now ignoring Landry completely, disappeared into the pantry, probably in search of a box. After several years of devoted, if bristly, service, the man was patently predictable.

"I'll take the pie over to Ria's place," Landry announced magnanimously, when his butler reappeared, sure enough, with a cardboard crate in his hands. "Wouldn't mind at all."

Highbridge sniffed. "If you want to give Ms. Manning a pie, sir," he said stiffly, "you'll have to bake it yourself."

With that, he got out the potholders again, placed the still-hot pie in the box, covered the works with a clean dish towel and headed straight for the back door. He grabbed the keys to his ancient Bentley from the hook on the wall and waltzed out of the house without another word.

"Well," Landry grumbled, to the empty kitchen, "*excuse* me."

THE STATELY CAR moved slowly along Ria's driveway, every surface polished to a proper shine, and, watching from her front window, she smiled.

Highbridge.

Ria turned and hurried back to the kitchen to put the kettle on in preparation for tea—the loose-leaf kind her friend preferred. The interstate shouting match with Meredith had left her with jangled nerves, and Quinn's crying fit, which had followed her lengthy shower, had done nothing to ease them.

In the course of that phone call, Meredith had insisted that Quinn *would* attend summer camp, and whether she liked the idea or not was beside the point. It was, she'd raged, the principle of the matter. She couldn't and wouldn't tolerate such flagrant defiance.

At first, Ria had tried to reason with Meredith. Why couldn't Quinn spend the summer right here on the farm, with her? Ria could use the help, she was willing to pay her niece a small salary and the separation would give both Quinn and Meredith a chance to regain their perspective.

But Meredith was having none of it. Quinn had disobeyed her, that was the crux of it all, and Meredith could not abide that. The girl would do as she'd been told, end of discussion.

Ria had finally lost her temper, quietly but tersely suggesting that Meredith was being stubborn, wanting her own way, just like always. Couldn't she understand how upset Quinn must have been, to endanger herself by taking to the open road the way she had? The girl had known the risks and she'd been desperate enough to *take them*—wasn't that proof enough that some changes needed to be made?

Instead of seeing the light, Meredith had retorted hotly that this was a *family matter,* now, wasn't it, and Ria ought to keep her nose out of other people's business.

"Damn it, Meredith, I *am* family!" Ria had shouted, as a complicated slew of old issues surged to the surface of her consciousness. They might have had different mothers, she and Meredith, but she was as much their father's daughter as her half sister was.

She would probably never forget—or forgive—Meredith's chilly response. "Get real," she'd all but snarled. "Your mom was a moneygrubbing tramp, a fortune hunter, a *bimbo* my father picked up in Las Vegas—and he'd never have married her if it hadn't been for you!"

With that, Meredith had slammed down the phone.

Ria had stood, rooted to the kitchen floor, the receiver still gripped in her hand, stricken and enraged and feeling horribly helpless.

Her mom, Evie, *had* been a showgirl in Vegas—one of the best, in fact. What Evie Dayton *hadn't* been was the home-wrecking slut Meredith made her out to be. Evie had been in love with Ria's father—genuinely and deeply—until she succumbed to a heart ailment, only six months after Frank's death.

Since then, Ria had bounced between mourning her mother and her young husband.

Ria's eyes had smarted and her sinuses had ached with the pressure of trying to hold back tears of fury and resounding sorrow. She'd adored her mother, depended upon her, wanted to be like her in so many ways.

The very air around Ria had seemed charged in those moments of lonely reflection, like the uncertain peace following a violent explosion.

Presently, Quinn had appeared in the doorway leading to the short hall, bundled in Ria's red chenille bathrobe, hair wet from washing, face pale, eyes huge, steam billowing all around her.

And there was Bones, damp from a bath of his own, standing small and loyal at the girl's feet.

Ria had simply shaken her head, at a loss for words, and Quinn had vanished into the office-turned-guest-room, Bones scrabbling to keep up with her.

A slamming door.

The heart-wrenching sound of a young girl sobbing without restraint.

Ria had followed her niece to that door, and she was about to knock and ask if she might come in so they could talk, but her hesitation had lengthened, and she'd finally lowered her hand instead, turned and walked slowly away.

Needless to say, Highbridge's unexpected visit was a welcome respite from the emotional storm. He must have taken his time parking the Bentley, because by the time he finally rapped at the back door, as he always did when he came over for tea and a chat, she'd worked through the worst of her angst by pacing and silently ranting at Meredith.

"Come in," Ria said, with a bright smile that trembled on her mouth.

Highbridge, peering at her through the screen door, worked the latch with one hand and entered, bringing a box with him. Whatever was in it smelled like prime acreage in downtown heaven.

"Yum," Ria said, barely able to restrain herself from hugging the man. "You've been baking again."

Highbridge spared her a smile, touchingly shy. Born in a bombed-out section of London shortly after World War II, he'd grown up under continued food and gas rationing, along with several brothers and sisters, his widowed mother struggling all the while to keep the family afloat. Although Highbridge hadn't spoken of being hungry throughout his childhood, Ria knew the privations he and his kin had suffered went far beyond what little he *had* confided.

It was a mark of his esteem for Ria that he'd told her as much as he had, and she'd felt honored by his trust.

"Cherry-rhubarb pie," Highbridge announced, hoisting the box slightly as evidence. "Your favorite."

The kettle began to whistle on the stove top, and Ria went over to take it off the heat. She filled her china teapot with hot water at the sink and let it sit for a few moments, so the boiling contents of the kettle wouldn't crack it open.

She used those few busy moments as an excuse to avert her face, so Highbridge wouldn't see how moved she was. Although her friend had been living well for years, the Bentley notwithstanding, doing without left its mark on people, and the cowboy's butler was no exception. A gift of food, coming from this man, was a special gift indeed.

"What's the occasion?" Ria asked, when she turned around at last, leaning against the counter and folding her arms. "It isn't my birthday—"

Highbridge surveyed her with kindly, knowing eyes. "I've been worried about you," he admitted. He glanced around, looking mildly uneasy. "If I'm interrupting something, though, I'll be out of here in a trice. I should have called before coming over—"

"Nonsense," Ria broke in, with a wave of one hand. "You're not interrupting anything, and you're welcome to stop in whenever the spirit moves you." She felt a surge of warmth for her friend as he stood awkwardly, with the pie box still in his hands. "Sit down, please. Make yourself at home."

"I can't sit down until you do," Highbridge retorted formally. "I *am* a gentleman, after all, and I will not take a seat while a lady remains standing."

Ria laughed and shook her head. "All right, then," she replied, "I'll hurry."

She finished brewing the tea, got out plates and forks and a knife to slice into the pie, carried everything to the table. As an afterthought, she went to the sideboard for a pair of linen napkins.

Finally, they sat.

Ria watched as Highbridge proceeded to cut into the luscious-looking pie, with its golden latticed crust and bubbling-up filling. "So," she said, after sucking in a preparatory breath, "you say you've been worrying about me." A beat passed. "Why?"

"Well, there *was* that incident with the runaway buffalo," Highbridge reminded her, after clearing his throat circumspectly. He scooped out the first slice for Ria, placed it on one of the plates and handed it across the table.

"As you can see," Ria said gently, accepting the fragrant delicacy, "I came through the ordeal quite nicely. Not a scratch on me, in fact."

Highbridge gave one of his ultradignified chuckles. It was impossible to imagine the man belly-laughing, holding his sides, snorting in the attempt to recover his breath after a fit of amusement.

"I am atoning for the unfortunate behavior of my employer," he said, dishing up his own slice of pie. He cleared his throat again, fork poised to dig in, as Ria had already done. "Mr. Sutton tells me he's apologized and—"

Highbridge fell silent and, by now, he looked embarrassed.

"And?" Ria prompted, very gently, to get him going again.

"Is it true that you've agreed to accompany him to a place called the Boot Scoot Tavern?" Highbridge lent the question so much gravity that Ria nearly laughed—with her mouth full. The result would have been disastrous, of course, at least in terms of good table manners.

Carefully, she chewed and swallowed, took a lei-surely sip of her tea. Before she could reply, though, Quinn showed up, accompanied by her faithful companion, Bones.

"Who asked you to go where?" the girl interjected. Her eyes were still puffy from crying and a brief sleep, but she was dressed in clean jeans and a red top, and her hair, now dry, had been brushed to a high shine and tugged back into a ponytail that made her look much younger than her seventeen years.

Highbridge slid back his chair and stood before Ria had a chance to answer. Indeed, before she'd even figured out an appropriate response.

"Highbridge," said the butler, by way of introduction, putting out one hand.

Quinn favored him with a beaming smile, walked over and shook the offered hand confidently. "Quinn Whittingford," she said. She glanced at the table. "Is that pie?"

"Have some?" Ria responded lightly, delighted and relieved that Quinn seemed to have rallied somewhat since the phone conversation with Meredith.

"Sure," Quinn said, finding herself a plate in the cupboard, helping herself to a clean fork from the dishwasher and returning to the table to take a seat.

Only then did Highbridge settle back into his own chair.

"Awesome," Quinn remarked, though whether she was commenting on the pie or the picturesque Highbridge and his elaborate decorum was unclear.

"Quinn is my niece," Ria explained, while the girl delved hungrily into the generous slice of pie in front of her. The fast-food lunch had obviously worn off.

"That explains the resemblance," Highbridge said, watching Quinn with a sort of tender amusement.

Ria, who did not see a resemblance, refrained from comment.

Quinn slipped Bones a small piece of piecrust, which he gobbled down quickly.

"This is seriously good," Quinn said. "The pie, I mean." Then she turned dancing eyes on Ria. "Back to my original question. Somebody asked you out. Who was it and where are you going?"

Highbridge chuckled again, took a sip from his teacup.

Ria fixed her niece with a mock glower. "What if I said it was none of your business, young lady?" she said.

Quinn beamed, plunging her fork into the succulent filling of the pie again. Her shoulders rose slightly, in a shruglike motion. "I'd find out anyway," she responded merrily. She swallowed and then peered at Ria across the table, as though searching a crime scene for clues. "You've met someone," she insisted. "Who is he? What's he like?"

Ria opened her mouth, closed it again.

She'd basically accepted a dare by agreeing to go out with Landry Sutton on Saturday night—it wasn't an actual *date* or anything. But how was she supposed to explain all that to a wide-eyed seventeen-year-old with a young girl's penchant for romance?

"He's—a neighbor," Ria finally replied, after exchanging a glance with Highbridge.

"Is he hot?" Quinn asked, her tone idle, matter-of-fact.

Highbridge choked on his tea but recovered admirably. "Hot?" he echoed.

"A hunk," Quinn translated amiably.

Highbridge looked baffled.

Ria, who was trying hard to come off as nonchalant, felt a surge of residual passion. For a moment—probably longer—it was as though Landry had just now kissed her; she felt the weight and warmth of his mouth on hers, the bold search of his tongue, the hard fire of his body against hers. The time-space continuum collapsed, and just as quickly reassembled itself again with a fierce jolt.

Was Landry Sutton "hot"? A *hunk?* Did porcupines have quills? Did squirrels climb trees?

"I haven't thought about that," Ria lied.

"Oh, please," Quinn countered, grinning.

Ria looked to Highbridge for help, but evidently, he wasn't in Sir Galahad mode at the moment. Either that or he was stumped for an answer.

"More pie?" he asked, after a moment of wired silence.

Bones rose on his hind legs, next to Quinn's chair, and rested his forepaws on her blue-jeaned thigh, clearly begging.

She laughed and gave him another snippet of piecrust.

"No, thanks, I'm good," Quinn told Highbridge, in belated reply. She smiled, pushed back her chair and stood, empty plate in hand. She set her dish and fork in the sink. "Would it be okay if Bones and I went outside for a look around?"

Ria nodded, distracted. "Sure," she said.

When the back door closed behind the girl and the dog, Highbridge cleared his throat yet again and remarked, with only slight reservation, "Delightful child."

"Yes," Ria agreed. "She is."

"You weren't expecting her," Highbridge guessed, his tone and expression mild.

"No," Ria admitted. "But I'd love it if she could stay here with me, at least for the summer."

Highbridge raised one eyebrow. "That isn't possible?"

"Her mother objects," Ria told him.

"Oh," Highbridge answered, and said nothing more, because he wasn't the type to interfere in private matters.

Family matters, Ria thought, recalling the verbal tussle with Meredith. Her shoulders immediately tensed up again.

"I've kept you long enough," Highbridge concluded, moments later, when it was clear there wasn't a lot more to say. He stood, fussing with the remaining pie and the attendant utensils. "I'll be on my way."

"Let me do that," Ria protested good-naturedly, taking over the table-clearing job. "Do you really have to leave so soon?"

"Neighborly visits, like pie, are best served in limited portions," Highbridge said wisely, with a slight twinkle in his eyes.

Ria smiled, rummaged through the many simple glass vases housed in one of the cupboards, found one, added water and led the way to the back door, waiting while Highbridge placed the pie carefully in her refrigerator.

"At least let me reciprocate with a few flowers," she told her friend.

Highbridge nodded, quietly pleased, and they walked toward the fields together. Ria, using the small set of clippers she carried in her shirt pocket, cut generous bouquets of zinnias and daisies, added carnations for pizzazz, thrust them all into the vase.

Just holding such beauty in her hands made Ria's heart sing, reassured her that life was good and Somebody was in charge, however confusing things might seem at times.

She wedged the thick bouquet into the vase and handed the works to Highbridge, with a smile.

"You," she said softly, "are such a good friend."

Highbridge took the vase full of zinnias and daisies and carnations, admired the display for a few moments before meeting Ria's gaze. "Thank you," he said moderately. With that, he turned to walk away.

Ria watched him until he'd settled himself behind the wheel of his vintage car. The whole picture gave her an odd, brief sense that she'd slipped through a wrinkle in the ordinary structure of things, into a realm of grace and tea and flowers that was, regrettably, long gone.

Highbridge gave the car horn a sedate toot, turned the machine around in a graceful sweep of polished fenders and shining chrome and set off up the road.

"I think the old guy's a little sweet on you," Quinn said, startling Ria, who hadn't heard the girl's approach. Bones, one row over, was chasing a butterfly, secure in the knowledge that he didn't have a chance of catching it.

Ria chuckled and shook her head.

Quinn elbowed her gently. "Tell me about the neighbor," she urged. "The guy who's taking you out, I mean."

Ria sighed. "His name is Landry Sutton," she said. "And he's not 'taking me out.' We're trying to be friends, that's all."

"How's that working out?" Quinn asked, bending to admire a red zinnia.

"I'm not sure," Ria replied honestly. Almost sadly. Highbridge and his Bentley were out of sight by then, but she kept her eyes on the billows of road dust they'd left behind.

Quinn's tone was incredibly gentle, remarkably

wise. "It's time," she said softly. "I know you loved Uncle Frank. I can understand how much you must miss him, even if I am only seventeen, but he's gone, Ria, and you're still young. You need a husband and children, a family."

Ria's throat thickened painfully, and the backs of her eyes burned, though there were no tears. *Husband—children—family.* The buzzwords of her soul, the things she wanted most in all the world, had always wanted. Was she wrong to long for that kind of love? Hopelessly out of date, politically incorrect?

"Nobody has everything, Quinn," she said, very quietly. She'd loved Frank so much, with every fiber of her being, in fact, and she'd lost him. Miscarrying their just-conceived baby when he'd died doing the thing he'd *lived* to do—fighting an apartment fire with his colleagues, defeating the destructive force, saving people and animals from death, only to perish himself.

Frank had been proud of his ten-year career as a firefighter, and justifiably so.

Still, when that blazing roof finally collapsed, there had been no one to save *him*.

"You deserve to be happy, Aunt Ria," Quinn insisted, and then she burst into tears. She'd always been too empathetic, too perceptive, for her own good. "You've got this great farm—I can tell you love the life you're living. But it isn't enough, is it?"

Ria swallowed, shook her head in glum admission. Quinn was right—even with blessings too numerous to count—it *wasn't* enough. While she wouldn't regard her time on earth as a failure if she never had the happy home and healthy family she longed for, she knew she'd feel deep regret when the end came.

Smiling now, having wiped away her tears with the knuckles of both hands, Quinn hugged Ria.

"Give it a shot," the woman-child urged, in a whisper. *"Take a chance."*

Ria finally collected herself enough to sniffle— had she cried, too, without even being aware of it?— lengthened her spine and pushed back her shoulders. "We'll see," she said. "In the meantime, let's go to town and do a little shopping."

Quinn looked concerned for a moment, as though she might be about to remind her aunt that she had little or no money, but then she gave a silent yet visible sigh and raised and lowered her shoulders. "Okay," she said.

Like Highbridge's visit and gift of pie, the small expedition gave both Ria and Quinn a lift. For a little while, at least, they could drive over country roads with the windows rolled down and the CD player blasting oldies at top volume.

Bones seemed content to stay behind, curled up on a folded blanket in a corner of the kitchen, a bowl of fresh water nearby.

At the giant discount establishment out on the highway, Ria and Quinn selected kibble and a bed for Bones, along with a leash and collar and some treats and toys. Since these purchases filled the cart Ria was pushing, Quinn returned to the front of the store for a second one.

The girl seemed to delight in choosing jeans and tops, sneakers and work boots, socks and underwear—at least partly, Ria suspected, because she knew her mother wouldn't approve of "cheap" garments. While sparing with her time and attention, when it came to her daughter at least, Meredith believed in "standards," wanted it known that *she* didn't patronize companies accused of running overseas sweatshops.

Oh, no. Meredith bought all of Quinn's clothes in high-end department stores, with the help of a personal shopper. The tailored suits Meredith herself wore were typically made by harried Hispanic, Russian or Asian women, recent immigrants all, working out of a cramped storefront in a part of Portland where windows and doors were barred and even the police were reluctant to visit, once the sun went down.

So much for boycotting sweatshops.

"This is fun," Quinn confided later, as they loaded bags and more bags into the trunk of Ria's car. But the glow had gone off her smile when she settled into the passenger seat, her shoulders dropping into a slight but noticeable slump. "Too bad Meredith's probably going to ruin everything."

Since she privately agreed—ruining things was what Meredith did best—Ria saw no need to comment. She fastened her seat belt, put on her sunglasses and turned the key in the ignition.

Quinn picked up the conversational ball. "If she'd just let me stay, I could work for you, on the farm, I mean. Pay you back for these clothes and the stuff you bought for Bones…."

Ria blinked a few times, afraid she'd cry. Her throat was tight—too tight for speech.

Quinn was quiet for a while. Then, softly, she said, "Aunt Ria?"

Ria managed a croaky "yes?" keeping her chin high and her eyes on the road. She wasn't sure how much the sunglasses would do to hide her emotions.

Quinn went on, her voice barely above a whisper. "If I have to go back to Portland—if I get sent to camp—will you keep Bones for me? He'd be safe with you, and I think he'd like being a farm dog."

That did it. The dam broke.

Ria pulled the car to the side of the road, shifted into Park, flipped on her blinkers and rested her forehead on the steering wheel. Her shoulders shook as great, silent sobs seized her.

CHAPTER SIX

IF RIA HAD made a list of the people she did *not* want to see her sitting alongside the highway in her dull and dusty car, having a personal meltdown while her poor niece looked on in helpless dismay, it would have been a long one, and Landry Sutton would fill the number one slot.

So, naturally, he materialized within moments, as though he and his big truck had been conjured by some hidden magician, tall and strong and solidly *present,* seeming to take up more than his share of space as he leaned to peer in at her through the driver's-side window, a worried frown creasing his forehead, his eyes slightly narrowed.

His fine mouth shaped the words *Are you all right?*

Ria's odd, silent sobbing fit was beginning to subside, thank heaven, but she was a long way from "all right." She rolled down the car window, knowing Landry would open the door if she didn't. He was firmly planted where he stood, and obviously not going anywhere.

While she tried to catch her breath, summon up

some shred of dignity by staring at the dashboard, Quinn bent forward in her seat in order to see around Ria and studied Landry before asking, on a single breath, "Is that *him?*"

Ria could only hope Landry hadn't heard the girl's question. If he had, he'd surely guess that he'd recently been the topic of discussion, and he might jump to the wrong conclusion.

"Having car trouble?" Landry asked mildly, as, out of the corner of one puffy eye, Ria saw him straighten. She knew he was still looking at her, though—she could feel his gaze in every nerve ending, every pore.

Ria shook her head, forced herself to meet those cornflower-blue eyes, darkening shade by shade as he watched her, waited for an answer. "No," she said, at once embarrassed and relieved that she'd regained enough equilibrium to speak at all. "We're just—"

She fell silent, stricken and confused and more than a little frightened—not of Landry, but of herself. In all her practical, left-brained life, she'd never fallen apart in quite the same way.

Certainly, she'd grieved a deep, soul-chafing grief after Frank died in the apartment fire—she'd loved him as completely as she'd known how to love anyone— and her season of mourning had lasted for a long, long time. Still, she'd always held herself together, when there were other people around, anyway.

For Ria, grief was a private thing, silent and subterranean, a dark night of the soul necessarily endured alone.

"Just what?" Landry finally prompted.

Bless her, Quinn finally came to the rescue, her tone cheerily matter-of-fact. "I think I upset Aunt Ria when I asked her if she'd take care of my dog—if I have to go back to Oregon, that is," she told Landry, leaning forward in the passenger seat to make eye contact. "I'm sure she'll be fine in a little while."

Ria rested her forehead against the steering wheel again and closed her eyes, though this time she didn't go mental. Instead, she was mortified.

"Okay," Landry agreed hoarsely, but he didn't sound convinced.

"I'll drive us home," Quinn announced brightly, pushing open her car door and stepping out. "I have my license."

"That's probably a good idea," Landry admitted, but he didn't move to walk away; Ria knew that without looking. She would have felt a shift in the very atmosphere if he'd gone, an actual void in the place where he'd been, like a major piece missing from a vast jigsaw puzzle.

Knowing it would be irresponsible to insist on driving in her condition, Ria got out of the car, let Quinn take her place behind the wheel. And then she just stood there, willing starch into her knees, not quite trusting her shaky legs to support her as far as the other door.

"Ria and I will be right behind you, in the truck,"

Landry said. The decision had obviously been made, and he didn't expect an argument.

Ria felt a swift flicker of annoyance, and took that as a good sign.

Quinn looked at Landry and then, with questions gathering in her eyes, at Ria. *Well?*

Ria nodded, the signal that she'd be okay riding home with Landry. "You know the way back to the farm, right?" she asked her niece.

Quinn rolled her eyes and grinned good-naturedly. "Sure," she replied. "I have a great sense of direction, you know."

"See you there," Landry told Quinn.

Then, with no warning at all, he lifted Ria into his arms and *carried* her back to his truck, seated her in the passenger seat and stood still for a long moment, studying her with pensive concentration.

"I'm really all right," Ria insisted. "Truly."

"You don't *look* all right," Landry replied flatly. "Buckle your seat belt."

With that, he shut the door and strode around to the driver's side, climbed in.

Ria, who'd left her purse in her car, suppressed an urge to grab hold of the rearview mirror, slant it her way and check her appearance. Did she look crazy? Sick?

She pursed her lips. She was *neither* of those things, thank you very much, and she wanted, in the worst way, to make sure Landry Sutton knew it, knew she wasn't a weak woman, prone to spontane-ous nervous breakdowns. Far from it.

"Who's the kid?" Landry asked presently, follow-ing as Quinn pulled carefully out onto the highway.

For some reason, the question prickled a little. "'The kid,'" Ria replied stiffly, keeping her eyes on the car ahead, *her* car, which, it seemed to her, lacked imagination and style, "is my niece, Quinn Whit-tingford."

Landry sighed audibly, but said nothing.

Ria was amazed to find herself rattling on, when silence would have been the most prudent course. She'd already made a fool of herself, and talking only increased the risk that she'd do it again.

Still, the words spilled out. "Quinn's seventeen. She ran away from home, and on her way here—to Three Trees, I mean—she found a little dog at a rest stop, evidently abandoned. If her mother forces her to come back home, which is a ninety-nine-percent probability, Bones will be dumped at some shelter within the first five minutes." Ria willed herself to shut up, found that she couldn't. There was some-thing freeing about confiding all this stuff to Landry, though heaven only knew why that should be the case, given their usual antipathy to each other.

Even more perplexing, her body had thrilled shamelessly to being carried in strong, protective arms, was *still* reverberating with odd sensations.

"So, anyway," she rushed on, aware of a need to be held in those same arms, just held, until she was herself again, and absolutely determined not to give in to that need, "Quinn asked if I'd take care of Bones, if she had to leave, and I'd already planned on it, but for some reason—for some reason—"

At last, Ria was running out of steam. A blush pulsed in her cheeks, and she swallowed miserably, audibly.

"For some reason," Landry said quietly, even gently, "you let down your guard, and the floodgates opened. It happens, Ria. In fact, it was probably good for you."

She stole a glance at him, savored his profile, the way the slight breeze coming in through his partly open window ruffled his hair, the strength of his hands, resting on the wheel, the almost Grecian perfection of his features.

"You don't think I'm crazy?" she asked, without intending to. The question was reflexive, and it sneaked out from behind her usual facade of sturdy pragmatism, fierce independence and unrelenting competence.

He looked her way, just briefly, and she saw a smile dance in his eyes before landing, almost imperceptibly, at one corner of his mouth.

A voice in her head warned, *Don't think about his mouth!* She'd already lost the best part of a night's sleep thinking about the man's mouth—and other parts of his anatomy—and she didn't want to repeat the experience.

Landry spoke solemnly, and with a certainty that

seemed to be rooted in the marrow of his bones. What would it be like to be so damn sure of everything?

"I think," he said, "that you're a flesh-and-blood woman, trying too hard to be too strong too much of the time. And right now I'd like nothing better than to lie down with you, somewhere dark and cool and quiet, and hold you close."

Fresh fire shot through Ria as though fired from a flame gun, burning in her veins, sizzling along the surface of her flesh, causing an achy, spilling sensation of expansion between her pelvic bones. Her reactions were so elemental, so primitive, that she wouldn't consciously register the fact that she'd just been thinking much the same thing only moments before until a lot later. When she would wonder, not for the first time, if Landry could read her mind.

Up ahead, Quinn signaled to make the turn onto Ria's twisting driveway.

Landry signaled, too, glanced Ria's way, gave a low chuckle and shook his head slightly. "No snappy comeback?" he teased, his tone husky, intimate, as though they were already lying in that "dark and cool and quiet place" he'd mentioned. She could almost feel his caresses, the seeking touch of his mouth as he slowly peeled away both her clothing *and* her inhibitions. "I'm surprised. Maybe even a little disappointed."

She said nothing; all her concentration went into

getting across the verbal and emotional mine field in front of her.

Quinn parked the car next to the house, while Landry brought the truck to a stop out front.

Ria rallied enough to unsnap her seat belt, shove open her door and say tersely, "Thanks for the ride." Then she fairly leaped to the ground, keeping her back to Landry, struggling awkwardly to shut the door behind her without turning around.

Something in his gruff chuckle made it clear that he knew he'd gotten to her again, just as he had with that outrageous kiss the day before, that the score had, once again, gone up a few notches. In his favor, of course.

"See you Saturday night," he said, in an easy drawl.

And then he drove away, leaving Ria simmering in her own juices. First, she'd had an emotional short circuit—or something—and Landry had turned up before she could pull herself together. He'd *carried her to his truck,* for pity's sake, and she'd *let him,* like some moony, eyelash-batting heroine in a silent movie, and then, *then* she'd sat there, like a lump, putting up with—no, *enjoying*—what could only be described as a kind of foreplay.

"That was the guy, right?" Quinn asked eagerly, having sprinted across the yard to meet Ria at the base of the walk. "The one you're going out with?"

Ria sighed. "Yes," she admitted wearily, having neither the will nor the strength to prevaricate.

Quinn's face softened, and she slipped an arm around Ria's waist as they headed toward the front steps. Inside the house, Bones was barking excitedly at their return. "He is *seriously* hot," Quinn said. "I mean, *wow*—"

In spite of her now-jittery mood, Ria had to laugh. "'He' has a name—it's Landry Sutton. And, yes, he *is* good-looking. But I think—well—he's sort of—out of my league." Seeing a protest brewing in Quinn's eyes, Ria hastened to explain as she unlocked the front door and pushed it open. "He's more sophisticated than I am, that's all. More *experienced* and—" She sighed as Bones launched himself at both of them, overjoyed. "I'm getting this all wrong, aren't I?"

Quinn bent, hoisted the little dog into her arms and nuzzled his furry neck while he squirmed with delight. "Yes," she answered. "You are. It isn't as if you *aren't* sophisticated yourself. *You're* experienced, too, *and* good-looking. Look in a mirror sometime, will you? You're *gorgeous,* is all."

"And you're prejudiced," Ria said, touched.

"You said he was out of your league," Quinn reminded her. "And that's so not true."

They gravitated toward the kitchen, the nerve center of any country house, and Ria dropped into her wicker rocking chair, next to a tall window, instinctively kicking off her shoes, breathing in the sight of her flower fields, soothed, as always, by the seemingly endless rows of vibrantly colored blossoms.

Quinn waited, still holding Bones in the curve of one arm, her free hand resting on her hips. By her expression, it was clear that she wasn't going to let the subject drop until Ria gave her a satisfactory answer.

"All right," Ria conceded, feeling an odd combination of invigoration and complete exhaustion, "I take it back. He's not out of my league."

It was true that she didn't feel inferior to Landry, which was probably what Quinn was fretting over. Ria liked and respected herself, was proud of the road she'd traveled, of the way she'd overcome so many obstacles along the way. Just the same, Landry definitely knew how to get past her primary defenses, how to touch her in her most vulnerable places with just a word or a glance. The unsettling truth was, she'd *wanted* everything he'd offered, and more.

Still wanted it.

If Quinn hadn't been visiting, if they could have been alone, even for a few hours, Ria knew she wouldn't have let Landry drive away; she'd have asked him inside, led him through the quiet little house and straight to her bed. She'd have lain with him, taken sweet shelter in his embrace, not resisting or hesitating but *reveling* in that first, small surrender, knowing all the while that it was only the beginning, that another giving in, wild and exultant and free, awaited them both in the heartbeat just beyond the inevitable moment when their mouths found each other.

"Okay, then," Quinn said, as though something

might or might not have been settled. "You just sit there and rest up. Bones and I will bring in the stuff from the car."

Ria, not wanting to be alone with her thoughts, insisted on helping with the task, and she soon realized she'd been right to do it. Physical activity nearly always untangled her thoughts, cleared her head.

And nothing jumbled her mental processes like an encounter with Landry Sutton.

After the purchases had been brought in and put away, Ria brewed a pot of tea while Quinn popped the top on a diet soda.

Just as they were about to sit down, take a break, the wall phone rang, a shrill jangle in the quiet heat of the afternoon.

Quinn and Ria looked at each other—a strange premonition prickled its way along the length of Ria's spine, and she sensed that her niece had felt something similar, because the girl went completely still for a few moments.

Then, with visible bravery, Quinn picked up the telephone receiver, with its twisty, overstretched cord. "Ria Manning's residence," she chimed, with a determined smile. But her whole face changed instantly, and her voice was shaky when she responded to whatever the caller had said. "Oh. Meredith. Hi."

Ria braced herself. She'd been thinking of heading outside to do some weeding and watering, but Quinn's expression and the sound of her half sister's name changed everything.

"Sure, she's here," Quinn said, after listening for a while. "Is something wrong? You sound strange—"

A blast of unintelligible words erupted on Meredith's end of the line, a kind of static, and Quinn looked at Ria, held out the receiver and waited mutely for her aunt to take over.

Ria got up from her chair, crossed the kitchen and spoke into the telephone, her voice calm and reasonable, her insides churning again. "Meredith? What's going on?"

Meredith's response stunned Ria. It was an outburst, an onslaught, almost a tangible force. And she was crying.

Meredith, made of far sterner stuff than her younger sister, *never* cried. Now a choked, soblike sound escaped her, raw and, for all the distance between them, both literal and figurative, painful to hear. "It's all collapsing!" Meredith cried, nearly hysterical. "Ria, everything's gone—*gone*—" She broke off to sob again, and the sound was terrible. "I had no idea what was really going on—I didn't know—I could shoot myself—"

"Meredith," Ria broke in firmly but gently. "Take a slow, deep breath. Take your time, get your bearings—you're not making sense."

Maybe, she thought, recalling her own recent meltdown while she waited for Meredith to get it together, *you and your sister aren't as different from each other as you'd like to believe, Ria Manning.*

Getting the story took a while, because Meredith kept stopping to swear or sob or cry out in pure frustration, but the gist of it was, the problem in the Seattle office was the least of Meredith's concerns. She'd just been confronted with irrefutable proof that two of her most trusted financial advisers had been quietly stealing from company accounts for years. Worse, even though they'd presented Meredith with federal and state tax forms right along, and she'd signed them all, they hadn't made the required payments. Since they'd kept the delinquent notices from her and fielded the phone calls, Meredith hadn't suspected a thing.

Now investors were clamoring for their money, and Meredith's legal advisers had strongly suggested shutting down all six of the firm's offices for an immediate and comprehensive audit. Creditors she hadn't even known about threatened to freeze her private accounts, as well.

At least she wasn't homeless. Yet.

Ria, listening, sank into her desk chair, trembling, the phone cord stretched to its limits, the receiver pressed so hard against her ear that it was starting to hurt. "What can I do?" she asked, when she was fairly sure Meredith had gotten it all out.

Meredith gave a bitter little laugh. "Do? What can you *do?*"

"Isn't that why you called?" Ria persisted gently. "To ask for help?"

Her sister was quiet for a long moment. Then,

with uncharacteristic meekness, she admitted, "I'm hoping that—well—that Quinn can stay with you for a while. Until—until things settle down, I mean."

Ria closed her eyes briefly, hurting for this sister who would not, even now, let her in. "Of course Quinn can stay here," she said carefully. Her niece, pale and wide-eyed, brightened a little when she heard this. "But, Meredith, you must need— What about living expenses—groceries—things like that?"

Meredith was immediately back on the defensive. "I'll manage," she said coldly.

How? Ria wondered. She certainly didn't have enough money to cover the company's back taxes, but she wasn't broke, either. She'd saved and invested and even though the farm wasn't earning a profit yet, and she still had to be careful with her spending, she could certainly afford to help Meredith out financially. Before she could find words to say any of this, though, Meredith was talking again.

"Just look after Quinn," she said. "Please."

"Certainly," Ria answered. "You'll let me know if—if—"

"I don't want your money, Ria," Meredith broke in. All vulnerability was gone now. "When I asked for your help, if you'll remember, you turned me down." She paused. "Tell Quinn I'll be in touch, probably by email."

"All right," Ria said lamely. What else was there to say?

Without so much as a goodbye, Meredith hung up.

"She's in trouble, isn't she?" Quinn asked, pale again.

"Yes," Ria replied. Some things couldn't, *shouldn't* be sugarcoated. Quinn was a young woman, after all, not a child, and this disaster was bound to affect her seriously, now and in the future. So Ria told the girl what she knew, which wasn't a great deal, adding nothing and leaving nothing out, and Quinn listened intently, intelligently, nodding once or twice to show that she understood.

"But I get to stay here, with you? With Bones?"

"Yes," Ria repeated. "For the time being anyway. Until Meredith gets a handle on things."

For a long moment, they were both quiet, juggling their own emotions.

Then, Quinn straightened her shoulders and beamed. "I get to stay here with you," she repeated, seeming to savor the thought.

Quinn glanced at the window over the sink. "There's still plenty of light," she said, with a brave resolution that stirred Ria's heart. "Let's go out there and get some work done."

Ria studied her niece for a few moments before giving a slow nod of agreement. "You know what?" she said, trying to shake off the echo of Meredith's words looping through her mind. *When I asked for your help—you turned me down.*

"What?" Quinn responded, the screen door creaking on its hinges as she tugged it open, ready to go.

"You've got backbone, Quinn Whittingford," Ria answered, meaning it. "And I'm very, very proud of you."

WHEN HE GOT HOME, the encounter with Ria very much on his mind, Landry fed his horses, checked on Bessie and the calf, placidly munching good Montana grass in the pasture, and decided he had too much free time. In Chicago, he'd worked sixteen to eighteen hours a day, six or seven days a week—one of the reasons, he supposed, that his chronically rocky marriage had finally crashed, burned and permanently disintegrated—and he wasn't cut out to be idle, not mentally, not physically.

Reluctant to go inside the house, he walked around the perimeter instead, taking in the solid parts, the ones with walls and windows and a sturdy roof overhead, but over half of the place was unfinished, framed in, but enclosed only by huge sheets of thick plastic and heavy tarps to keep out the weather.

He reckoned a shrink—or a mystic—would probably say the structure was a reflection of his psyche, if not his soul, and he wouldn't be half-wrong.

Landry sighed, shoved a hand through his hair. He was double-minded, that was his problem—part rancher, part type-A money mogul—with one foot in the old life and one in the new.

It was time, as both his brother Zane and Highbridge had been saying for a long while, to make a choice and stick by it. Go or stay. Be a rancher or head back to the city and the art of the deal.

Both scenarios had their upsides—he loved the peace and the open space of the ranch, but he missed the pace of city living, too, the way it used him up, left him with little or no time to think about his personal life.

Until today, Landry hadn't believed he was on the fence at all, whatever Zane and Highbridge thought. He was *there*, wasn't he? In Parable County, Montana, raising buffalo, keeping horses, riding bulls and bucking broncs when he got the chance and driving the requisite big truck?

He was over Susan, had been since before he married her that first time. The unflattering truth? She'd been just another status symbol, a trophy, like his collection of classic cars, his tailored suits, his expensive watch and all the rest of it.

Susan was a smart woman, as well as a world-class beauty. She must have known all along that he didn't love her, and that had to have hurt. Okay, so he hadn't been the best husband; he'd never been unfaithful—that would have meant he was like his father, and, as motives went, it was admittedly dicey. He'd showered Susan with expensive gifts, taken her on glamorous vacations, dutifully attended her endless charity events even though he hated being stuffed into a monkey suit and making small talk with her rich friends.

They'd had next to nothing in common, he and

Susan—except for Ingersoll Investments, of course—and for all his success, deep down, he'd still been a waitress's kid, a gypsy, always feeling as though he was one step ahead of some calamity. Home, when they had one, was a rented trailer, a cheap motel room, somebody's living room floor.

Susan, on the other hand, had been raised in mansions and penthouses. She'd attended the best boarding schools, with the sons and daughters of senators and even presidents, sailed all seven seas on yachts, flown all over the world in private jets.

For all that, she'd actually loved him. She'd wanted to have his babies. Once upon a time anyway. Basically, he'd given her nothing she couldn't have gotten for herself—nothing at all. Instead, he'd used her.

I'm sorry, he told Susan silently, over the months and the miles, over the intangible but real wreckage the two of them had left in their combined wake. Fat lot of good being sorry now did, he reflected.

High above his head, above the clouds and the orbiting space junk and the ozone layer, stars were beginning to pop out, stars so old and so far away that some of them had been dead for millions of years. Still, their light traveled on, silvery and ghostlike, and bright enough to chart the routes of ships and airplanes.

"Sir?" The voice came out of the twilight.

Highbridge.

"What?" Landry asked, none too graciously, though he was actually grateful for the distraction.

The butler cleared his throat, approached with tentative steps. "Are you quite all right?"

"Why wouldn't I be all right?"

Highbridge didn't even flinch at Landry's abrupt tone, which only made him feel more like an asshole than he had before. "Well," the older man ventured stalwartly, "you generally dine at six, and it's already seven-thirty."

Landry gave a ragged burst of laughter. "That's why you're worried? Because I'm late for supper?"

"I didn't say I was worried," Highbridge pointed out.

"Aren't you supposed to be off duty by now?" Landry walked slowly toward the man he'd hired, after the most recent divorce, when Susan made it clear that she no longer required the services of a butler. It hadn't seemed to bother her that Highbridge had been a faithful family employee for twenty-plus years—she was ready to dump him and move on.

"Quite," Highbridge admitted, somewhat huffily. He straightened his perfectly straight string tie and stiffened his shoulders. Turned to walk away.

"Highbridge," Landry said, with quiet respect. "I owe you an apology."

You and Susan and a lot of other people.

"Nonsense, sir," Highbridge protested, still walking. With those long legs of his, clad in his usual formal suit of clothes, he resembled a crane doing a bad imitation of a penguin. "Your meal is warming in the oven."

Landry caught up, walked alongside the other man. "That's good," he said. "Thanks."

Highbridge stopped when they rounded the corner of the house, such as it was, and regarded Landry with solemn patience. "There's no need to thank me, sir. It's my job to prepare your meals."

Actually, it *wasn't* Highbridge's job to feed him, but they'd had this discussion many times, to no avail, so Landry let it pass. "I wish you wouldn't call me 'sir,'" he said, and that wasn't new, either.

"Wish to your heart's content," Highbridge replied, with consummate dignity and the merest hint of a lilt in his voice. "Sir."

Landry laughed. "Damn, you're cussed," he said.

Highbridge favored him with a little bow. "Thank you," he replied, serious as a heart attack. Then he sucked in a breath and added, "If that will be all, Mr. Sutton, this is bingo night, and it's my turn to drive. Miss Cleo will have my head on a spike if I'm late picking her up."

Landry pictured his butler in the basement of some church or lodge hall, bent over a row of bingo cards, the kind with little sliders that opened and closed over the numbers, and smiled at the paradox that was Highbridge.

"Say hello to Cleo for me," he said as Highbridge headed resolutely for his polished Bentley.

Highbridge didn't answer.

Inside, Landry washed up at the kitchen sink, took his dinner from the oven and peeled back the tinfoil. Lasagna, one of his favorites, along with garlic bread and, waiting in the refrigerator, a green salad.

If he'd followed the dictates of his mind, Landry wouldn't have eaten at all. His body, though, demanded fuel.

So he sat down at the table, with a can of very cold beer, and ate his lonely supper. His stomach eventually registered gratitude, though he never actually *tasted* a single bite of any of it. With grim amusement, he recalled Susan's Zen phase, a few years back, when she'd meditated regularly, burned incense and insisted on doing everything "mindfully," from brushing her teeth to making love. During that all too brief interlude—Susan was nothing if not changeable—Landry had slowed down a little himself, not been quite so driven, and he'd enjoyed experiencing the much-touted present moment. Especially when sex was involved.

Ah, yes, sex. How long had it been? Better not to calculate.

Landry sighed and, finished with his meal, cleared the table, rinsed his plate and utensils, stowed them in the dishwasher, then crushed the empty beer can and dropped it into the recycling bin.

After that, he found himself at a loss for something to do.

It was too early to hit the sack, he wasn't much for watching TV and he felt too jangled to read. So he prowled the inside of the house in much the same way as he'd done the outside, earlier in the evening.

He took in the massive living room, with its beamed cathedral ceiling, the hardwood floors, the natural rock fireplace and the floor-to-ceiling windows. The well-equipped bar in the corner didn't call to him, so Landry let his gaze drift past it without pausing.

There were a few pieces of mismatched furniture, stuff that had seemed fine in his Chicago penthouse but looked downright pretentious here in rural Montana.

The walls were bare—Susan had laid claim to most of the photographs and all of the paintings— and the floors always felt cold, whatever the season, when he walked across them without boots.

Beyond that echoing expanse lay Landry's bedroom, as cell-like as its counterpart when it came to decoration, but spacious, too. Here, there were built in bookshelves, the fireplace was as big as the one in the next room and one whole wall was composed of tall, arched windows. The master bath was downright hedonistic, with an enormous tub, a fancy shower stall with multiple sprayers, intricately designed mosaic-tile floors and marble countertops, but, like other finished parts of the house, it had all the warmth of a narrow scrub-brush canyon on a winter night.

Yep, Landry concluded, it was time to make some

decisions. Chicago or Montana. The fast lane or the slow one.

Walk away from Ria Manning, once and for all— or get her into bed and see what, if anything, happened after that...

Fireworks or fizzle?

There was, of course, only one way to find out for sure.

CHAPTER SEVEN

THE FOLLOWING SATURDAY morning, Ria was up and dressed before dawn, in anticipation of the weekly farmers' market, held at the fairgrounds over in Parable, running from early spring to late in the fall.

Content, finding peace in routine, she puttered, letting Bones out and then, after a few minutes, in again. She fed the dog, and made a cup of coffee for herself, debating whether to let Quinn sleep a little longer or go ahead and rouse her to help cut zinnias and daisies and carnations, place them in plastic buckets and load the works into the back of the elderly pickup truck parked in the old tractor shed.

With luck, it would be a busy day, what with making the thirty-mile drive to Parable, setting up in the usual booth, chatting with other vendors and eventually customers for eight to ten hours, counting out change and wrapping bouquets in damp newspaper.

She decided to give Quinn another fifteen or twenty minutes before waking her.

There was no huge hurry, after all, and besides, Ria cherished those early hours of the morning, when the sun was still snuggled behind the eastern mountains and the resounding silence was a soul symphony, in and of itself. The grass remained damp with dew—delicious under bare feet—and the night creatures were just starting to turn homeward, to find their nests and holes and hollow logs. The birds, meanwhile, stirred and blinked in their twig-and-twine havens under the eaves of barns and houses, high in the branches of trees, preparing themselves to sing in a new day.

Ria smiled at Bones, busy chowing down on his ration of kibble. He added his own special nuances, warmth and humor and easy devotion, and she wondered why she hadn't adopted a dog or a cat long ago.

Down the short hallway, the guest room door creaked on its hinges, and Quinn, clad in shorty pajamas, padded past on the way to the bathroom, without a word or a glance, her hair rumpled and her movements slow and scuffling, like those of a sleepwalker, or someone blindfolded.

Ria chuckled, remembering that her niece was not a morning person.

She brewed a second cup of coffee, hoping that would revive the girl.

In the near distance, the toilet flushed, and water ran in the sink, stopping with an audible squeak when Quinn turned the faucet handle. The plumbing rattled.

A couple of minutes later, the girl meandered into the kitchen, hair tamed by a quick brushing, face pink from splashes of cold well water. She took the coffee Ria offered with a little moan of beleaguered thanks, raised the mug to her mouth with both hands and sipped.

"It can't be morning," she complained, after licking her lips and squinting at the nearest window. "It's still *dark*."

Ria laughed. "It's morning, all right," she answered. "Are you hungry?"

Quinn shook her head, blinking the sleep from her eyes. By now, Bones was scrabbling at her right knee, demanding a greeting, and the girl giggled and bent to pat his head. "I make it a rule never to eat unless I'm fully conscious," she told Ria.

Again, Ria smiled. "Good idea," she said. "I usually get breakfast at the farmers' market, after setting up for the day," she said. "There's a concession wagon, and you can have pancakes, bacon or sausage, scrambled eggs or cereal. Even French toast and crepes. The coffee's good, too."

Quinn drank more of the brew Ria had just given her, looking more alert after every swallow. Bones, having finished his kibble, lapped up some water and bid his mistress an enthusiastic good morning, was at the back door again, wanting to go out.

"Hmm," Quinn said noncommittally, crossing to open the way for Bones to hit the yard. "I guess I should hurry," she added, watching the dog through the screen door. "What was it Uncle Frank used to say? 'We're burning daylight'?"

Ria felt a soft, bittersweet stab at the memory. "That was it," she confirmed.

Being a firefighter/EMT, Frank had worked four days on, three days off. When he didn't have to be at the station, ready around the clock for the inevitable calls that summoned him and his colleagues to action, he liked to get out of the city, go fishing or hiking or, in summer, water-skiing, and, since they were apart when he was on duty, he wanted Ria right there at his side. Once in a while, if it was raining, for instance, he could be talked into visiting an indoor flea market or taking in a movie, but for the most part, Frank had needed to be doing something physical, preferably in the open air.

And Ria had gone along. Not that there weren't plenty of times when she would have preferred to do something else, but she mostly hadn't minded. Even-tempered and perennially cheerful, sometimes to an irritating degree, Frank was good company, and he was smart, not to mention funny. Old-fashioned as it seemed in retrospect, Ria had loved making her husband happy.

Oh, yes, she thought now, biting her lower lip. She'd definitely been in love with love back then.

But had she really and truly loved *Frank?*

Yes, she decided, in the space of an instant, but no marriage was perfect and she'd stopped trusting him, consciously or unconsciously, after the slipup. He'd been away from home, attending a special two-week training seminar, and one night, when he'd had

too much to drink with some buddies in the hotel
bar, he'd been a little lonely and a lot depressed. He'd
wound up in bed with a classmate, a paramedic from
another state, named Carly.

Back home, he'd told Ria what had happened—
they'd agreed never to keep secrets from each other,
no matter what—and sworn he'd never cheated on
her before and would never do it again. He'd pleaded,
with tears in his eyes, for a second chance.

Of course Ria had been hurt—not just hurt, she'd
been wounded to the core of her spirit—but she'd
known that Frank didn't have it in him to lie. He'd
proved that by telling her what he'd done. A lot of
men wouldn't have confessed, fearing the fallout,
perhaps even coming to the convenient conclusion
that it would be kinder to say nothing.

Slowly, painfully, she'd forgiven him. Or, at least,
she'd *thought* she had. Now, as the old ache pulsed
like a bruise to the heart, she wondered.

She and Frank had moved on, put the incident behind them as best they could, but something in Ria
had been fractured, irreparably. Without the bedrock
of trust, she'd found, love changed, eroded—little by
little, in her case.

And that distrust, that subtle cynicism, was part
of the reason she was so wary, even testy, around
Landry Sutton, in spite of—or was it *because* of?—
the breathless, cliff-edge attraction between them.
Very possibly, she thought, with a sense of aching

sadness, she'd never be able to trust *any* man, Landry or anyone else.

Discouragement swamped her as she considered the ramifications of it all: no happy family for her. No husband and no babies. Deliberately, and with considerable difficulty, Ria shifted her focus from these dismal thoughts and sent her brain hurrying along another path, though admittedly one that ran parallel to the first.

Since Quinn had spent a lot of time with Ria during the Portland years, an arrangement Meredith had encouraged, the girl had often accompanied her aunt and uncle on their day trips, grumbling but happy when Frank clapped his hands in the guest room doorway to wake her up at the crack of dawn, declaring in a booming voice that they were burning daylight and vowing to sing every chorus of the National Anthem if he didn't see some action, immediately.

Since Frank was no singer, it wasn't an empty threat. And he'd had other methods of waking up the household, if not the neighborhood, as well. Once, after digging his high-school-band trumpet out of a box in the attic, he'd dusted the thing off, positioned himself in the hallway between the two bedrooms of their apartment and played reveille.

Reveille. Furthermore, he'd not only played the notes loudly, he'd played them badly, the horn emitting an earsplitting screech throughout.

He hadn't pulled that particular stunt again, since Ria and Quinn had yelled at him, and the people living above, below and on both sides of them had pounded on their walls and ceilings and floors in earnest protest.

Frank had shrugged his powerful shoulders and returned the trumpet to the attic, but he hadn't really reformed. When the next outing rolled around, and his wife and niece "lollygagged" in their beds, he'd crowed like a rooster. That drew similar complaints, of course, so he moved on to squirt guns, stupid jokes and, in Ria's case, tickling.

Noticing that her parallel mental paths had merged, Ria purposefully regrounded herself in the current moment, but she smiled, albeit a bit wistfully, at the memories.

Quinn, meanwhile, had refilled her coffee mug, gone back to her room and presently emerged again, wearing jeans, a pink T-shirt, sneakers and a lightweight jacket, all things they'd bought together the night before. With Bones frolicking around them, and pink light spilling over the rims of the mountains, Ria and her niece armed themselves with clippers and buckets half-filled with water, and headed into the fields.

In the dim predawn light, they cut armloads of flowers, choosing the brightest, freshest ones, just reaching the peak of their beauty, arranged them by color and variety in more buckets, topped off the water so the blooms wouldn't get thirsty on the drive ahead.

Finally, Ria backed the farm truck out of the shed,

engine rattling, exhaust pipe blasting intermittently. She offered the usual prayer of thanks that the rig was still running. She'd bought the contraption from one of the neighbors, when she was still new in the community, with a little money and a lot of faith. The truck ran well enough, unless the temperature dropped below thirty-two degrees, as it often had that past winter, and the odometer, apparently having used up its allotment of numbers years before Ria came along, had ground to a halt at some point, the last numeral forever stuck between a five and a six.

Quinn laughed when she saw the truck, shouted to be heard over the thundering chortle of the motor. Mysterious things clattered under the hood, and the exhaust pipe popped several more times, like a round of bullets fired in quick succession. "What a relic!" Quinn shouted, grinning. "Is there an actual *color* under all that rust?"

Ria pretended indignation; then she laughed, too. She got out of the rig, shaking her head, and teased, "The truck happens to be blue, for your information. What do you say we get the flowers loaded up?"

Frank's voice echoed in her head. *We're burning daylight.*

Quinn pushed up her figurative sleeves and went right to work alongside Ria. When they were done, and the pickup bed was filled with flowers and buckets, the girl asked tentatively, "Bones gets to go with us, doesn't he?"

She seemed to be holding her breath, waiting for

Ria's answer. Had Meredith ever said yes to this child? Quinn was clearly braced for a no.

Ria refrained from comment, since she'd always tried not to criticize Meredith in Quinn's presence, and nodded in the affirmative. Bones was welcome to come along. "*But,*" she clarified, holding up an index finger to make her point, "he'll have to have his collar and leash on at all times. We can't have him wandering off or bothering the customers or the other vendors."

Quinn lit up with delight, promised she'd keep an eye on Bones the whole time they were away from home and dashed inside to fetch his leash and collar, along with two plastic bowls for water and kibble, transporting the latter in a sealed storage bag.

Soon, the three of them were rumbling along winding country roads toward town.

"How far away is Parable?" Quinn asked as they passed through Three Trees a few minutes later. All of the businesses and most of the houses were still dark, though a light shone in the occasional window.

"Are you rethinking breakfast?"

Quinn shook her head no. "Just curious," she said.

"Good." Ria grinned. "Because none of the diners or the fast-food places will be open before six. And to answer your original question, it's about thirty miles from here to Parable."

They drove on in pleasant silence for a while, each thinking their own thoughts.

Then Quinn ventured carefully, "Will *he* be there?"

"He?" Ria asked, though she already knew who her niece was referring to.

"Landry Sutton," Quinn said mildly, in a tone meant to convey the fact that she wasn't born yesterday.

Until then, Ria had been keeping thoughts of Landry, and the forthcoming night at the Boot Scoot Tavern, safely at bay. Now here he was, in her face, metaphorically speaking. If she wasn't careful, she'd start imagining ahead of time what it would be like to dance with him in a dim and crowded bar lit mainly by a jukebox and the neon beer signs that probably hung in every bar in the country.

A hot tremor went through her at the prospect of being held close against that hard, sculpted chest, those muscled thighs....

Whoa, Ria told herself silently, sitting up a little straighter in the lumpy, duct-tape-mended seat of that old truck, jutting out her chin a smidgen and squaring her shoulders with such force that they ached slightly. By then, to her chagrin, she'd succeeded so well at distracting herself that she'd forgotten Quinn's question.

Grinning, Quinn repeated it. Would they be running into Landry at the farmers' market?

"Probably not," Ria answered, her voice coming out hoarse, like the croak of a frog. She paused to clear her throat, shore up her dignity again. "Sometimes his brother Zane and his wife, Brylee, show up, though. And you might get to meet some of my other friends, too—the market's a popular place."

Quinn's expression turned thoughtful. "*Zane* Sutton?" she asked, her voice soft with sudden awe. Bones, blissfully unimpressed by celebrity, it would seem, lay curled up on Quinn's lap now, catching a nap. "The *movie star?*"

"That's him," Ria said, enjoying her niece's obvious amazement. For all their phone calls, emails and texts, she'd never mentioned knowing anyone famous—it would have been wrong, in her opinion. One of the reasons Zane Sutton and Casey Elder had come to Parable County in the first place, after all, was that they wanted to live quietly, out of the limelight. "Turns out, we have several celebrity neighbors. Casey Elder, the country singer—around here, most people either call her by her first name or 'Mrs. Parrish,' if they're not well acquainted—lives just down the road from us, with her husband, Walker, and their children."

Quinn's mouth dropped open, and her eyes went wide. "No *way*," she marveled, when she'd recovered a little.

Ria chuckled. "Way," she countered. "But don't expect a lot of razzle-dazzle. Casey and Zane are both down-to-earth types, and they like to be treated like everyone else around here—like ordinary people."

"Except they're *not* ordinary," Quinn reasoned.

"You might be surprised," Ria replied, thinking with warmth of Zane Sutton, who was considerably nicer, in her opinion, than his brother. And then there was Casey—always smiling, always ready to help when there was a need and as solidly *un*pretentious as anyone Ria had ever known.

She told a few stories, and the thirty miles between Three Trees and Parable rolled beneath the wide tires of the old truck quickly, and the sun was up when they pulled into the parking lot at the fairgrounds. The space was already crowded with cars and pickups and people unloading their wares.

Two boys appeared immediately, and insisted on lugging the heavy buckets, filled with water and flowers, inside the long building that served as an exhibition hall during the rodeo and the county fair, and along the sawdust-covered aisle to Ria's usual booth. They both wore battered jeans, clean but well-worn cotton shirts and the straw cowboy hats that were so ubiquitous in Montana.

Ria introduced the teens to Quinn simply as Shane and Nash, saving last names and family relationships for later, and they touched their hat brims in acknowledgment, said "howdy" and grinned shyly.

Quinn was clearly charmed—it would have been impossible to miss the admiring glances coming her way—though as soon as the pair had finished the unloading, gotten acquainted with a very receptive Bones, politely refused to accept payment for their help and finally disappeared, she whispered a com-

ment. "Very cute, but *way* too young for me." A
pause, a mischievous lift of her eyebrows. "Do they
have older brothers, by any chance?"

Ria grinned, busy rearranging the flower buckets
and fluffing out their vibrantly hued contents. "Actually," she said, "Nash is Zane and Landry Sutton's
younger brother, but that's it for siblings, as far as I
know, so no luck in that quarter, I'm afraid. And Shane
just has an older sister and two baby brothers—strike
two."

Quinn made a face, conveying mock disappointment, and said nothing.

The crowd was already pretty thick, Ria noticed,
early as it was. Not surprisingly, a lot of folks around
the county, whether they lived in town or out in the
countryside, raised their own flowers, as well as vegetables, but there were enough nongardeners and
tourists to sustain the market throughout the summer, and right on to the end of October, when pump-
kins were the biggest draw.

There were other things for sale, too—everything
from organic herbs to handmade quilts, soap and
candles, beautifully tooled leather items like belts
and bridles, vintage and home-sewn clothing, colorful aprons and screen-printed T-shirts, modest an-
tiques, rusty farm equipment and old books. In early
spring, seedlings appeared in some of the booths,
growing out of cardboard egg cartons and small peat
pots, and, even now, shimmering jars of jam and jelly
lined some of the improvised counters and shelves.

Ria loved the place and the people. The money she usually earned, not a lot but certainly enough, by her standards, would add up over the course of the season.

When Ria heard her niece's stomach rumble, even over the noise of chitchat and down-home sales pitches, she sent the girl to the concession wagon to buy breakfast, *any* breakfast, for both of them. She'd sold several bouquets before Quinn returned with foam boxes containing French toast, drenched in syrup, along with link sausages thrown in, as she put it, "for a shot of protein." There was coffee, too, piping hot when it arrived, but stone-cold long before Ria finally got a chance to take even one sip. And she hadn't done any better with the food, unlike Quinn, who'd somehow managed to gulp down a fair portion of hers.

"Phew," Quinn commented, during a brief lull that felt like an indrawn breath soon to be exhaled, "are there always this many people?"

"No," Ria replied, after flipping through a mental calendar. "The rodeo starts next weekend. It's a big deal, a kickoff to Independence Day, which is sacred around here, and visitors come from all over the state—and farther away—to get in on the fun."

"Next weekend?" Quinn asked, after selling a bouquet of pink gerberas and making change for a twenty-dollar bill. "Aren't they showing up a bit early?"

The lull was over.

Ria worked, smiling and selling more flowers, even as she answered, "Some of them are on vacation, visiting relatives or camping out. Some of them sell food and souvenirs and stuff, and there are the carnival people who set up the rides and the fireworks specialists, too. Their preparations are fairly complicated. Others come to sign up and compete in one or more of the rodeo events. The motels, here and in Three Trees, fill up fast, obviously, and the early birds get the rooms."

Quinn absorbed all this information as she sold more flowers.

When the foot traffic finally died down a little, Quinn took Bones for a walk, refilled his water bowl from a faucet above one of the horse troughs and came back to the booth just in time to meet Casey and Walker Parrish's daughter, Clare.

Clare was only a year or so younger than Quinn, a pretty redhead with her famous mother's lively personality, arresting green eyes and quick smile and, it was rumored, her talent for music.

Not the least bit shy, Clare, clad in regular jeans, a ruffled green top and scuffed boots, extended a hand to Quinn, across the buckets of flowers lining the counter, a board stretched between two wooden barrels, and introduced herself by name.

Quinn tried not to look impressed, Ria noted with amusement, but she'd definitely recognized Clare, probably by her strong resemblance to Casey. Or, perhaps, it was because Clare had made the tabloids herself, a couple of years ago. Early on, she'd been the original wild child, but Casey and Walker were good parents, in for the duration, and as she'd adjusted to living on a ranch instead of in fancy hotel suites and luxurious tour buses, she'd settled down a lot.

"Hi," Quinn greeted the other girl, relaxing a little. "I'm Quinn Whittingford."

Clare's smile was warm and a little mischievous. She smiled a hello at Ria, then turned her attention back to Quinn. "I'm throwing a slumber party at our ranch tonight," she said. "Whisper Creek? Anyhow, we're going to have a ginormous tent, plenty of music and a barbecue to remember. Want to come?"

Quinn actually blushed a little, she was so pleased—and probably surprised—by the invitation. Ria knew Meredith normally kept the girl on a short rein, back in Portland, and, since she could be sure Casey and Walker would be keeping a close eye on the evening's proceedings, she certainly wouldn't forbid her niece from going.

"Could I bring my dog?" Quinn asked, after a few moments of awkward silence.

Ria, still busy making sales, followed the conversation between the two girls without missing a beat, pleased that Quinn was already making friends in a new place.

"Sure," Clare said readily, with another dazzling smile. "We have all kinds of critters running around at our place. One more won't do any harm."

"Would it be okay with you?" Quinn asked Ria. "If I went to the slumber party, I mean?" Again, the girl seemed to expect a flat refusal.

Ria's smile took in both Clare and Quinn. "I don't see why not," she said. "It sounds like lots of fun."

Quinn glowed like a pair of headlights on high beam.

Clare, meanwhile, returned Ria's smile and said she'd pick Quinn up at the farm around six-thirty, if that wasn't too early.

After another careful glance at Ria, who nodded to indicate that six-thirty would be just fine, Quinn told Clare, still a bit shy, that she'd be ready to go.

The next several hours flew by and, since they ran out of flowers around four in the afternoon, Ria decided to close up early. She and Quinn loaded the now-empty buckets, having dumped the remaining water into the dirt outside the exhibition hall, gave the booth a swift cleaning and left, stopping at various points on the way to the exit so Ria could introduce her niece to some of the other sellers and a few of the shoppers.

After giving Bones a short spin around the parking lot, just in case, they all climbed into the truck, ready to head for home.

At least, *Quinn* was ready. Ria, on the other hand, was getting more and more nervous, because tonight was the night. A simple date would have been unsettling in itself, but this was more than a date. Landry had basically *challenged* Ria to go out with him, to resist him. The egomaniac.

Backing out wasn't an option, however well-advised it might seem. That would be the same as admitting that Landry was right, that she was afraid to get too close, afraid to be vulnerable, afraid of just about everything.

The irony? She *was* afraid.

But she was going to the Boot Scoot Tavern with Landry Sutton anyhow, mainly because her pride overruled her common sense.

There was an ominous grinding sound when Ria turned the key in the truck's ignition, then—nothing. Not even a faint purr or a tiny buzz.

She tried again. Same result.

Much in need of a shower and a few minutes to put up her feet and do nothing at all, Ria sighed in frustration and swore under her breath.

Quinn rolled her eyes, Bones standing on his hind legs in her lap, smudging up the passenger-side window, but she didn't say anything.

Before Ria could offer her niece any reassurance that she wasn't going to miss Clare's party, she spotted two familiar male figures approaching from different directions.

Her close neighbor Walker Parrish, she noted with relief, and Slade Barlow, the former sheriff of Parable County, who lived on a ranch just outside Parable, with his wife, Joslyn, and a flock of kids, as well as a sizable herd of cattle and numerous horses.

The men met in front of Ria's truck's hood; both of them offered her a slanted smile, through the windshield, and tugged at the brims of their hats.

"Knights in shining armor?" Quinn asked, with a note of hope. Of course she was still fretting about not getting home in time to get ready for the shindig, not to mention a good chance to get to know some kids her own age.

Ria was already rolling down her window. "Something like that," she replied with a little smile.

Slade pushed back his hat, scratched his head thoughtfully and popped the rusty hood. As it rose with a whine of rusted hinges, Walker approached Ria's side of the rig.

"What's the trouble?" he asked, unperturbed. Just another cowboy, taking another problem in stride. No sweat.

"I don't know," Ria said. "It just won't start."

Walker nodded, acknowledging Quinn, but he was the proverbial man of few words, pretty much incapable of small talk, and so was Slade, so neither of them spared the girl a verbal "hello."

"We'll see what we can do," Walker told Ria, before heading around to the front of the truck.

With the hood in the way, both men were blocked from sight.

"Are *all* the guys in this town hot?" Quinn asked, in a loud whisper.

Ria chuckled and shushed her.

After a few minutes spent examining the engine

with Slade, Walker sprinted off toward his truck, returned in moments to park the rig close to Ria's pickup. Jumper cables were strung between the two vehicles.

At a wave from Walker, Ria turned over the ignition again.

A low growl, but no start-up.

For her part, Ria thought being stranded had its advantages, because it meant she'd have a viable excuse to call off an evening with Landry without chickening out, but she knew Quinn couldn't get home soon enough. She was biting her lower lip, stroking Bones with one hand and staring wistfully off into space.

On the next try, after a second signal from Walker, the truck's ancient engine came to life with a lusty roar. The hood came down with a thump, latching itself in place.

So much for fate giving her an easy out, Ria thought, surprised to find that she wasn't all that disappointed. In fact, there was a disturbing little tingle of anticipation quivering in the pit of her stomach, another at the back of her throat, still another suspended midway between her hipbones.

Blushing because of the images tumbling into her brain in response to that damn tingle, she thanked Walker and Slade for their help. They simply nodded, spoke briefly to each other and went their separate ways.

"What are you going to wear?" Quinn asked as

they cruised through Parable, headed for the high-way that led to Three Trees. "On your date, I mean?"

Ria swallowed the throat tingle, though the others wouldn't be quelled, and countered, "Let's talk about *your* evening instead. You'll need a sleeping bag—I think I have one in the storeroom in the basement—not that you'll do all that much sleeping probably."

Quinn grinned, but the twinkle in her eyes con-veyed the message that she wasn't fooled, even if she *had* allowed herself to be sidetracked. "I can't believe I get to do this," she marveled quietly.

"Surely you've been to slumber parties before—"

But Quinn shook her head. "Nope," she said. "Meredith thinks overnighters are a threat to civili-zation as we know it."

Pleasantly tired from a day's work, mentally flipping through the unremarkable contents of her closet for the right outfit to wear to a cowboy bar, Ria laughed out loud.

And it was a sound of pure joy.

CHAPTER EIGHT

LANDRY, HAVING SPENT most of the day over at Zane and Brylee's place, helping to herd cattle from one patch of grazing land to another, then riding a few fence lines for good measure, got home in time to do his own chores and grab a long, hot shower.

He stepped into the kitchen, wearing clean clothes and a pair of boots he reserved for things that didn't involve mud or manure, like funerals or supper at somebody else's house. While he wasn't the sort to play hard-to-get, he didn't want to seem too eager, either, when he knocked at Ria's door half an hour from now.

He'd been a little overgenerous with the aftershave, he supposed, and he'd about brushed the enamel right off his teeth before rinsing with a healthy slug of mouthwash—god-awful stuff that tasted like kerosene—but the effects would probably be subtle.

Highbridge, seated at the kitchen table in front of his personal laptop, raised both his bushy eyebrows at the sight of Landry. His nose twitched slightly as he caught the scent of aftershave.

"Ah," the venerable butler said, without inflection, his long face bland, "Saturday night. Time to cut a rug, so to speak, on what passes for a dance floor at some cowboy dive with smoke in the air and sawdust on the floor."

Landry grinned. "That was a colorful description," he replied, crossing to the cupboards, taking out a tall glass and filling it with cold tap water. "In fact, I can't recall the last time I heard the phrase 'cut a rug.' Shall I assume you still don't approve—as usual?"

With that, he raised the glass to his mouth, swilled down half the water inside. The stuff took away some of the taste of mouthwash, and anyway, a day on horseback, rounding up stray cattle and checking for breaks in the fences, left a man feeling thirsty.

"I have nothing against cowboy bars," Highbridge replied, his tone lofty, his diction deliberate. "It is not the kind of place men of my generation took a lady. A lightskirt, perhaps, but not a lady."

A "lightskirt"? Quaint terminology that, but then, that was Highbridge all over—quaint.

Taking special care not to laugh, lest he choke to death or spew water in all directions, Landry concentrated on swallowing, emptied the glass, set it down next to the sink with a mild thump. "Well," he said, "since we missed out on last night's bingo game and there don't seem to be any ice cream socials or formal cotillions on the horizon, I guess the Boot Scoot will have to do, just this once."

Highbridge huffed out a small, exasperated sigh. "Ria Manning is a fine woman," he said.

Landry nodded. "That she is," he agreed.

Highbridge pushed back his chair and turned away from his laptop screen, though he didn't stand up. "Don't forget it," he replied evenly.

Landry let the warning roll off his back, then gave a snappy salute, but the thought of the box of condoms he'd tucked away in the glove compartment of his truck earlier did cross his mind. He'd had them for a while, and he hoped they were still good—not that he figured he had a chance in hell of using any, not this early in the game, anyhow.

The game?

Good thing Highbridge couldn't hear his thoughts.

Landry intended, absolutely, to get Ria into bed, the sooner the better, but he wasn't playing around, the way Highbridge seemed to think he was. Whatever else she represented, Ria Manning was serious business.

Highbridge, his formerly expressionless face a mask of disapproval now, got to his feet, snapped the laptop shut and tucked it under one arm, a signal that he was done suffering fools for the duration. Sure enough, he started for his quarters, in back of the kitchen, but midway, he stopped, turned his head and favored Landry with a long, warning glare.

The way the man was acting, Landry thought, with a slight touch of annoyance, a person would have thought he was Ria's father, or maybe an over-protective big brother or uncle, instead of a much-older friend. "I shall bid you good-night, sir," the butler said, every word starched fit to stand up on its own.

Landry couldn't resist a mild gibe. "Don't wait up," he replied.

ARRIVING HOME FROM the farmers' market, Ria parked the truck in the equipment shed, unloaded the buckets and stacked them in a corner. Quinn gave Bones some time to run around the yard, pee against the rose arbor and generally unwind after a full day of being a very, very good dog.

Inside the house, Ria washed her hands at the kitchen sink, glanced at the clock and felt her nerve endings jump, all at once.

The big date.

It's really going to happen.

She'd been an idiot to accept Landry's dare, Ria knew that only too well, but there was no going back now without coming off as a coward, so she might as well prepare as best she could, steel herself to resist some serious temptation.

Trying to stay in the present moment, she searched for and found the sleeping bag she'd promised Quinn, unrolled and unzipped it and hung it over the clothesline in the backyard to air out a little.

When Ria came inside again, she could hear the shower running. *Don't use up all the hot water,* she thought ruefully. As usual, her workday had left her feeling grungy. Her practical self would have chosen a hot bath, a light supper and a book over a date with the hottest cowboy in Parable County, if not the whole of Montana, but another part of her had the upper hand, and *that* part wanted to play with fire, dance on the edge of a high precipice, spread her wings and soar.

Landry Sutton, up close and personal. Resisting him would be a real challenge, and she *would* resist him, just to prove that she could. They'd made a sort of informal wager, she and Landry, and Ria intended to win.

Since she couldn't go back in time and refuse the initial invitation, which would have been her first choice, there was nothing else to do but feed Bones his supper and brave the wilds of her closet in search of something to wear.

Ria didn't own anything that would be called sexy—just cotton sundresses, an outfit she reserved for church—when she *went* to church, that was—a few lightweight cardigan sweaters, half a dozen T-shirts, two summer tops and a whole lot of denim.

As for footwear, she had sneakers, house slippers, work shoes, some high heels, remnants of her previous incarnation as an accountant at Meredith's company, and one pair of black Western boots she didn't remember buying.

Talk about uninspiring.

Okay, so she wasn't out to stun Sutton with glamour, but she didn't want to look drab, either.

She finally selected her newest pair of blue jeans and a faded yellow print top, sleeveless, with a modest neckline and a few ruffles, laid the garments out on her bed, along with fresh underwear and a pair of thin socks.

When Quinn finally came out of the bathroom, trailed by billows of steam and one small and very attentive dog, Ria grabbed her sensible blue chenille bathrobe, hoping the water in the shower wasn't running cold, because she wanted to wash her hair as well as scrub herself spotless.

As it turned out, the water wasn't actually cold—just lukewarm—and Ria made quick work of sudsing up, shaving her legs and finally shampooing and rinsing. Stepping out of the shower stall, she wrapped her shivering self in a towel and moved to stand in front of the mirror above the sink.

By the time she was finished, the water had taken on a distinct chill. At least there hadn't been any steam to cloud up the glass, she thought, amused, even as goose bumps broke out all over her body. She hadn't had to share a bathroom in a very long time, and it would take some getting used to, living with a teenager.

After deciding on just a skim of makeup—tinted moisturizer, a swipe of mascara, some blusher and lip gloss—Ria brushed her teeth, blow-dried her dark hair and went back to her room to get dressed.

The jeans were still right where she'd put them fifteen minutes before, and so were the boots, underwear and socks. The yellow cotton top, however, had mysteriously disappeared, to be replaced with something clingy and pink, with a V-shaped neckline.

"Quinn?" she called.

Her niece opened the door, stood on the threshold, grinning. "That shirt looked like an upcycled flour sack," she said. "So I swapped it out for one of mine."

Ria frowned. "What do you know about flour sacks?" she asked, apropos of nothing much. It was a handy way to stall, though, to hold off the moment when she and Quinn would have to mention The Date. "I'll bet nobody's even *seen* one since the 1960s."

"Au contraire," Quinn replied pertly. "There was a whole big *pile* of them at the farmers' market today—in the quilting club's booth. They're billed as 'vintage fabrics' and they sold like crazy."

Ria sighed, eyeing the pink top again. She must have bought it for Quinn the night before, along with piles of other clothes, though she didn't recall it specifically. It was a mere snippet of shimmery softness, and it would look sweetly innocent on Quinn. On her, however, it would be about as subtle as a billboard reading "Take me now, cowboy—I'm all yours."

"I can't wear this," she protested, albeit weakly. The color of the top reminded her of cotton candy, or the delicate petals of spring tulips, and it felt silky between her fingers…

She let go of the garment, drew back her hand as though she'd been burned.

Quinn giggled. "Why not?" she asked lightly. "It'll look great on you."

"Maybe I don't want to look 'great,'" Ria suggested, with a sour glance at her niece. She was already wavering, though, and Quinn probably knew it.

It might be kind of nice, wearing something wispy and ultrafeminine for once.

"Just try it on," Quinn urged sweetly. And then she stepped back and closed the bedroom door without waiting for a reply.

Ria hesitated for what seemed like a long time, though it was probably a matter of seconds, and finally, fretfully, gave in to temptation and pulled the top over her head, marched over to the mirror above her dresser.

She looked—well—not like her usual T-shirted self. Her skin glowed, and even though she hadn't put on any makeup yet, her cheeks were a pretty shade of very pale apricot. Her eyes shone, strikingly blue, and her freshly washed hair gleamed ebony, softly framing her face. And there was something sultry lurking there in her reflected self, too, hidden for now but waiting for just the right moment to jump out at her—or, more likely, at *Landry*.

"Yikes," she whispered.

Bones began to bark excitedly just then, and Ria heard the sound of a car or truck out front, coming to a stop. One door slammed, then another.

Quinn's ride to the party at Whisper Creek had

arrived, and Ria had to go out there and say hello, at least. Also on her immediate agenda: remind Quinn to (1) have a great time and (2) behave herself.

She kept the pink top on and wriggled into her jeans before hurrying toward the living room.

Quinn was ready to go, the sleeping bag brought in from the clothesline, rolled up neatly and resting on the floor next to the front door, her backpack beside it, Bones stationed nearby, quiet now that his personal goddess had told him to hush.

Footsteps sounded on the porch, the decisive tap of a man's boot heels, the lighter step and rubbery squeak of a young girl's sneakers. Quinn opened the door before anybody could knock.

Walker Parrish stood in front of the screen door, with Clare at his side. A company pickup waited at the base of the flagstone walk, the engine still running.

Walker smiled at Quinn as she fumbled to unlock the screen; then, looking past the girl, he smiled at Ria, too.

"Long time no see," he quipped, stepping inside.

Ria laughed, but a part of her was wondering if Walker knew about her date with Landry. Quinn might have said something to Clare back at the farmers' market, without Ria's knowing, of course. Word could be all over the county by now, given the way news traveled in small communities—at the speed of light.

"Your dad is one of the guys who got the truck started for us, over at the fairgrounds," Quinn remarked to Clare. In her world, the big city, Ria supposed, most of the people you encountered were strangers, and offers of help were suspect. With good reason, unfortunately.

"It's a small world," Clare replied, eyes sparkling with laughter and, probably, the prospect of all the fun ahead.

"Around here anyway," Quinn answered, looking just as excited as her new friend.

Walker bent to pick up the sleeping bag and the backpack. "Guess we ought to get on with it," he said, with a slight grin. "We have a few more stops to make."

Ria was focused on Quinn again. She wasn't the girl's mother, but she felt responsible for her just the same. "Enjoy the party," she said, kissing her niece's forehead. "And be good."

Quinn nodded, a little rushed, and gathered Bones in her arms. He was still wearing his collar, and the leash was looped over his mistress's left wrist.

"And you be good, too," Ria said, shaking one index finger in front of the dog's small black button of a nose.

Clare and Quinn practically stampeded out of the house, across the porch and down the steps, feet barely touching the front walk, chattering to each other as they made a beeline for Walker's flashy extended-cab truck.

He paused on the tattered welcome mat, holding the sleeping bag and the backpack and looking benignly rueful, no doubt thinking, as Ria was, that children grew up too fast. "We'll look after Quinn," he said, quite unnecessarily. "And either Casey or I will bring her back home tomorrow, probably after lunch, since these shindigs generally last till dawn. Then everybody conks out, and it takes a cannon blast to wake them up."

Ria nodded, enjoying the image, but that odd thickness was in her throat again, making it hard to speak. "Thanks, Walker," she said. "My best to Casey."

Walker replied with a nod of his own, tugged at his hat brim one more time and walked away. Ria watched until he was in the truck, with the girls and the dog, and then, very softly, as though reluctantly marking the end of something, she closed the door.

Alone, she turned her back to that door, leaned against it, closed her eyes and let out a long, slow breath.

Here goes nothing, she thought.

WALKING UP TO Ria's front door, with a bouquet of red, yellow and white blossoms purloined from his sister-in-law's garden in one hand—coals to New-castle, as Highbridge would have said, since this was, after all, a flower farm—Landry felt his palms go damp and the pit of his stomach lurch a little, as though he stepped off something solid onto thin air.

He was thirty-four years old, but right about now, he might as well have been fourteen, he was so nervous.

What was *that* about? He'd been with plenty of women, before and after Susan, even if the pickings *had* been a little on the slim side since he lit in Montana and decided to stay awhile, see if he liked the place. There had been a few sexual skirmishes—he was no monk, after all—but he'd been careful to confine most of his adventures to Missoula or Great Falls, where he could expect some anonymity. In Parable County, sleeping around was bound to stir up gossip, given that practically everybody knew everybody else's business, and while loose talk wouldn't have bothered him all that much, those of the female persuasion tended to take a different view. They had reputations to consider, and they mainly wanted wedding bands—engagement rings at the very least.

Ria was obviously independent, and not in the market for a husband, but she was still a woman. And what other people thought mattered to her.

Unbidden, a vivid picture of Ria, deliciously naked, sweetly willing and therefore his for the taking, loomed in Landry's mind—a phenomenon that had been happening a lot lately. Landry's groin tightened painfully, like powerful machinery seizing up for lack of proper oiling, and he lowered the bouquet to waist level, just in case there was visible evidence of how much he wanted her.

Telling himself he was being stupid, if not downright juvenile, he tightened his jaw, ratcheted up his resolve and paused for a long moment before raising one hand to knock briskly on the woodwork surrounding Ria's door.

"Just a second," she called cheerfully, from somewhere inside.

Landry waited.

Ria opened the door, let her eyes drop to the bouquet, sent them zip-lining right back up to Landry's face. "Hi," she said, after a short delay.

She was wearing a top, a pink thing with no more substance than a whisper in the dark, trim jeans and boots, too, and, unless he was seeing things, lipstick and eye makeup, too.

Landry's spirits rose a little. Unfortunately, so did something else.

"Hello," he said, several beats after he should have spoken.

"Come in," Ria replied, a bit too brightly, stepping back to admit him. "I'll just put those flowers in water before we leave."

Landry ground out a gravel-paved "all right," then nodded for good measure, kept the things below his belt buckle as he stepped into the house. Redundant or not, he was damn glad he'd brought the blossoms—what had Brylee called them?—because it felt as if he'd shoved a chunk of firewood down the front of his pants, and he definitely needed something to take cover behind.

He followed Ria through the small house, noted that it was tidy and almost as sparsely furnished as his own place. When they wound up in the kitchen,

Landry took care to stand behind one of the ladder-back chairs surrounding the table.

"Peonies." Ria smiled, accepting the bouquet from his outstretched hand and taking a moment to admire them. "Mine are already dropping their petals."

Peonies. That was what the things were called. Silly word. Landry swallowed hard, still feeling like a kid.

He couldn't just stand here; he had to *say* something. "Brylee tells me they're a special variety," he croaked out. *Shit,* he thought. What was next? Cracks in his voice? A spontaneous outbreak of teenage acne?

Determined, Landry cleared his throat. "They bloom late," he finished, still quoting Brylee, because he didn't know a damn thing about plants. She'd been pleased, his sister-in-law had—a little *too* pleased, as a matter of fact—when he'd shown up at her and Zane's place about twenty minutes ago and asked for a few flowers.

Get a grip, he told himself silently, wondering where his usual generous allotment of self-confidence had gone.

Ria had had her back to him during the first minute or so, taking a vase from high up in a cupboard, so she had to stand on tiptoe to reach, then adding water at the sink, trimming the stems of each peony before adding it to the vase, all of which gave him a little time to—well—*deflate.* He hadn't quite completed the process when she finally turned around, but luck was with him, as it turned out, because Ria was focused on the flowers, setting them in the center of her table, fluffing them out, rearranging this one and that.

When all that was done, she looked at Landry again, and a little frown puckered the perfect skin between her perfect eyebrows.

"Is something wrong?" she asked, her gaze dropping to the whitened knobs of Landry's knuckles, where he still gripped the back of the chair.

Landry cleared his throat again, summoned up a flimsy grin, meant to come across as cocky. "Nope," he lied. "I'm just fine and dandy."

"Then why are you holding on to that chair for dear life?" Ria persisted reasonably. "If you're not feeling well, we could postpone—"

What Landry was *feeling* just then was that he was a real dope, on a steep and slippery decline into something even worse.

The insight pricked at his pride, caused him to buck up and start acting more like himself. He consciously released his clenched fingers. "I'm fine," he said.

Ria was still studying him, still looking concerned.

"I'm fine," Landry repeated grimly. He wasn't as hard as before, but he still had a bulge where there shouldn't have been one. Damn, but he wished he

hadn't left his hat in the truck. He could have used it as a kind of shield, like he had with the flowers.

"You don't have to be a grouch about it," Ria pointed out, bordering on peevish now. "If you'd rather not go out, just say so. It would be fine with me."

That said, and without giving Landry a chance to answer, she sashayed past him, though where she was headed, he had no clue.

All he knew was that he couldn't let her go, not yet.

So he caught Ria by the elbow, careful not to hurt her but not about to let her walk off and leave him standing in her kitchen like a damn fool, either.

Touching her had been a tactical error—but he realized that a heartbeat too late.

He might as well have closed his fingers around a live wire as taken hold of Ria Manning; the voltage was high and hot, jolting him, jolting her, too, arcing back and forth between them like invisible lightning.

The next thing Landry knew, he'd pulled Ria against him, buried the fingers of one hand in her silky cap of dark hair and tilted her head back so he could look directly into her eyes.

He expected her to stiffen in resistance, break free or even slap him across the face, hard. Instead, she gave a throaty little whimper, part sigh, and stared up at him with wide eyes.

"What the hell *is* this?" Landry muttered, thinking aloud, not expecting a reply.

But Ria gave one. She thought for a moment, then shook her head slightly. "I have no earthly idea," she admitted in a breathy whisper.

Against his own better judgment, Landry kissed her then. He kissed her gently at first, and then with growing heat and fervor.

And she rose onto her toes, draped her arms around his neck and kissed him right back.

There was some tongue action then, and Landry figured he was a goner for sure.

Yet, perhaps because they were both starved for oxygen, their mouths parted suddenly, as if by unspoken agreement, and they were both gasping like divers surfacing with no air left in their tanks.

Landry held Ria by her shoulders, which were trembling a little, and took half a step back to give her some space.

"I guess we'd better go," he said huskily, when he finally caught his breath.

Ria nodded. "I think so," she concurred, clearly flustered.

Despite their mutual resolution to break it up before things went even further, neither of them moved for what seemed like a full minute.

Landry was hard all over again, but there was nowhere to hide. Since the situation wasn't likely to improve anytime soon—unless they went straight to bed, of course, and got this fixation, or whatever it was, out of their systems—he'd just have to tolerate the discomfort, ride it out.

At just about any other time in his adult life, Landry would have steered things in the direction of the nearest soft, flat surface, without a second's hesitation. But Ria was different from every woman he'd ever known, let alone bedded.

When he made love to her—and he knew it would happen eventually, sure as death, taxes and the on-going incompetency of Congress—he wanted it to be by conscious choice, something she *knew* she wanted, not because she was dazed and distracted, like now. He could have swept her away, he had no doubt of that, but when the sex was over and the haze had lifted, she might hate him. And herself, as well.

Both possibilities were unacceptable, as far as he was concerned.

Landry still needed to touch her, though, and he ran the backs of the knuckles in his right hand down the side of her face, very gently, sobered by the sure knowledge that he'd never wanted a woman as much as he wanted this one, and probably never would.

Common sense and instinct did battle inside him; he felt his resolve slipping a little. *Right here, right now,* urged the dark side of his conscience, where the shadows were. Landry's better angels won the battle, as it turned out, but it was close.

He turned Ria around, placed a hand on the small of her back and steered her out of the kitchen, back through the living room, out onto the porch, into the lingering light of a summer evening.

Her keys jingled as she tried to lock up.

Landry suppressed an urge to lean down, just a little, and brush his lips along the narrow channel of the nape of her neck, visible because her head was tilted forward, causing her hair to part in back as she concentrated on a simple task that had inexplicably turned difficult.

Instead, Landry took the keys from her hand, locked the front door and then ushered her toward the passenger side of his truck. He hadn't thought to wash the rig, but it looked passably clean, so he decided not to worry about it—although even that distraction would have been welcome at the moment.

There was an awkward pause when Ria stepped up onto the running board, tripped and nearly tumbled backward into his arms. From there, it would have been a short fall to the soft grass at their feet, Landry thought, with amused resignation, and that would have meant all bets were off, since there was nobody else around.

Things didn't come to that, though. Fortunately.

Or *un*fortunately.

Landry steadied Ria, and she climbed, blushing, gaze pointed straight ahead, into the seat. Time stopped, once again, it seemed to him, freezing them both in a moment he never wanted to end.

During the drive to Parable, much to Landry's relief, the atmosphere wasn't quite as sexually charged as before, for whatever reason, and they both settled down a little.

Ria rolled down her window and let the breeze

dance in her hair, eyes closed, a smile of content-
ment on her lips.

Landry would remember the way she looked just
then, remember the scent of her skin and hair, the
peaches-and-cream glow of her skin, for the rest of
his long life, and pinpoint that exact instant, when
he fell in love with Ria Manning, hard and deep
and forever.

CHAPTER NINE

RIA DIDN'T KNOW whether to be worried or relieved when she and Landry pulled into the crowded parking lot adjoining the Boot Scoot Tavern, a battered and unpainted structure that had not only seen better days, but better decades, even better *centuries,* since the place dated back to the 1880s, according to local legend. The saloon probably hadn't changed much since the old days, and it was as much an institution in the town of Parable as the courthouse or the Pioneer Cemetery, where generations of regular customers were buried, along with teetotalers, of course, and all those who fell somewhere in between the two.

Now country music blared into the dwindling light of day, a river of sound rolling through a rustic entrance, the double doors propped open with beer kegs. Partiers came and went, women in skimpy summer tops and jeans, rhinestones flashing on their back pockets and fancy stitching on their many-colored boots, men spiffed up cowboy-style, in their best pair of jeans, crisply ironed cotton shirts, long-sleeved without exception, hats they wore to go out on the town, but never when they worked. The spit-shined boots were a given, plain in comparison to those the ladies sported, invariably brown or black, with square toes, as opposed to pointy ones. Those, Ria had learned about five minutes after she drove across the Montana state line for the first time, were for dudes and wannabes.

No real cowboy would be caught dead in them.

These observations had kept Ria's jitters at arm's length for a few minutes, but they'd arrived, and it wasn't possible to ignore the fact for very long.

Thinking their own thoughts, not looking at each other, she and Landry got out of the truck and headed for the entrance.

Just before they would have stepped inside, however, the artificial calm Ria had so carefully cultivated suddenly deserted her. Instantly, she was wary, as out of her element as a goldfish expelled from its bowl, flopping around on dry carpet. She thought of the cowgirls, glittering with rhinestones, and suffered by comparison. She was definitely under-blinged, she thought glumly, with not a single sparkling stone anywhere on her person. And did *all* the female patrons of the Boot Scoot Tavern wear size-minus-two jeans? It didn't help, reminding herself that her own pants were eights that glided on easily, right out of the dryer.

Finally, Ria thrust out an audible sigh, well aware that she was being silly, and made a brave effort to shake off her misgivings.

With a slanted grin, Landry glanced down at her, as they stood there in the gravel just a few feet from the threshold, and took her hand, squeezed lightly once. She might as well have had a digital display embedded in her forehead, Ria thought, because if he hadn't guessed exactly what she was thinking, he'd come pretty darned close.

"I may have failed to mention it before," he told her, in a low drawl, meant for her ears alone, "but the way you look tonight makes it hard to draw an even breath."

She narrowed her eyes, grateful for the surge of adrenaline the remark gave her and, at the same time, patently suspicious. Was that a line? she wondered. If it was, it just might work.

And if it *wasn't*—if Landry had actually meant what he said...

A sweet, piercing tremor zipped through Ria.

Watching her face, Landry chuckled. "You're even prettier when you're asking yourself what I'm up to," he said. Then he tightened his grip on her hand and squired her into the dim, noisy, throbbing heart of the Boot Scoot Tavern.

Ria's eyes took a few moments to adjust to the shift from fading daylight to a sort of cozy gloom, but when her vision returned to normal, she saw that the legendary watering hole was almost exactly as she'd imagined it would be. The space was jam-packed with people in moods ranging from sullen to out-and-out jolly, the high volume of the jukebox shook the walls and the floor like a giant pulse, and multicolored lights flashed from the top of the music machine, putting Ria in mind of a strange alien craft either coming in for a landing or getting ready for liftoff.

Waitresses in skinny jeans and sexy tops wove their way among several tables, deftly balancing beer bottles and cocktails on tiny round trays, laughing and joking with the clientele. Couples danced, wherever they could find an open space amid the throng. Pool balls clicked smartly somewhere nearby.

Already overstimulated, Ria blinked, uneasy but, at the same time, fascinated. She'd been in bars before, of course, but this one had its own rowdy charm, seeming mysterious somehow, and not quite part of the real world, a secret place within a secret place. *Brigadoon,* with boots and cowboy hats instead of kilts.

She breathed the whole scene in, savoring it, unsettled by it.

Things *happened* here, Ria thought, things began and ended. People fell in love, and sometimes out again, within these walls, beneath this rickety ceiling. There were stolen kisses and fistfights. Promises were made; promises were broken.

Landry finally nudged her out of this strange reverie, and that was a mercy, because Ria was starting to scare her solidly pragmatic self with all those woo-woo thoughts. She only missed the magic, wished she hadn't let go of it, for the tiniest fraction of a second.

"Let's get something to eat," Landry suggested, close to her ear. "I have a feeling we're going to need our strength."

Miraculously, a table for two was open, and Landry, still holding Ria by the hand, led her through the crowd, nodding as folks greeted him, swapping actual "hellos" with some of them.

Although Ria had lived in Parable County as long as Landry had, and knew many of the people they encountered, he seemed to be acquainted with every single one of them, male *or* female. The odd sensation that she didn't belong, that she was essentially a stranger in a strange land, returned, with a vengeance, crashing over her like a tidal wave.

Ria, normally a sensible person, tried to identify what she was feeling—was she excited, scared? Neither and both. Clearly, self-analysis was getting her nowhere.

When they finally reached the table, which was small and round, tucked into a corner and splashed with colored light from the jukebox, and Landry had pulled back Ria's chair, playing the gentleman, she allowed her knees to do what they'd been threatening to do from the moment she'd opened her door to him earlier in the evening—which was buckle like a couple of overcooked noodles.

Now that she was seated, somewhat breathless from the crossing, Landry moved to the other side of the table and sat.

They were facing each other, and their knees were touching.

Ria half expected to spontaneously combust, from just that much physical contact, and perspiration tickled the skin between her breasts, itched between her shoulder blades. She squirmed a little on the vinyl-seated chair, bit her lower lip while she considered scooting back an inch or so, in order to break the charged connection coursing between her body and Landry's, then back again, as though they were playing catch with a ball of lightning.

There was a problem with the plan, of course. *Two* problems, actually.

The move would be too obvious, especially in such a small space, and Landry might take it as a concession of some kind, count it as another victory, like the two kisses—had there really been just two?—that had stopped the earth, at least for Ria. On top of that, there wasn't that much room to maneuver—her back was to the wall, figuratively *and* literally.

"Relax," Landry said, watching her with amusement in his too-blue eyes. Or had he only mouthed the word, or even just *thought* it, employing some telepathic version of texting? It was hard to tell, now that she'd evidently fallen down the rabbit hole. *This way to Wonderland.*

A smiling waitress approached, dressed like all the other women in the bar, but chubby enough to shoot down the size-minus-two theory. She asked if they wanted food, and handed them each a stained vinyl menu when Landry answered with a yes.

Realizing she had about as much personal autonomy as a single sock tumbling end over end in a clothes dryer—or Alice, plunging toward a place where rabbits wore pocket watches and playing cards painted roses red—Ria was reeling again. Hoping no one would notice, she pretended to be absorbed in the list of specials paper-clipped to the inside of her menu. The words scrambled in her brain, backward, upside down and all-around unintelligible. Was it possible to become dyslexic between one moment and the next?

Ria might have gone right on obsessing, in the privacy of her own head, that was, for the rest of the night, if Landry hadn't reached out, taken her menu, set it aside and closed strong hands over hers.

"Ria," he said—or mimed, or thought— "take it easy, will you? Everything's all right, I promise."

His touch soothed and riled her up another notch, both at once. Now that their hands were linked *and* their knees were touching, the circuit was complete, and the electricity went from *crackle* to *zap*.

The waitress, who must have slipped away into the noisy void at some point, resurfaced with a tray holding two draft beers bubbling and foaming in glass mugs big enough to serve as umbrella stands.

Ria's eyes widened. She didn't recall ordering a drink, mainly because she *hadn't*. She'd gotten sick on red wine back in college, and had steered clear of alcohol ever since.

Landry must have ordered for her while she was zoned out.

Not that she'd zoned back *in* yet. Here in Briga-saloon, or Wonderland, or whatever it was, the rules were different. *She* was different.

Landry smiled at her, left his hands right where they were, his palms warming all ten of her fingers, and exchanged a few words with the waitress, who nodded, returned the smile and disappeared again.

"I hope you like fish and chips," Landry said, leaning in until his face was just a breath from hers. His aftershave, subtle and probably expensive, suffused her senses, made her a little dizzy. And the electricity was getting stronger, circulating faster, almost *visible*.

"Fish and chips will be fine," Ria replied briskly, straightening her spine. As if she actually had any say about anything.

Landry grinned, watching her intently, seeing, she feared, everything she was trying so hard to hide, now that she'd officially lost her everlovin' mind. One glimpse of the Mad Hatter or the Red Queen, Ria thought, and she was out of there. *Gone*.

Having made up her addled mind about that much, at least, she freed her hands, used them to lift her mongo mug of ice-cold beer and hold it out a little way, as if to say "Cheers." Then, after taking a deep breath and letting it out slowly, she took a big swig of the stuff. It wasn't bad, actually, so she followed that gulp with another. And another.

Landry, his eyes reflecting the grin resting light as a hummingbird's feather on his sexy mouth, lifted his own mug in response. Unlike Ria, he took his brew in sips, not mouthfuls, seeming to savor each one.

Easy enough for *him* to do, Ria thought, drinking way too much, way too fast. He wasn't on edge, wasn't the least *bit* rattled, now, was he? No, sir. Landry Sutton was at home in the Boot Scoot Tavern; he knew everyone there, was completely at ease in his own skin. And he wasn't guzzling his beer, either.

She, by contrast, wanted to take a swan dive into hers, and she was unquestionably rattled, a regular maraca keeping time with a fast beat.

After a few minutes, the beer began to fulfill its promise, calming Ria down a little, smoothing out some of the rough edges, pushing back the thumping music and the madding crowd. Which, by the way, surely exceeded the legal limits of occupation, and therefore presented numerous hazards.

Where was Sheriff Boone Taylor when you needed him?

The food arrived, interrupting Ria's most recent spin cycle. The meal consisted of chunks of breaded fish and gigantic fries intermingling on greasy deli sheets tucked into plastic baskets dulled by long and consistent use.

Having downed most of her beer by now, Ria ordered another.

Landry didn't comment—not that she could have heard him over all that ruckus if he had. The jukebox had been silenced, only to be replaced by a live band, equipped with amplifiers, electric guitars and belting out some serious twang.

The lyrics were familiar, poignant and oddly comforting—faithful old dogs breathing their last, trucks breaking down, train whistles piercing dark and lonely nights, Mama passing on before she ever got that washing machine she'd been promised and, of course, the inevitable prison term, admittedly deserved.

Landry did raise an eyebrow when another five-gallon drum of draft beer came to rest in front of Ria, and one corner of his damnably kissable mouth quirked up, too. Then he sighed visibly, if not audibly, and began to eat.

Ria nibbled at her meal—it was quite tasty, if you didn't mind trans fats, salt overload and plenty of preservatives—but she mostly concentrated on drinking more beer. She was starting to feel *good*.

Where had this stuff *been* all her life anyway?

Presently, the food baskets were removed, Ria's barely touched, and Landry, looking cheerfully rueful, pulled Ria to her feet and elbowed out a place for them on the dance floor. He held her close, and she allowed herself to enjoy the hardness and the heat of him, the masculine scent of his cologne and the skin beneath it, the sensation that he was not only guiding her through a slow dance, but holding her up.

Not, of course, that she was *drunk*. Far from it—she couldn't remember the last time she'd felt this bold, this free, this *sexy*.

Landry's breath was a warm tease against her ear, and sure enough, the tingling started up all over again. "Maybe we ought to get a little fresh air," he whispered.

"I like *this* air," Ria replied. The Boot Scoot, for all its strange magic, was neutral territory.

If Landry Sutton thought she was going to fall for the old "fresh air" trick, he was way off the mark. Did he actually think she didn't know that, once he got her outside, under the stars, he'd probably kiss her?

And if that happened, Ria knew only too well, she'd soon find herself on her back in that extended-cab truck of his, saying yes when the right answer was definitely no.

Landry laughed again, and she felt the vibration of it, a rumble rising in his chest.

"'This air,'" he countered in a husky drawl, his mouth close to her ear again, "isn't going to sober you up."

"Are you insinuating that I'm—intoxicated?" she asked, offended.

"I'm not 'insinuating' anything, woman," Landry answered. "I'm flat-out stating a fact. You're not just intoxicated, you're looped, three sheets to the wind, half in the bag, in your cups—"

"Are you through?" Ria inquired, swaying slightly. "Or are there *more* clichés coming my way?"

Just then the music stopped on a vibrating drumbeat that faded slowly and left a still-quivery hush in its wake.

Landry was grinning at her. "Probably," he replied easily, "but none of them come to mind just now. I could check the thesaurus app on my phone if you're curious."

"I am *not* curious," Ria informed him coolly. "*And* I want to sit down."

She was relaxed, yes. She could admit that, at least to herself. She might even be a little tipsy. But she was most certainly *not* drunk, she was sure of that, even though she'd never felt precisely this way before and thus had nothing to measure her present delightful condition against.

Well, there *had* been that one incident in college, but that surely had been a fluke, a youthful lapse of judgment. She'd had too much red wine at a party and, by the grace of God and a legion of guardian angels, she'd landed—alone—in her narrow dormitory bed, willing the room to stop spinning and tilting from side to side and, okay, praying for death.

This was a different situation. Years had passed, and she wasn't that shy girl trying so hard to fit in anymore. She was a grown woman now, strong, sure of herself, in control.

Back at the table, fresh mugs of beer awaited, thin sheaths of ice slipping down their sides. That waitress deserved a big tip, in Ria's opinion.

Landry sat her down in her chair—it *was* a little disconcerting that he felt the need to do that—then took his own, across the table from her.

Their knees were pressed together again. Ria, skittish before, allowed herself to enjoy the sensation. Actually, she *reveled* in it. Wanted more.

The band riffed its way into a soft ballad, underscored with a buzz of static from the amplifiers.

"Highbridge was right," Ria thought she heard Landry say, just as he shoved the splayed fingers of one hand through his hair, arousing a sharp desire to reach out and retrace that same path with her own fingers.

"About what?" she shouted, in order to be heard. She cared what Highbridge thought of her, after all.

Landry pretended to wince, but a kind of sad amusement flickered in his eyes. "He said this was a bad idea," he answered.

Then, with a rueful shake of his head, he pushed back his chair abruptly and stood, pried some bills from a front pocket of his jeans and dropped the currency on the table. It was plenty, for all the beer and the food, the accountant in Ria noted, from a remote and rational nook in her brain, even including a generous gratuity.

Clearly, she concluded, they were leaving. Well, good: The place was loud and hot and way too crowded, and if she *had* an inner cowgirl, there'd been no sign of her tonight.

Just to remind Landry that he didn't give the orders, Ria stalled, chugged more of her beer, thinking it would be a shame to waste the stuff, with all its medicinal properties.

Finally, Landry gently removed the mug from her hands, set it back on the table and escorted her through the blue-jeaned, booted multitudes, out the door and into the parking lot.

That first buffeting faceful of cool, fresh air clarified matters with a wallop.

Ria couldn't deny it now—she was *definitely* drunk.

What she *wasn't* was sorry, because, for once, nothing hurt. Over the past few years, Ria had gotten so used to hiding a broken heart that she'd almost stopped noticing the ever-present ache.

"You need coffee," Landry told her, wrapping an arm around her waist and half carrying her back toward his truck. "The more the better."

Ria looked up at the stars, billions upon billions of them, and marveled as though seeing the night sky for the first time in her life.

"So beautiful," she said.

They were beside Landry's truck a moment later, and he'd been occupied, supporting Ria with one arm and releasing the door locks with his free hand. When she'd spoken, though, he'd gone very still, and looked down at her for a long time. Then, his voice grave and gritty as sandpaper, he'd said, "'Beautiful'? Absolutely. It doesn't even begin to describe what I'm seeing right now, though."

The remark confused Ria, but she was still blissfully blotto, so she didn't ask Landry what the heck he'd meant by it.

Maybe she was afraid he'd come right out and tell her. For now, all she really knew was that she didn't want the coffee he'd offered moments before. She didn't want to sober up, either—not yet. Her heart and brain were swathed in soft bunting, she had a pleasant buzz going, and, for the next little while anyway, all was right with the world.

Landry shook his head, as though he'd asked himself a silent question and not liked the answer, opened the passenger-side door and hoisted Ria unceremoniously onto the seat. He leaned across her to catch hold of the seat belt, buckled her in.

She started to sing.

Landry shut the door, sprinted around to his side and got behind the wheel. "If you have to throw up," he said quietly, even gently, "give me some warning so I can pull over to the side of the road."

"Well, *that* was certainly a romantic thing to say," Ria replied, between choruses of the only drinking song she knew—"Ninety-six bottles of beer on the wall, ninety-six bottles of beer—"

Landry chuckled, started the truck's engine. "You skipped ninety-seven," he said as gravel crunched beneath the tires and the headlights pushed back the sultry darkness.

Ria started over from ninety-nine.

Landry gave a groaning laugh and drove out of the parking lot, onto the street beyond.

Besides houses and a couple of trailer parks, they passed at least one café, called the Butter Biscuit, without stopping, so Ria figured Landry must have changed his mind about the coffee, which was fine with her, because she didn't want any. Besides, happy as she was, and compelled to sing at the top of her lungs, she knew she was in no condition to set foot in a public place.

She had a reputation to consider.

She'd gotten all the way to seventy-four in her beer-on-the-wall song when Landry suddenly pulled into the drive-through at a burger place. There were no other vehicles in line.

"Stop singing," he said, not unkindly, before he rolled down his window to place an order at the speaker box.

Ria stopped, and it was kind of a relief, though she was concerned about losing her place in the song. She settled back in the seat, heard him ask for two coffees, black with a shot of espresso, just before her eyelids drifted downward and she slipped into a dream she wouldn't remember.

LANDRY DROVE, letting his own coffee cool in the cup holder, right alongside Ria's. He'd added two bottles of water to the order, as an afterthought, and tossed them onto the backseat.

The road between Parable and Three Trees was dark and the fabled big sky was popping with stars. He wished Ria were awake, so she could see them, too. Once or twice, he said even her name, but softly.

She stirred when she heard his voice, so he knew she was alive, but she didn't wake up.

If Highbridge ever found out about this, Landry thought, with grim humor and a persistent ache in the neighborhood of his heart, his name wouldn't be Landry Sutton anymore. It would be just plain "Mud."

Being nobody's fool, Landry wasn't about to go into any details concerning his "date" with Ria, not to the butler or anyone else, and ten would get you twenty she wouldn't say a word about it, either. That part was more than okay with him, but what was he going to do if Ria woke up in the morning, head throbbing and stomach churning, just one big hangover-wearing skin, and decided it was *his* fault she'd guzzled all that beer?

Couples with a lot going for them had gone their separate ways over lesser things, and that was for sure.

Moreover, while he hadn't forced Ria to drink like somebody trying to put out a fire in their belly, he *was* at least partly responsible, no getting around that. He'd been the one to come up with the bright idea to take her to the Boot Scoot Tavern, after all. He'd looked at it as a sort of cultural immersion, he supposed. Thought it would be a place where Ria could loosen up.

She'd sure as hell done *that,* all right. But Landry doubted she'd cherish the memory, once she was sober again.

Irritated with himself, he thrust a hand through his hair and jammed on the brakes when he spotted a doe and two fawns about to run out in front of the rig, their eyes eerily aglow in the glare of his headlights as they sprung across the road.

A belated glance at Ria assured Landry that she hadn't been startled out of a sound sleep by the sudden stop.

A smile crooked up the corner of his mouth. If Ria had done much drinking up till tonight, he'd eat his hat. Still, she'd done things up right, so to speak. And by the time morning rolled around, she'd be hungover and thoroughly pissed off, just on general principle.

Landry's smile faded, like the highway receding into the gloom behind them.

Yep, Ria was bound to hate herself, once the sun came up, if not before then.

Then she'd start remembering things, piecing them together, and hate him, too.

They were less than a mile from the bright lights of Three Trees when Ria suddenly sat up very straight, opened her eyes wide and whimpered a single word: *"Stop."*

Landry complied, jumped out of the truck and sprinted around to Ria's side, opening the door for her.

She groaned and tried to get her footing on the running board, which was, of course, between her and the ground, but she slipped.

Landry caught her by the waist, set her on her feet a yard or so from the truck and barely managed to shift himself out of the line of fire before she bent double, groaned plaintively and retched, once, twice, three times, into the rocky dirt alongside the asphalt.

Agonized because there was nothing he could do, Landry kept a firm hold on the waistband of Ria's jeans with his right hand, the bare skin of her spine warm against his fingers, not wanting her to take a header into the ditch, on top of everything else. With his free hand, he smoothed her hair back from her forehead and her cheeks.

When she was done heaving up her socks, Ria looked up at him, her face as pale as a full moon in a black, starless sky, and her lower lip quivered.

"Oh, my God," she said, as though surprised to find herself where she was.

Landry had nothing to add, so he waited until he figured Ria was steady enough to stand on her own, then reached into the backseat of the truck for the bottled water he'd bought earlier. It wasn't exactly cold, but it was wet.

He unscrewed the cap and handed Ria the bottle.

Her hand trembled as she took it, raised it almost to her mouth and then lowered it again.

"Turn around," she said, with a shaky but stubborn kind of dignity. "I don't want you looking at me."

Landry refrained from pointing out that she was a little late with *that* request, turned his back and waited.

He heard her gargle and spit, gargle and spit again.

He couldn't help smiling, so he was damn glad she couldn't see his face.

"Okay," she said, after a brief interval of silence. "I'm through."

Landry turned to face her again. She looked small and miserable and more like a girl than the woman he was all too aware she was.

His heart turned over in his chest, and something tender shinnied up his throat. He'd blown this one big-time, he thought, with genuine sorrow. Why hadn't he listened to Highbridge, taken Ria to a nice restaurant or a movie or someplace like that? *Any place* but the Boot Scoot Tavern?

Ria moved to climb into the truck, saying not a word and avoiding Landry's eyes, but she let him help her onto the seat again. That was something, wasn't it?

Neither of them spoke again as they passed through Three Trees and then onto the narrower, more winding road that led home.

At some point—Landry wasn't exactly sure when—Ria started to cry, very softly, as if she didn't want him to know.

"I can't believe I did that," she said, in a husky whisper.

Landry didn't have a clue what to say, besides "Did what?" which would have been a stupid question, given that she'd been stating the obvious, so he just kept driving, his grip on the wheel so tight that his knuckles went numb.

Ria recovered her composure gradually, but with admirable effort, and kept her gaze fixed on the road ahead, far ahead, beyond the long reach of the headlights.

When Landry turned onto her driveway, he hit every rut and pothole, it seemed, even though he'd made up his mind to avoid them, keep the ride as smooth as possible, since Ria had been through enough for one night, thanks, in no small part, to him.

He stopped the truck at the foot of her front walk, came around to open her door and help her down, bracing himself for what he knew was coming. Damn it, he wouldn't even be in her good graces until morning—she'd already started hating him.

Now she'd tell him to stay the hell away from her, from now until the crack of doom, and who could blame her?

She didn't move, evidently wasn't inclined to chat, either.

So they stared at each other, Landry standing on the ground, Ria sitting sideways on the passenger seat. In the harsh glow of the truck's interior light,

Landry saw that her face was still pale, and she'd cried the mascara right off her lashes and onto her cheeks, where it left smudges. Her lower lip wobbled.

Time stopped, started again. Landry was starting to get used to the phenomenon.

Finally, he offered his hand to help her down, and when she didn't take it right away, he figured he'd already touched her for the last time, back there on the side of the highway, and something vast and bleak opened inside him at the thought. Not touching Ria, ever again, would be like living on the dark side of the moon, all by himself.

"Come in for a while?" she asked, very solemnly, at last taking his hand, which, Landry realized, had been suspended in midair for some seconds, forgotten.

When Ria was standing on the ground, Landry cocked his head to one side, sure he must have heard wrong. "Did you just say—?" He finally managed to get out *most* of a sentence, which seemed like an accomplishment, since he hadn't been sure if his vocal cords had rusted over or not.

She smiled, a sad, soft smile, nodded once. "I could use some company," she said. Then the pallor in her mascara-stained cheeks gave way to a fragile shade of pink. "Don't worry—I won't keep you long."

She swayed slightly, just then, and her eyelashes fluttered. Acting on pure instinct, thinking she might be about to faint, Landry lifted her into his arms, just

as he had that other time, when he'd come upon her
on still another roadside, and he carried her up the
walk and the porch steps, right to the door.

By the time they were standing on the welcome
mat, Ria's face was pink all over. "You can put me
down now, please," she said primly. "The keys are in
my shoulder bag, and that's behind me, which means
I can't get to it from here."

Awkwardly, bearing the imprint of said shoulder
bag where it had been caught between them, Landry
set Ria on her feet, hoping she hadn't felt a whole
other kind of imprint.

Her purse was small, basically a leather envelope
with a strap, and she fumbled with the flap for a few
seconds, rummaged inside and produced a key ring.

Without a word, she handed the works to Landry.

He recalled that the long brass one fit the front
door. He inserted the key and turned the lock, noticing, as he hadn't when he'd picked her up for the
date from hell earlier that evening, that the place
was quiet.

No barking dog. No teenage girl, glued to the
modest TV in the living room.

"Quinn's over at Clare's—at a slumber party,"
Ria said, evidently reading the curious expression
on Landry's face. "Bones went with her."

"Oh," Landry said, silently declaring himself a
total dumb-ass.

"There's a coffeepot in the kitchen," Ria said, with

another shadow of a smile. "Why don't you help yourself, while I grab a quick shower?"

First, she'd told him straight out that they were alone, at least until morning. Then she'd mentioned a shower. Was it wishful thinking, Landry wondered, or was she suggesting something more than a cup of coffee? Landry didn't know, and he wasn't about to ask.

So he just nodded, deciding to take things as they came, and went on to the kitchen, once Ria had vanished through an arched doorway.

Landry's heart was beating double time as he flipped on the light switch, scanned the scrubbed countertops for the coffeemaker, found it and extracted a couple of pods from the metal basket nearby.

He heard the plumbing clatter, like a distant train rattling along the tracks, and then the sound of water running, full blast. An image of Ria, stripping off her clothes and stepping under the spray, was just starting to take shape in his mind's eye when he purposely derailed the thought and concentrated on his assignment, which was making coffee.

The machine was the one-cup kind, similar enough to the one he had at home that he had the java brewing within seconds. He scouted for cups, found them on a cupboard shelf and took out two.

With that done, Landry was suddenly in need of distraction, since the water in the shower was still running, and it would be oh so easy to imagine—

He fairly thrust himself into motion, walking over to the small desk in the corner, where Ria's computer stood, clad in plastic covers. The equipment was old-fashioned, if not completely obsolete, a fossil of a thing, with a big monitor and a tower to boot.

Just as he would have turned away, in search of something less personal to occupy his mind, Landry noticed the framed five-by-seven photograph, almost out of sight, there in the shadow of the mammoth monitor.

He picked up the picture, looking at the frame first. It was cutesy and probably cheap, made of cast resin and edged with Dalmatians, each one sporting a bright red fireman's hat and a toothy grin.

There was a heart at the top, red like the dogs' hats but dusted with glitter.

Landry felt his throat thicken as he finally let his eyes take in the picture inside, a black-and-white shot of a smiling man, probably around thirty years old, decked out in full firefighting gear.

Looking into that open, honest face, Landry recalled the wedding band he'd seen on Ria's ring finger, not just on the morning after the buffalo debacle, but before that, too. He hadn't been looking for the ring tonight—he'd been too wrapped up in its wearer—but that didn't mean it wasn't there.

He'd wanted distraction, and he'd gotten it. He hadn't heard the water in the shower stop running, and he flinched, imperceptibly he hoped, when Ria spoke from just behind him.

"He was my husband," she said matter-of-factly. "His name was Frank."

Landry had known she'd been married, known she was a widow, too. So why did Ria's statement strike him in the solar plexus with the force of a ramrod?

Carefully, he set the picture down, turned around. His gaze went straight to the ring finger of her left hand. The band glowed, wide and golden, as if marking a claim, reminding him that she belonged to a dead man.

Landry cleared his throat. Forced himself to meet Ria's eyes.

She'd scrubbed away the blotches of mascara and put on a pair of flannel pajama bottoms and an oversized gray sweatshirt long enough to reach her knuckles.

"I'm sorry," Landry said, because he was, and not just because he'd taken her to the Boot Scoot Tavern and let her drink too much beer.

He was sorry for everything bad that had ever happened to her, in her whole life, and would have given anything, in that moment, if he could go back, year by year, heartbreak by heartbreak, and mend all the broken places.

Ria glanced at the picture, then looked at Landry again. "Don't be," she said. "Pictures are meant to be looked at." A smile quirked at both corners of her mouth, a little twitch. "No coffee?" she added.

Landry recalled his original mission and pointed

to indicate the cup he'd brewed and forgotten, while he was trying not to think about Ria naked in the shower, with beads of water clinging to her eyelashes and her skin....

While he was looking at Frank Manning's face and flat-out envying the guy, even if he *was* six feet under, because Ria had loved him. Loved him so much, in fact, that she was still wearing his wedding ring.

Landry cleared his throat. "I think I'll skip the coffee," he said. "Get out of here so you can rest."

But when he took one step, Ria planted herself directly in front of him.

"You said you'd hold me, if I wanted you to," she said, in a murmur. "Does the offer still stand?"

CHAPTER TEN

RIA WAS SURE she could guess at least *some* of what Landry was thinking in those strained moments after she'd blocked the speedy exit he'd been about to make—from her kitchen, from her house, from her *presence*.

She suppressed a sigh and stood her ground. Okay, she *had* basically asked the man to spend the night with her, but they were both adults, weren't they, she widowed, he divorced? Not to mention that *Landry* had been the one to make the initial suggestion, the one who'd told Ria boldly that she needed holding and he was ready and willing to fulfill that need.

So what was the big deal? It wasn't as if she'd specifically offered sex, after all, though she certainly wasn't ruling it out, either. She'd said, "Hold me," that was all.

Under other circumstances, Ria might have been insulted by Landry's reaction. Because he was always so damn sure of himself, so used to being right, she could only conclude that he'd decided a few things: that she, Ria, didn't know that she wasn't quite herself, that she might *think* she was sober, when she was actually still very much under the influence, that she was missing her husband and wanted a temporary stand-in for Frank, not Landry himself.

All of which, in his lofty opinion, would make her vulnerable, defenseless and, therefore, off-limits. Well, Ria thought, if she'd read Landry correctly, his reasoning was faulty.

First of all, she'd *never* been herself in quite the way she was right now, standing barefoot in her shabby but clean kitchen, heels dug in, because Ria wasn't playing around. Her mind was razor sharp, her attention focused enough to ignite anything or anyone in her path. For once in Ria's up-and-down life, she wasn't self-conscious, a miracle in and of itself. She knew she looked about as *unglamorous* as possible, without a ratty bathrobe, a head full of curlers and a thick layer of goopy face cream to complete the look, and she didn't give a damn.

Second, although Ria knew she'd suffer for over-indulging, that was a simple matter of cause and effect, of science, not sin. Alcohol didn't agree with her; she'd known that and gone ahead and chugged down about a gallon of the stuff anyway, and in very short order.

But damn it, she was *inside this body,* thinking with this brain, feeling with this heart, looking out through these eyes, and she knew she wasn't merely sober, but *stone-cold* sober, as surely as if she'd suddenly been snatched out of a hundred-year nap by a giant hand—

just call her Sleeping Beauty—summarily immersed
in a star-splattered northern sea, between icebergs, and
then just as quickly plucked out again, jolted awake by
the chill, keenly aware of everything around her and
wanting to live, *really* live. For so long she'd been in a
trance, surviving, though just barely, putting one foot
in front of the other with no permanent destination in
mind, marking time while she waited for—what? A
celestial wake-up call?

And now she'd heard that call, that hey-you from
heaven, somewhere between a neon-lit honky-tonk
in a small Montana town and all that throwing up
alongside the highway, and she wasn't going to ignore it.

That wasn't all, though. There *was* a third thing.

Yes, it was true that she missed Frank, sometimes
with a vengeance, and maybe she always would. But
she wasn't in the market for a substitute, as Landry
seemed to have surmised after seeing the photograph
she kept on her desk.

There had been only one Frank.

And there was only one Landry Sutton.

What *did* she want? Right now, in this moment?

That one was easy. Ria wanted a solid, flesh-and-
blood man to hold her close through what remained
of the night, make her feel safe and cherished in his
arms while she sorted out all these new insights.
And, okay, she wouldn't mind some hot, feverish
sex, if it seemed right at the time.

Not just *any* man would do, of course—Ria

needed more than a warm body beside her in bed. She needed Landry Sutton, hardheaded, stubborn, arrogant *Landry Sutton*.

And darned if she knew why.

She smiled, seeing the consternation in Landry's face as he stood there, waiting her out, too cussed to initiate the next stage of conversation, determined not to budge until she spoke again. No matter how long it took.

Finally, Ria spoke. "Stay," she said, and that was all. Just that one word. It wasn't a plea, and it wasn't a command. It just *was*.

Having said what she wanted to say, plainly and simply, with no hidden meanings, nothing but the bald truth, Ria turned and, with all the dignity she possessed, left the room. There was nothing more she could do.

Maybe Landry would follow, maybe he wouldn't.

It was up to him.

"HELL," LANDRY MUTTERED, alone in the kitchen. He felt like a cross-tied bronco, unable to go in one direction or the other.

Go or stay, cowboy? he thought. *What'll it be?*

After long deliberation, which pretty much got him to the same old nowhere, he sighed, crossed the scuffed linoleum floor, switched off the lights and made his way to Ria's room, moving slowly, but toward, not away. The glow of a lamp spilled softly into the short hallway, guiding him like a faint beacon.

Even then, almost consumed by the wanting of her, a primal drive, powerful beyond anything he'd ever felt before, Landry knew he wouldn't make love to Ria, not tonight, maybe not ever.

He would simply hold her, no matter how tempted he might be to go further, because of one thing and one thing only: the golden band on her finger.

In her heart, Ria was still another man's wife. She wasn't ready to let go of her lost firefighter, and that, Landry decided, had to be okay with him, like it or not, because for him, there were lines that couldn't be crossed.

It was that simple.

And that complicated.

He paused in her doorway, raising his arms, gripping the framework.

Ria was already in bed, but she was sitting up, pillows propped behind her, leaning back against the white iron headboard, an ornate thing with a bewildering variety of leaves, birds and curlicues. She watched him serenely, her hands folded in her lap.

Landry might have caved, for all his resistance, because she was so beautiful, and he wanted her so badly. But he looked at her hands again, saw Frank's wedding ring, glinting in the lamplight. *No trespassing.*

"Just hold me," Ria said, guileless as an angel. "That's all I'm asking you to do, Landry. Hold me, this one night. I need to remember what it's like not to be alone."

Landry swallowed hard. He could identify with that—there'd been plenty of nights when he'd have borrowed against his very soul to love some good woman, and be loved in return.

Just hold me. I need to remember what it's like not to be alone.

Oh, yes—Landry understood where Ria was coming from, all right. Did she realize what this kind of restraint would cost him?

Probably. But did she *care?* That question wouldn't be so easy to answer.

"I'm not Frank," Landry said, in a low, rumbling voice that chafed his throat raw with every word. The statement was beyond obvious, of course, but it needed saying anyhow.

"No," Ria affirmed softly. Reasonably. "You're not Frank."

Landry hesitated for another moment, but then he went ahead and approached her, not because he had any fewer misgivings than before, but because he couldn't leave Ria alone. Not tonight.

He sat down heavily on the edge of the mattress, with his back to Ria, kicked off one boot, then the other.

"Thank you," Ria said. And then she switched off the light.

"Don't," he answered hoarsely, lying down beside her, fully clothed and determined to remain that way.

"All right," she agreed, in a whisper with no more substance than the touch of a butterfly's wing.

Ria snuggled close against Landry's side, rested her head on his shoulder.

Landry wrapped his arms around her, a fairly awkward proposition, since he was on top of the covers and she was underneath. He let his chin rest on the crown of Ria's head, and her hair was like silk against his beard-stubbled skin, and the wanting got significantly worse, though he would have sworn, only a heartbeat before, that such a thing wasn't possible.

He drew a long, deep breath, released it, trying to settle down a little, get his bearings, establish some kind of defense.

The room was country-dark, with just a thin shaft of moonlight shining through the window and pooling on the foot of the bed, reducing everything else to shadowy, indistinct shapes.

And that was a good thing, since Landry had the hard-on of all hard-ons and he preferred to keep the information to himself.

"How did he die?" he asked, after a long time. He hadn't planned on saying anything at all, but there it was.

Ria's breathing was slow and even, but he knew she wasn't asleep. Presently, she answered, "Frank was killed in a fire."

"I'm sorry," Landry said.

"Me, too."

"Did you love him?"

"Yes," Ria replied. A pause followed, one that seemed to have its own pulse. "Did you love your wife?"

Landry might have been amused by this question, deft turning of the tables that it was, if he hadn't felt like a multiple-injury nine-car pileup right about then. "I thought I did," he answered, when he was ready. "Later on, I had my doubts."

There was another brief silence, while Ria absorbed the information. Then, tentatively, she asked, "Was she faithful to you?"

It was a reasonable question, Landry supposed. He just hadn't expected it to be at the forefront of their first real conversation.

"Probably," he said.

"Were you faithful to her?"

"Yes," Landry said. "Maybe for all the wrong reasons, but—yes."

He didn't usually engage in this kind of personal discussion, but he was invisible in that dark room, and he liked the way Ria felt, warm and soft and scented with her own perfume, lying so close, one arm slung across his chest.

It was nice, even without the sex. But sex would have been better.

"What reasons?" Ria asked.

It would be so easy to kiss her—to put a stop to the soul probing by opening the door to all the pleasures his body was craving, even as he willed himself not to want her. And it would be so wrong.

"The usual ones, I guess," he said, when he thought he could trust his voice not to betray him. "I worked long hours, and she was restless, always traveling to some spa or retreat or shopping mecca—so we were apart more often than we were together. And I guess we never had much in common to start with."

"But you never cheated? Not even once?"

Odd that she kept homing in on the fidelity issue, Landry thought, but he couldn't track the observation through his brain, wrestle it down and examine it, because not making love to Ria Manning took all the energy he could muster up.

"Not even once," he finally replied. "Which is not to say I was never tempted."

"You were pretty unhappy," Ria surmised sadly, splaying the fingers of her left hand over his heart. The wedding ring burned right through his shirt, like a laser, or the business end of a tiny, red-hot branding iron.

Landry caught a ragged breath. He needed a cold shower, and bad.

"Yeah," he said. "I was unhappy. But so was Susan."

Another pause on Ria's side—sad. Tender, too. "Not a match made in heaven?"

"More like a match made in the boardroom," Landry answered.

"Then why on earth did the two of you get married?"

If only I knew. "It seemed like a good idea at the time, I guess." Then, after a long interlude of silent self-discipline, Landry decided it was his turn to do some quizzing. "That sweatshirt you're wearing—was it Frank's?"

"That's a strange question," Ria said mildly, sounding puzzled, rather than annoyed.

"No stranger than the ones you've been asking me," Landry pointed out.

"No," Ria admitted, with a philosophical sigh, and Landry thought he heard just the faintest note of amusement in the response.

She yawned lustily, snuggled closer, blissfully unaware, he would have bet, that she was making bad matters worse with every move of that sumptuous body of hers, no matter how slight. "I guess not," she said.

"Then—?"

"No," she relented, rightly concluding that he wasn't going to let this go. "I used to wear Frank's shirts sometimes, after he was gone, but it was a phase."

Ria began to move her hand on his chest, round and round, in slow circles.

Landry bit back a groan. The hard-on was at full mast now, but still, incredibly, getting bigger, and, *damn it,* it hurt like hell. If this kept up, he'd probably blow a blood vessel or something.

"Then whose is it?" he asked. He was pushing, but he couldn't help it. The shirt was big, made for a man with some bulk to him, not for a slip of a woman like Ria.

"That's essentially none of your business," Ria purred, after another expansive yawn. Her hand kept making those slow circles, her fingers catching on one of his shirt buttons once in a while, pausing for a split second, as if she might be deciding whether to undo it or not.

God help me, Landry thought.

"True enough," he answered gruffly, awash in sweet and absolute anguish by then, "but I still want to know."

She chuckled, a sultry sound, a *womanly* sound, as far from a girlish giggle as east was from west. "It belonged to a guy I knew in college," she said. Her hand paused at his collarbone, and she ran a single finger down the row of his shirt buttons, all the way to his belt. And went right on talking, just as if she hadn't split the atom. "Ted was a jock. I was a number nerd, so we were probably doomed from the first. Things were hot and heavy for a while, but then we both got bored and went our separate ways. I got custody of the sweatshirt because it happened to be in my laundry hamper when the music stopped." Her finger trailed along the edge of his belt now, drawing a fiery line.

Landry was silent, mainly because he knew if he

opened his mouth, if he sucked in a much-needed breath, he'd exhale it as a groan.

"What is it?" Ria prompted, with a sleepy smile in her voice. The finger followed its crisscross path.

Landry caught hold of her hand, stopped the exploration. "Have mercy, woman," he rasped. "I'm tough as hell, but, *damnation,* I'm not invincible."

She laughed. "I never thought I'd hear you say that," she said. "That you aren't invincible, I mean."

He didn't let go, but closed his fingers around her wrist instead, partly because he liked the way it felt, and partly because he didn't trust her not to push him over the edge.

"Go to sleep," he told her, long after she'd spoken.

"Is that an order?" Her tone was teasing, amused. She was definitely smiling, he knew it, even though he didn't look at her to verify the suspicion.

Landry ground his back molars together before replying, "It's a suggestion."

Another chuckle, followed by a mischievous "Do you know what I think, Landry Sutton? *I* think you want to make love to me."

Damn. The woman didn't know when to quit.

Still, Landry wasn't going to lie. "Of course I want to make love to you," he said evenly, glaring up at the ceiling. "I'm a *man,* Ria, not a safety-test dummy."

Her response? An impish "So what's stopping you?"

Landry growled a swearword. "This is *not* going

to happen," he vowed, with a finality that didn't quite ring true, at least for him.

Ria turned the screw, purred, "You don't find me attractive?"

"Hell, yes, I find you attractive," Landry bit out. "I do have a set of working eyeballs, you know. Not to mention a few other parts clamoring for a say-so."

A breathy giggle. "Then why not—?"

"Stop it, Ria. *Now.* It wouldn't be right, and you damn well know it!"

"Why wouldn't it be right?"

Landry thought hard; strange to feel so desperate to avoid the very thing he wanted, right then, more than anything else in the world. What he came up with was an admittedly lame "Because, when you're in your right mind, you don't like me, and, some of the time, I don't like you all that much, either."

Ria didn't deny what he'd said, but she also didn't give up, either. "But you want me? Physically, I mean?"

He was at the end of his patience, ready to snap, ready to show Ria Manning just how much he *did* want her, followed by how much he knew about pleasing a woman, with a few new tricks thrown in for the hell of it.

"What do you think?" Landry demanded. "The blood in my veins is as red as any other man's." He lightened his grip on her wrist, in case he was hurting her. "Now, one question. And I'm serious here,

Ria. Are you torturing me for some viable reason, or just because it's fun?"

Ria laughed again, a chiming sound, joyous and, no getting around it, brazenly bold. "I'm not trying to torment you, Landry," she said, when her laughter had dwindled to a series of hiccups. "I'm just feeling a little—receptive."

"You're also a little *drunk*."

"Am not."

"Are, too."

Now, *there* was an adult exchange.

Suddenly, Ria yanked free of his grasp, sat bolt upright with the speed of a cannonball shot from a rocket launcher and switched the bedside lamp back on, nearly blinding Landry in the glare.

Flirty only seconds before, the woman was suddenly rigid with anger and naked frustration, her arms folded tight across her amazing chest—oh, to divest her of that damn sweatshirt and get down to business—her eyes snapping.

"Some women," she informed him curtly, "would be insulted by your behavior."

"And some women," Landry retorted, just as furious as she was, and horny as hell on top of that, "would have sense enough to know when *some man* was trying his damnedest to do the right thing."

"The key word," Ria pointed out, reddening attractively and still mad as all get-out, "is *women*. I *am* a woman, Landry Sutton, not some nineteen-year-old airhead with rhinestones on the back pockets of her jeans!"

Landry sat up, too. He was still irritated, but the emotion was giving way to utter confusion. *Women.* They might not be from Venus, as that old book title proclaimed, but they sure as *hell* weren't from earth, either. "What does *that* have to do with the subject at hand?" he demanded. "And who said anything about buckle bunnies with rhinestones on their butts?"

Wisely, Landry withheld the observation that those butts were usually fine to look at, and to hell with the rhinestones.

When Ria didn't answer, but simply looked tight-lipped, he finally caught the drift, his temper in the red zone again, and ranted on, though he did make a real effort to keep his voice down.

"If I had a taste for 'nineteen-year-old airheads,' as you put it, I wouldn't be here right now." A pause, a raspy breath. "As it happens, lady, I prefer *grown women.*"

Instantly, Ria raised a hand to her mouth and, for one terrible moment, Landry thought she was going to start crying again, which made him feel like a complete jerk, about to graduate from Asshole U with honors. Then he realized, clued in by the twinkle frolicking in her eyes, that Ria wasn't on the verge of tears at all. She was trying not to laugh.

He was both relieved and royally bent out of shape. "You think this is funny?" he drawled, his voice as rough and dry as a dirt road in a drought.

"No," Ria said, with a quick shake of her head. "Of course I don't." But she still felt a need to cover her mouth, he noticed. Her shoulders were shaking a little, and that light was still in her eyes.

Landry swung his legs over the side of the bed, turning his back to Ria in the process, and looked around for his boots.

Enough, damn it, was enough.

But Ria laid a hand on his shoulder, and everything came to a wrenching halt.

"Don't go," she said.

Landry stiffened, then thrust out a sigh, braced his elbows on his thighs and lowered his head, shoving the fingers of both hands into his hair.

Up was down. East was west. The sun would probably shine at night from here on out, while the moon took over the day shift.

And, damn it all to hell, when was the last time he'd gone to bed with a woman and kept his clothes on for the duration? *Never,* that was when. Was he possessed or something?

If nothing else, Landry had always been a man who knew his own mind, a man who thought his decisions through carefully but quickly, made them and didn't look back. Now, all of a sudden, he not only didn't know his mind, but he didn't know his ass from a hole in the ground. He was coming undone, falling apart at the seams, morphing into somebody he didn't begin to recognize. And it scared him shitless.

If Ria had been on the verge of a giggle fit a few minutes before, she was in a very different mood now. He felt her shift, knew she was kneeling behind him now, and when she spoke, her voice was sad and soft and somehow it fractured Landry's heart.

"I'm sorry," she said. "I *was* messing with you, and that's not right."

Landry unclamped his jawbones, but he didn't turn around, didn't look at her. He didn't dare move.

"Forget it," he replied.

She went right on talking—that was a woman for you. When a man wanted a little peace and quiet, she wanted to "communicate." When he asked her if something was wrong, though, she invariably said "nothing," meaning exactly the opposite, and then she clammed up, operating on the crazy premise that if the jerk de jour really cared about her in the least, he'd *know* what the problem was, without having to ask in the first place.

There was no winning *this* game.

"Listen to me, please," Ria continued, massaging his shoulders now, quietly turning Landry inside out. "Either you think you're saving me from myself, because the 'little woman' doesn't know what's good for her, or all that stuff about wanting me was just so much fast-talking bullshit." A beat passed, and then she went in for the kill. "Which is it?"

He turned around then, saw that he'd been right, that Ria was on her knees on the mattress, but she wasn't playing the supplicant. Her blue eyes were clear and serious. She might have been baiting him before, he thought, but she was on the level now. She wanted a straight answer, that was all.

"You're not ready," he said flatly. The truth, he reflected, with disjointed reason, might set a person free, as the Good Book said, but it sure wasn't easy to face sometimes.

Ria tilted her head to one side, studying his face. "How can you possibly know whether I'm ready or not?" she asked.

Landry took hold of her left hand, held it up between them, used the pad of his thumb to turn the wide wedding band gleaming on her finger.

"*This* is how," he said, with real sorrow.

Ria closed her eyes. All the starch seemed to drain out of her, and she lay down again, turning away from him this time, curling up like a night flower closing itself against the break of day.

Landry ached, everywhere. "Ria—"

"Go away," she murmured. "Please. Just go."

He stood, grabbed up one boot, then the other.

Carried them out to the darkened kitchen, where he plunked down on a chair to pull them on.

He'd started out with honorable intentions, he brooded, in glum silence, and he'd *still* managed to botch things up.

It was a gift, he thought, with jaw-clenching irony. And then he did as he'd been told.

He left.

THE SUNSHINE WOKE Ria the next morning, but not gently, the way it usually did. Oh, no. It glowed red as the fires of hell through her eyelids, and immediately kick-started the mother of all headaches, the thump-thump kind, a biological metronome. No, a jackhammer.

She groaned. She'd expected this rush of misery, and she was down with the overwhelming likelihood that she deserved to suffer a little, but knowing something wasn't the same as being at all prepared to cope.

Ria sat up, blinking. Dizzy.

Landry.

She stiffened, squeezing her eyes shut again. *No, don't think about him. Not now.*

Even her hair hurt, and that wasn't all. Her tongue was thick and nasty-tasting and dry as cornstalks left over from Halloween, and her stomach—well, it was out of control, off the rails, careening toward complete rebellion.

Ria groaned again, arms crossed tightly as though her insides might tumble out if she wasn't careful, and groped her way to the window. The light was a continuing torment, a gong sounding in her brain, right along with the steady *rat-a-tat-tat* of the jackhammer.

After fumbling with the cord for a few agonizing seconds, she was able to close the blinds. It helped, but only a little.

She stumbled to the bathroom, stood gracelessly

in front of the commode, not sure what would happen first—would her head explode, or would she heave up the lining of her stomach? Could go either way.

In the end, it went *this* way: Ria managed to rummage through the medicine cabinet and then every drawer in the bathroom vanity until she finally found a bottle of aspirin, wrestled off the cap, swallowed two tablets with a gulp of water—and *then* threw up. Repeatedly.

She was on her knees, too weak to stand, when the convulsions finally stopped. When she was sure that part of the ordeal was really and truly over, and not just regrouping for a fresh attack, she *crawled* back to bed, hauled herself up onto the mattress and burrowed under the covers.

Birds began to sing and, for the first time in her life, Ria wished they'd just shut the hell up so she could feel sorry for herself in peace.

They didn't, of course. Instead, they seemed to be rehearsing for a performance of Handel's *Messiah*.

She would just go back to sleep, then. Except her head hurt too badly and her poor stomach alternately cramped up, charley horse–style, and then became a rumbling void, demanding food.

Food. God, no.

Ria was glad Landry had gone home, that he wasn't there to see her like this—until she *wasn't* glad. The bastard. She wouldn't be in this situation if it wasn't for him.

Presently, Ria thought she heard a door open and then quietly close. Quinn must be home, she decided.

She'd pretend to be asleep if her niece looked in on her, wondering, as she surely would, why Ria was still in bed, since she usually rose ridiculously early.

Ria heard the footsteps then—boot heels on bare wooden floors. Not Quinn. Of *course* not Quinn—she'd probably been up all night, with Clare and the others. By now, they'd both be dead to the world, slumber-party veterans sprawled among their fallen comrades.

A burglar, then?

She should be so lucky.

Landry was back.

Ria waited, eyes closed too tightly, ready to do her Sleeping Beauty number.

Except that Landry didn't come to the bedroom. He was in the kitchen, opening and closing cupboards, banging pans around—was he *trying* to kill her?—rummaging through the refrigerator.

Dear God, was he going to *cook*?

Hungry as she was, one look at food, one *whiff* of it, would have her racing for the bathroom again, retching the whole way.

Silently, she willed him to go away, leave her to suffer in private.

It didn't work, of course. Even if she'd had that

kind of mind power at her disposal, Landry would have been impervious to it.

He'd won another round, and now he was going to rub it in.

CHAPTER ELEVEN

LANDRY SUTTON KNEW a thing or two about hang-overs, so he stepped as lightly as he could, without taking off his boots anyway, when he let himself in through Ria's unlocked front door the next morn-ing. He was there on a mission of mercy—or so he liked to believe—and he took care to keep a lid on unnecessary noises, making just enough to her know she wasn't alone.

He searched the cupboards until he found a medium-sized saucepan, set it on the burner with a slight *thump,* meant to carry, though he had yet to decide what kind of grub he'd put into the thing yet.

If somebody made a list of his strong points, Landry thought, with a grin quirking up one side of his mouth, "culinary genius" would be nowhere on it.

Knowing Ria probably felt as though she'd been chopped up and run through a blender on high speed, he hoped she was perceptive enough to figure out that she wasn't in danger, wasn't about to be con-fronted by a prowler or a serial killer or some other lowlife. Landry had never heard of a crook who cooked, a sneak-chef, if you will—and he was fairly sure Ria hadn't, either.

In need of an eye-opener, he brewed himself a cup of coffee, his first of the day. He'd been in a hurry to get out of the house before he encountered High-bridge, knowing there would be a serious run-in if that happened.

Taciturn as he was, the butler never hesitated to meddle in Landry's business, or to preach an impromptu sermon with a lot of unwanted opinions woven through it, like threads in a sheet. Therefore, he'd paused just long enough to feed his horses, turn all but one out to pasture for the day and saddle up.

First order of business: make sure Bessie and her so-called calf were where they were supposed to be—in the southern pasture.

The buffalo were minding their own business, grazing placidly in the first purple-tinged light of a late June morning.

After that, he'd just ridden for a long time, aim-less, letting the big sky and the trees and all that space untangle the knots in his brain—and else-where. Then he'd stopped by Zane's place, found his brother doing chores in the barn and asked to borrow a horse. Specifically, a tame one—his were all either too green to be trusted or too spirited for a rider with morning-after issues.

Not that he went into all that much detail.

Zane had looked him over in amused appraisal, making it damn good and clear that he knew more than Landry wanted him to, including why he wanted the second horse, but in the end, he'd been gracious enough to withhold his usual pithy comment, saying only, "Help yourself."

Landry had left his own gelding loosely tied at the water trough, gone inside and chosen a fat little sorrel mare from the lineup in the long row of occupied stalls, assessing her as more likely to plod than run, considering her girth.

After that, he'd picked out a likely-looking saddle and a blanket to put under it, thickly cushioned with sheep's wool, along with a bridle, lugged the works out of the well-equipped tack room, saddled the mare in her stall and then led her out into the still-cool breeze of a summer morning.

Zane was standing next to Landry's gelding by then, stroking the animal's neck and carrying on a one-sided chat. He had a way with critters, Zane did. Kids, too. And, of course, women, though these days he reserved all that rodeo-bad-boy charm for one specific female—his wife, Brylee.

Love had sure settled *him* down, and that might have been discouraging if he and Brylee hadn't been so happy.

Landry stopped in his tracks for a moment, swallowed a rush of envy, and finally got going again when the mare bumped into him from behind.

He'd wanted to say one thing to his brother—that he was in deep with Ria Manning and he wasn't sure whether he ought to stick with his present course or run like all hell in the opposite direction—but he and Zane, though they'd made strides over the past year, still weren't close enough for that kind of honesty.

So Landry said something else instead. "What the heck are you feeding this horse? She practically waddles."

Zane looked back at him over one shoulder, chuckled. "We call her Butterball, for obvious reasons. As for what I'm feeding her—grass hay and just enough grain to make life worth living." He patted the gelding once more, then turned around to face Landry full on. "I bought her two days ago, at a livestock sale in Missoula—you might say it was a mercy purchase."

Landry grinned at that observation. He'd barely slept the night before, of course, getting home late the way he had and everything, horny and pissed off and deeply worried about Ria on top of it, and he'd woken in a funk, without a trace of good humor in him.

The long ride had revitalized him, though.

And so had being in his brother's company, awkward as it was.

"I'll take it easy on her," he'd promised, and then felt the backs of his ears heat up a little, realizing the statement could have been taken two ways. He'd been referring to the mare, not Ria—Zane's quick grin reconfirmed Landry's suspicion that there were no secrets in either half of Hangman's Bend Ranch—but clarifying the matter would have been worse than clumsy, so he didn't make the attempt.

"You do that," Zane had responded, in an amiable drawl. He stepped up to hold Butterball's reins while Landry swung up onto the gelding's back, handing them over when the time came.

Landry had frowned slightly. Then he'd tugged at the brim of his hat, reined the gelding toward the county road and ridden out at an easy trot, Butterball jogging along behind him.

Reaching Ria's place, he'd left both horses in the shade of a tree, well away from any flower beds, and left them to graze on dew-kissed grass green enough to make a man blink if he looked at it for too long. His own mount wasn't likely to run off, and he figured the mare didn't have that much initiative.

Now here he was, standing in the woman's kitchen as if he had every right to be there—obviously, she hadn't unfurled herself from the fetal position after he'd left the night before and locked the front door—trying to figure out what to do next.

Highbridge would have made tea, he supposed, the herbal kind most likely, in place of his favorite loose-leaf brand, and suitably weak, giving Ria a fighting chance to keep it down.

Landry, on the other hand, reasoned that she probably needed something with a little nourishment value, if she was going to get her strength back.

So he rummaged through her small pantry until he found a red-and-white can of chicken noodle soup. He removed the lid with an electric can opener—

more noise—set the can on the stove next to the
waiting pan and proceeded to hunt down a colander.

He found one, after a lot more opening and closing of cupboard doors, placed it on top of the pan and
dumped the soup into it, congratulating himself for
sensitive forethought and watching the thick broth seep
through the little holes, leaving noodles, some micro-
scopic vegetable parts and a few minuscule chunks of
chicken behind. That done, he set the colander aside
in the sink without disposing of the contents, filled
the soup can at the sink and sloshed water in on top of
the broth to thin it down to a manageable consistency.

Damn, he was good. A regular Fred Nightingale.

Humming under his breath by now, he located the
knob that corresponded with the right front burner
and turned it to medium-high. Mission almost ac-
complished.

"What do you think you're doing?" a wan voice
asked, startling him out of his mild hubris. Ria, of
course.

He smiled, turned away from the stove to greet
his unwilling patient.

Ria had swapped out the pajama pants and that
dude's sweatshirt for a long cotton nightgown. Over
this, incongruously, she wore a snappy blue blazer—
probably the first cover-up that came to hand before
she came out here to raise hell.

"Good morning to you, too," Landry said cheerily, with the suggestion of a bow.

"Go away," she replied, standing there stiff as a

fence post, with her arms folded. Then, as if she'd decided an explanation was called for—generous of her—she went on. "I hate you. I hate myself. Right now, in fact, I think I hate just about everybody."

"I'm not going anywhere," Landry said, unruffled. "And you'll probably get over hating yourself and 'everybody' sooner or later. As for hating me—" He paused, shrugged and gave her his cockiest grin. "Why change horses in the middle of the stream? Liking me all of a sudden would be rash."

Ria narrowed her eyes, a tender shade of blue, although red-rimmed to be sure and a mite on the puffy side, as well. Her skin, normally peaches-and-cream, had turned a pale shade of green, like split-pea soup with too much milk in it. "And far be it from me to be *rash*," she replied pointedly.

Sarcasm? Probably. She'd been impetuous—make that frisky—the night before. And she didn't like remembering that.

Too bad.

Landry chuckled, pulled out a chair and, taking a light hold on her shoulders, pressed her into it.

She sat, reluctantly, then peered past him, at the pan on the stove.

"I'm not going to eat," she announced.

"That's what you think," Landry replied amiably.

She scowled.

He ignored her. The chicken broth was going from a simmer to a rolling boil, so he took the pan off the heat and ransacked the cupboards again, deliberately making a ruckus, until he found a good-sized mug. He squinted at the inside, as though he figured it might not be clean, and, to his abject satisfaction, he saw Ria bristle, there at the far edge of his vision.

Good. He'd gotten another reaction. With this particular woman, that constituted progress—however questionable.

Hiding a smile, Landry poured the contents of the pan into the mug, carried it to the table and set it down in front of Ria.

She sat watching the steam roll up from the mug, as if she were hypnotized or something. Then, rather than recoiling, or maybe throwing the whole works in his face, as Landry had half expected her to do, she looked at the broth with a sort of hopeless yearning.

Watching her, he felt something flip in the center of his heart.

"I can't," she said miserably. "Anyway, it's too hot."

"Sure, you can," Landry answered, gently now. He took the mug over to the fridge, added a couple of ice cubes, set the soup in front of her again. At least if she decided to throw it at him after all, he wouldn't have third-degree burns to show for his good intentions.

He scraped back a chair of his own then and sat down across from Ria. "Start with a sip, and take your time."

"It won't stay down," Ria mourned. "Even water—"

"Try," Landry persisted, very quietly.

She raised her eyes to his face then, and he caught a glimpse of the Ria he knew, the one who, though she seemed to enjoy giving him what-for at the slightest provocation, was in full control of her renegade emotions.

That was definitely a relief.

"Quinn will be back any time now," she said, concentrating on the ice cubes floating in the mug, serious as a prosecutor laying out a strong case in court. "And if she finds you here, she'll think I— you—we—"

"Slept together last night?" Landry finished for her, delighting in the healthy color flooding her cheeks. "Well, that's easy enough to remedy." With those words, he stood up and headed for Ria's room, with the deliberate certainty of a man who knew exactly where it was. There, he closed his mind to all the sense memories and the rapid-fire images of what might have been, appropriated one of the pillows from her bed, along with a knitted cover-up thing he found draped over the back of a chair, and made the return trip to the kitchen. He paused just long enough to hold them up and say, "I spent the night on the couch. That's my story, and I'm sticking to it."

Ria's jaw tightened visibly, but she said nothing.

Moving on to the living room, Landry tossed the pillow and the cover-up onto the couch and jumbled them up a little, so they'd look properly messy, as if he'd tossed them aside when he woke and never given them a second thought.

Brilliant, he thought.

Okay, so the setup wouldn't explain, even to the most casual observer, why there were two horses outside, he allowed, only slightly less pleased with himself, but maybe Quinn wouldn't notice them.

Yeah, right, Landry thought. Invisible horses.

Still, the ruse was worth a try—heaven forbid they simply tell the kid the truth—so he left the tangle of bedding right where it was and went back to the kitchen.

Ria was still sitting at the table, but he suspected she'd tasted the broth while he was out of the room. She couldn't have been any more stubborn if her skull had been cast from molten bronze.

"Bottoms up," he said merrily, sitting down again and indicating the mug of watered-down soup in front of her.

"Are you being *deliberately* obnoxious, or does it just come naturally to you?"

Landry remained happily intractable. After all, Ria wasn't the only one around here with a hard head.

"Drink the broth."

"I just want to go back to bed and quietly die," Ria protested, but instead of following through, she curled her fingers around the mug handle and hoisted it an inch or so off the tabletop.

"Going back to bed isn't an option," Landry informed her, "much less dying. We're going riding as soon as you choke down some of that broth and put some clothes on."

Ria looked horrified. "*Riding? On horses?*"

"On horses," Landry confirmed, immovable.

"*Out* of the question," Ria said, with a sniff. "I'm sick. I need rest."

"Wrong on both counts," Landry answered, folding his arms, leaning his chair back on two legs and grinning at her. "You're not sick—you're hungover. There's a difference. And what you need is fresh air and a little exercise, not 'rest.' That'll only keep you thinking about how bad you feel."

"You are *insufferable.*"

Landry smiled broadly. "Thank you," he said.

Ria made an exasperated sound, took a couple of cautious sips from the mug, waited a second or two to see if any kind of physical calamity would strike and, when one didn't, kept drinking.

"If I finish this, like a good girl," she said acidly, between sips that were getting progressively bigger, "will you go away and leave me alone?"

"Not a chance," Landry answered. "You look better already." He couldn't resist. "The blazer is a nice touch, I must say. Who'd have thought to pair one up with a nightgown?"

"Shut up," Ria said, but she didn't sound as though she had high hopes that the request would be granted. She was looking straight at him, though, and her eyes were shooting sky-blue fire. "Get this through your thick head, Landry Sutton—I am *not* going any-where, *especially* not with you!"

"Yeah, you are" was his casually confident re-sponse. "You just haven't accepted the fact yet." He pushed back his chair, rose to his feet again. "Finish the soup. Since you seem to be stuck in neutral gear, I'll rustle up some clothes for you and—"

Ria seethed.

He loved it when she seethed. It was proof that her blood ran hot, a distinct advantage in bed. Pro-vided they ever *got* to bed, that was.

"Forget it," she told him. "You can't *make* me get dressed."

"No," Landry admitted, on his way back to the bedroom again, "but I can do it for you if you're going to be stubborn."

"I'll call the sheriff," she shouted after him, but Landry could tell she was bluffing.

"Do that," he called back. The house was small. They probably didn't need to yell, but there it was. Their personal communication style. "My guess is, once he hears the whole story, Boone will be on my side."

Ria gave a small, strangled scream of sheer and unadulterated frustration and stomped after him, only to find him not riffling the contents of her closet or bureau, but sitting smugly on the side of the bed, waiting for her.

"All right," she said. "But if this damn fool idea kills me, it'll be on your conscience!"

Landry didn't laugh, but it wasn't easy. Damned if the woman wasn't beautiful, even when she was mad as a wet cat and hungover as hell, both at once.

He held up both palms, in a gesture of peace, and kept his mouth shut.

"Get out," she told him.

He glanced at the door. No lock, and that was good, because she wouldn't be able to shut herself away, thus creating a standoff. He could be forceful when the situation called for it, but kicking in the door would be going too far.

Wouldn't it?

Landry sighed, got up and left the room.

Ria slammed the door behind him, hard.

He took up his post in the hallway, leaning idly against the wall.

Inside the bedroom, drawers opened, banged shut again. There was a lot of foot stomping and some pretty colorful muttering.

Landry simply waited, calm as a Zen monk in deep meditation, his expression amiable. The fact of the matter was, he was enjoying every moment of Ria's muffled tirade.

The conclusion he'd come to the night before, on the way to the Boot Scoot Tavern, surfaced again. He loved Ria Manning, God help him.

And he definitely wanted her. But as long as Ria wore her late husband's wedding band, he wouldn't do anything more than kiss her—there had to be *some* reward for all this nobility and self-control, didn't there? And there were certainly plenty of ways to make her want him.

It was a challenge, and Landry thrived on those. A little mental foreplay, plenty of Sutton charm and Ria would be his in no time.

Landry's native confidence wavered, very slightly and very briefly.

He sure hoped she'd come around anyway, because if she didn't, he'd be fresh out of bright ideas.

RIA WAS FEELING better with each passing moment, which was great in every way but one: it made her wrong and Landry right. Again.

She practically yanked on her clothes—fresh underwear, jeans and a T-shirt, socks and her one pair of boots. Then she swiped deodorant into her armpits, brushed her teeth for the second time that morning—the first pass had been more about desperation than hygiene—and ran a comb through her hair, briskly dispensing with a bad case of bed head.

What was wrong with Landry Sutton anyhow?

He'd seen her at her worst—silly drunk, throwing up alongside the road and, this very morning, dressed like a homeless person and so ornery that she was starting to offend *herself.*

She sighed once, heavily, hoping to vent at least some of her frustration, and stood still in front of the mirror above her vanity table, studying her reflection and wondering what the hell Landry saw in her.

Frank's ring caught a stray beam of light just then,

and Ria remembered how Landry had taken her hand
the night before, when she'd made an idiot of herself
by asking why he wouldn't make love to her, held it
up in front of her nose and said, *"This is why."*

Now she fidgeted with the band—even started to
take it off—but something stopped her. What made
her hesitate?

Love for a man she would never see again?

No. She'd accepted Frank's death long before she
got to know Landry; she realized that now. What
she felt for her brave, goofy, lost husband was fond-
ness, not love.

The truth was, the ring was a kind of shield, a
magical talisman that kept men from getting too
close. For a long, long time, Ria not only hadn't
wanted that kind of intimacy, but she'd feared it.
Her soul had been too raw, her heart and mind and
faith too bruised, to open herself up to such pain by
taking a chance on trusting somebody.

Who, after all, should have been more trustwor-
thy than Frank?

Unable to help herself, Ria went right on looking
backward, into the unreachable past. At first, people
had left her alone, respected her grief and her fierce
need for solitude, for time to think and remember
and sort through a lot of paradoxes—like the fact that
Frank had loved her very much, she knew he had,
and yet he'd risked everything for a one-night stand.

Sure, he'd tried to clear the air. He'd wept, something she'd never seen him do before, and he'd apol-

ogized and promised to be faithful from then on. On some level, Ria had believed him. She'd taken him back into her heart, tried to pretend nothing had happened, eventually convinced herself that nothing had to change, that she and Frank could just go on as before.

When she was truly honest with herself, though, Ria knew she hadn't carried off this feat of self-deception, simply because the pain of being betrayed by the person she'd trusted most, the person who had made sacred vows in front of an altar, had never actually gone away. She'd submerged it, that was all, and then Frank was dead, and sorrow buried her as surely as if the whole side of a mountain had given way, come down on top of her, crushed her.

Come what may, there was no changing the fact that Frank had, for one night at least, forgotten that he loved her.

Ria drew a deep breath, let it out and left the wedding band right where it was, on her left-hand ring finger. Weird? Maybe. But, like it or not, she still needed that thin golden boundary. Without it, she could be swept away all over again and, eventually, *hurt* all over again.

One betrayal by a man she loved had nearly destroyed her. Another would finish the job.

Finally, Ria turned away from the mirror, vaguely troubled by the woman she'd seen looking back at her in the smooth glass, and left her room.

Landry was waiting in the hall. She made a face at him.

He laughed.

And, remarkably, that was the beginning of a good day.

Leading the way outside, Landry untied the mare and introduced her to Ria as Butterball.

It was a fitting name, but the horse was a sweetheart, and Ria, who'd ridden a little when she was younger, taking weekly lessons until the phase passed, took an instant liking to the animal.

She managed to mount Butterball, with just a leg up from Landry, and the cloudless blue sky, the cool breeze and the sight of acres of flowers seemed to saturate her entire being as she looked around. Even the sun, her worst enemy when she'd been forced to open her eyes that morning, seemed benign now, blanketing her in gentle warmth.

"You're not half-bad at this," Landry commented, keeping his eager gelding reined in so Butterball could keep up without giving herself a heart attack from overexertion. "Riding horseback, I mean."

Ria laughed. "Thanks," she replied. "I think."

For the next hour or so, they simply rode, through meadows and woods, along the banks of the Big Sky River and, finally, back around to Ria's farm.

Quinn was sitting on the front steps when they arrived, Bones cavorting in the grass at her feet. The girl grinned and waved, then bounced up off the step and hurried toward Ria and Landry, though her attention was mainly fixed on the horses.

Watching her niece, Ria reflected that, against all odds, she'd had a wonderful time on the ride, at least partly because she and Landry had avoided serious talk. He'd told her funny stories about growing up on the road, and some of the things he and Zane had done, which were the stuff of memoir, in her opinion. He'd described a gypsy's childhood, often low on money or gas for the car or even food, but none of that seemed to bother Landry—he didn't say so outright, but he'd been a happy kid. Yes, they'd moved from town to town, this hapless little family, the boys starting school in a new place every year, but their mom had always managed to spin the next challenge as an adventure. Listening, laughing now and then and tearing up at times, too, Ria had found herself wishing she'd known Maddie Rose Sutton—clearly, she'd been one heck of a woman.

Ria came back to current reality, somewhat reluctantly.

Quinn, who'd evidently been prattling away right along, patted Butterball's damp neck while Ria climbed down from the saddle, doing her best not to wince when her feet hit the ground.

"Can I ride sometime?" Quinn asked eagerly.

Landry smiled, his face shadowed by the brim of his hat, but he didn't reply.

"We don't actually own a horse," Ria reminded her niece, with gentle humor. Lord, but she was going to be sore after this ride, and Quinn was bound to notice, but, to Ria's way of thinking, that was still better than if she'd witnessed her aunt's hangover.

"Clare's family has a whole bunch of them," Quinn pointed out, beaming. "Her dad is a stock contractor. He goes to rodeos all over the place, and sometimes Clare goes with him, too. He used to take her brother and leave her at home, but—"

The girl blushed and fell silent. If she'd been texting a girlfriend, she probably would have explained her sudden hesitation this way: TMI.

Too much information.

"Lots of ranchers around here," Landry said quietly, addressing Quinn but looking at Ria—all of Ria, if the nerves jumping under every inch of her skin were any indication. "It shouldn't be too hard to scare you up a horse."

"Great!" Quinn crowed, over her brief spate of chagrin. "How about now?"

Ria gave the girl a mock glare. "How about later?" she countered. "It may be Sunday, but we have chores to do—fields to water, weeds to pull."

Landry chuckled at that, tugged at the brim of his hat and waited while Quinn gathered Butterball's reins and handed them up to him. He took them, nodded farewell and turned both horses away, heading slowly along the driveway, toward the road.

Shading her eyes with one hand, Ria watched him go.

Funny about this Landry thing. That morning,

before the broth and the horseback ride, she'd done everything she could to run the man off. Now she wished she could call him right back again. She was like a magnet, it seemed to her: one side repelling Landry, the other pulling him to her and holding him there.

Another wave of pure heat went through Ria then.

Quinn finally nudged her lightly to get her attention. "If I were you," the girl said, grinning, "all grown up and stuff, I mean, I sure wouldn't have made a guy like *that* sleep on the couch."

"Quinn Whittingford!" Ria scolded, but she couldn't help laughing a little. "What kind of talk is that?"

"The straightforward kind," Quinn replied. "I'm seventeen, remember? We had sex education way back in sixth grade—all the gory details—so it's old news. Besides, my generation isn't hung up on stuff like that." The grin widened, and her voice dropped to a confiding whisper. "I saw the pillow and afghan on the sofa when I went inside to put my things away."

Embarrassed, caught out on something she hadn't actually done, Ria steered her niece toward the house, where they could grab some bottled water and put on a little sunscreen. She'd find out more about Quinn's views on sex later, when she'd thought of a way to broach the subject. Hopefully, the girl had enough sense to abstain for a few more years.

"So," she asked, "did you have fun at Clare's party?"

Smiling, and using the word *awesome* a lot, Quinn was in verbal overdrive again, spilling all the delightful details.

CHAPTER TWELVE

HIGHBRIDGE WAS IN the kitchen, as usual, when Landry finally couldn't delay going inside any longer. He'd returned Butterball to her stall in Zane and Brylee's barn, brushing the animal down and checking her hooves for rocks or other irritants before he patted her on the nose and took his leave.

If anybody besides Cleo had been around, he might have stayed awhile, just to burn through another hour or so, but the housekeeper explained that (1) some folks had to work for a living, so she didn't have time to sit around jawing for half the day, if that was what he had in mind, (2) Brylee had gone over to her company, Décor Galore, for a meeting of some kind, no telling when she'd be back, and (3) Zane and his darned dog were off someplace, up to God only knew what brand of fresh foolishness, and young Nash had gone with them lest they find themselves one fool short.

Well, that pretty much sized things up.

So Landry had tipped his hat to Cleo, hiding a grin, turned away from the screen door he'd just had the bad judgment to knock at, crossed the porch and the yard and gotten back on his horse.

Now, all too soon, he was home.

Highbridge turned his head at Landry's entrance, gave him a generous dose of the stink-eye and went back to what he'd been doing—peeling and chopping vegetables to add to the big Crock-Pot waiting on the counter next to the sink.

Although he'd hoped to cut a wide swath around his disapproving butler before, the attitudinal winds had shifted. Landry's back was up; it was past time for a showdown, and he was damned if he'd leave the room without one.

Highbridge seemed to guess that. He heaved a great, long-suffering sigh and turned to face his employer, wiping his hands on a ruffled apron that would have struck Landry as damn funny—if he hadn't had his tail in such a twist.

"It's good to know you're alive and well, sir," Highbridge remarked as an idle aside, delicately barbed.

Game on, Landry thought. *Bring it.*

"You were in doubt?" he countered dryly.

Highbridge's thin shoulders rose and fell in a faint pantomime of a shrug. "Not really," he said, and just when Landry thought the old coot had finally seen fit to drop the "sir" from the tag end of just about every sentence he ever uttered, he tacked it on after all. Went on to say, "You made your intentions quite clear yesterday. And from the gossip zipping around the internet, you made good on them."

Landry narrowed his eyes. "What gossip?"

Highbridge sighed. "Don't tell me you're surprised, sir," he said, moving to set the plug in the Crock-Pot and settle its lid in place. "Many of your fellow revelers felt compelled, evidently, to chronicle your escapades at the—" here, the intrepidly nosy butler paused to sniff in refined disdain "—the *Boot Scoot Tavern*—some of them even took photographs."

Landry lifted one hand, increasingly miffed by Highbridge's tone and a few other things, too. "Hold it a second—you've lost me. I'm stalled out back there at the word *escapades*. What, exactly, did you mean by that?"

Highbridge regarded him dolefully for a long time and then completely ignored the question and asked one of his own. Maybe Landry wasn't the only one around here who wanted to have this out, once and for all.

Had the Englishman been a younger man, they'd probably have been outside by now, having themselves a good old-fashioned brawl.

"How could you, sir?"

"How could I *what?*"

"How could you have gotten Ria Manning *drunk*—and in such a public place? I can assure you, *sir,* that the lady in question isn't going to like some of those photographs. Or the harm they may well do to her reputation."

Landry lowered his eyebrows and slitted his eyes in pure consternation. "Maybe I'd better have a look at these pictures before we continue this conversation," he said in a taut undertone.

"Maybe you should," Highbridge allowed, making a show of being busy placing handfuls of vegetable parings in his countertop compost bin.

"Then we're agreed." Landry sighed. "Where do I find these scandalous images?" he asked, and though he might have sounded cocky, he said those words at some cost to his pride.

Highbridge didn't turn around. "I sent you the links," he said primly. "Via email."

Email. What was the point in bouncing messages up to some satellite and then right back down again, into a computer in the same damn house?

Shaking his head, but with a burr of dread stuck in the pit of his stomach, Landry headed for his home office, fired up the desktop, logged on and clicked his way straight to his mailbox.

The butler's communiqué was at the top of the list.

Highbridge, not normally a technical whiz, had been thorough; his links were neatly separated, each with its own bullet point, each leading to one of half a dozen different social-media sites.

Every picture was cockeyed, or blurry, obviously snapped on the sly, but they told a story, all right. Each and every one of them showed Ria looking bewildered, distracted, harried—and somewhat rumpled, as though she'd been given a date drug and didn't know it yet. For all that, she was beautiful. Heartbreakingly so.

In one particularly memorable shot, she appeared to be draped on Landry while they danced. He, on the other hand, looked sober, in charge and pretty damn smug in the bargain. To wrap things up, there was a short video of him carrying Ria across the Boot Scoot's seedy parking lot to his truck. She appeared to be limp as a rag doll, while, in point of fact, she'd been gearing up to sing every chorus of "Ninety-Nine Bottles of Beer."

Thankfully, the free-range camera bugs hadn't caught her throwing up alongside the road. That was some consolation, but not much.

Landry made a mental note to trace every one of the pictures back to the sender, not to blitz him with kamikaze emails—that wasn't his style—but as fair warning that he'd be around presently—in person—looking for explanations.

In the meantime, he had other things to take care of, so he logged off, rose from his desk chair and returned to the kitchen.

By then, Highbridge was browning stew meat in an electric skillet, still wearing that silly apron and as indignant as ever. He sniffed again, and refused to look at Landry.

"Okay, so the shots aren't all that flattering," Landry admitted, with an edge to his voice. "Ria went a little overboard with the beer, but so what? She's of legal age, and it was probably good for her to loosen up a little."

Maybe, if you didn't count the throwing up, the hurt in her eyes, Landry corrected himself in grim silence. *Topped off, of course, with a miserable night and that monster hangover that was waiting to pounce when she opened her eyes this morning.*

Regret, no stranger to him these days, ground through Landry like a giant set of jagged gears that refused to mesh, snagging on each other instead.

Highbridge began spearing pieces of stew meat, with exaggerated stabs of his cooking fork. It was no great trick to guess whom he'd like to stab.

"You're absolutely right, sir. One bad night in a barroom shouldn't ruin Ria, not in this day and age—and heaven knows she wasn't the first person to make an error in judgment—but what about the remainder of the evening? What about what happened after that oh-so-dignified exit from—that place?"

"Aren't you jumping to a conclusion or two here?" Landry asked. "Not to mention way over the line between what's your business and what's mine?"

"Let's just say I didn't find it difficult to surmise the rest," Highbridge responded, ignoring the reference to his blasted meddling.

Landry wanted to explode, to defend Ria *and* himself, to say he hadn't slept with the woman, but his pride wouldn't let him.

"So, basically," he said instead, in a remarkably

even tone, considering the tornado gathering force inside him, "you're saying I deliberately got Ria drunk, carried her off like a caveman and had my way with her as soon as we were alone."

"You said it, sir. I didn't."

Landry couldn't contain the storm any longer. He doubled up one fist and slammed it down hard on the tabletop, releasing the worst of it with that single burst of furious energy.

Highbridge didn't so much as flinch. He did raise his eyebrows slightly, though, a clear indication that Landry had just confirmed all his suspicions.

"Look," Landry half growled, when he had enough control to risk speaking at all, "if your opinion of me is as low as it seems to be, why the hell do you stay here? Why did you follow me out here from Chicago in the first place?"

Highbridge looked mildly surprised by the inquiry. "Why, that's quite simple, sir. You needed me."

"I'll be *damned,*" Landry marveled, half under his breath.

"Most likely not," Highbridge observed, before going on. "Contrary to what you apparently believe, I happen to think very highly of you, sir. You can be quite full of yourself, it's true, and you seem to have only two speeds—full throttle and dead stop. You often act before you think—I give you the move to this ranch and the buffalo-herd-that-isn't as examples—and yet—"

"Yet?" Landry prompted dangerously. Was there a

favorable opinion hidden someplace in Highbridge's latest speech?

The other man actually smiled. "And yet," he went on, "you are highly intelligent, you genuinely care about people, I think, and you're gentle with animals, even those great, lumbering bison of yours. I've never seen you turn away from hard work, or any kind of challenge—be it in the boardroom of a Fortune 500 company or on the range. When somebody needs help, you're there to lend a hand." A pause, probably for dramatic effect. "Finally, I believe you possess a very high degree of integrity, as well."

"Gee," Landry drawled, with all the conciliatory goodwill of a splash of battery acid, "thanks heaps. Now I know I haven't lived in vain."

Highbridge spread his hands, one of which held a meat fork with a chunk of beef on the end of it. "Splendid," he said, paying no mind to Landry's sarcasm. "I shall rest assured, henceforth, that my point has been properly made."

"Until I piss you off again," Landry qualified.

Highbridge clucked his tongue. "Sir, sir, sir. Such language does not become you."

"I give up," Landry muttered.

"Excuse me, sir?" Highbridge asked. The pretentious old geezer—he hadn't missed a word Landry had said. He had the acute hearing of a hawk and the eyesight to go along with it.

"Never mind," Landry bit out.

Flustered, he retreated to his private space, took

a long, hot shower, pulled on a pair of sweatpants and then fell facedown across his bed, finally giving in to the exhaustion he'd been sidestepping all day.

Landry awoke several hours later, more rummy than rested, but hungry as a Montana grizzly coming out of hibernation at the ragged end of a long, hard winter. He lay there, sprawled across the mattress, for several minutes, waiting for the decomposition of deep sleep to reverse itself and render him from a collection of subatomic particles to a solid human being again. Then he rolled out, visited the bathroom and finally set his course for the kitchen.

When he got closer—it was a big house, even with fully half of it unfinished—he caught the savory scent of Highbridge's hopped-up version of beef stew. It was his specialty, served only when he was either celebrating or trying to restore domestic tranquility after a dustup of some kind. The Brit was even a little vain about the concoction, with ample reason, in Landry's opinion.

The stuff was magnificent.

Highbridge guarded the recipe the way the Secret Service guarded an incumbent president, though he did admit to adding a whole bottle of burgundy when he was feeling—as he put it—"a bit on the adventurous side."

Landry's stomach rumbled in anticipation, and his mouth had been watering since he caught the first whiff. Stew was stew, but when Highbridge upgraded the ingredients, it was a gesture.

Hopefully not a *farewell* gesture.

Even if he *was* probably the only cowboy in the world who employed a butler, and suffered a degree of secret embarrassment over it, Landry was fond of Highbridge, would hate to see him leave.

He was brooding over that disturbing possibility when he lifted one palm to shove open the kitchen door, meaning to find out what the real deal was and end the suspense, when he caught the timbre of a voice that was at once strange and familiar.

Landry forgot all about being hungry as he froze, having pegged the speaker's identity almost instantly.

It was Jess Sutton—his father.

Landry hesitated long enough to draw a deep breath and let it out slow and easy.

Then he pushed open the swinging door and strode into the kitchen as if he owned it. Which, of course, he did.

Sure enough, there was his dad, looking older than the last time Landry had seen him, his clothes a few years out of date, the hair plugs furrowing his crown and the gold chain hanging around his neck dead giveaways that he still considered himself a ladies' man.

Highbridge sat across the table from Jess, and they were playing cards, most likely gin rummy, since Highbridge didn't go in for poker or blackjack—church-basement bingo was *his* pet vice. Seeing Landry, the butler cleared his throat, politely excused himself from the game and beat a quick retreat to his quarters.

Jess stayed right where he was. He tossed down his hand of cards and regarded Landry with a faded version of his own blue eyes, and Zane's, as well. A little smile quirked the corner of the old man's mouth, but that must have been mostly reflex, Landry thought, because the man did not look happy.

For a few long moments, father and son simply watched each other, both of them waiting stubbornly for the other one to speak.

It was going to be a long, *long* wait, as far as Landry was concerned.

Finally, Jess gave in, with the usual air of magnanimity, and ended the stalemate with a low, gruff chuckle and "Well, boy, I didn't expect a welcome-home party, but I thought you might be able to scrape up a simple hello."

Landry headed for the slow cooker on the counter. Lifted the lid, drew in the aroma. "All right," he said, replacing the lid and keeping his back to the unwanted visitor. "Hello."

Jess chuckled again, a raspy sound, probably the result of years of chain-smoking and cheap whiskey. "You're every bit as ornery as your brother," he said. "But you don't have his kind of self-control. Guess that's because he's older."

Landry turned around, leaned against the counter and folded his arms. He wasn't going to argue.

"What do you want?" he rasped.

"Why is that always one of the first questions you or Zane ask me?"

"Because you *always* want something," Landry replied. "What is it this time? And don't tell me you blew the five grand I sent you and need another 'loan' to save your neck, because if that's the case, *Dad,* you're shit out of luck."

Jess leaned back in his chair, hands raised to shoulder level, palms out, as though expecting a knuckle sandwich, but his eyes belied the gesture. As little time as Landry had spent with his father over the years, he knew how to read the man's eyes—a kid on the fringes learned the skill early—and they indicated a combination of shrewd amusement and a sort of bland sorrow.

"I'm not here to ask for anything, son," Jess replied, when he was ready. "I did what I said I'd do with that five thousand dollars—I paid my gambling debts and put as much distance between me and the poor man's Las Vegas as I could—as quick as I could. Since you wouldn't believe me anyhow, I'll spare you the speech about how much I appreciated what you did."

Landry frowned—it was a given that he wasn't buying Jess's assertion that he "wasn't there to ask for anything." Reno wasn't exactly on the other side of the world, but it was a long way for a guy like his dad to travel, especially now that he was aging. Never able to hold on to a car—or a job, for that matter—when Jess Sutton decided to hit the road, whether out of necessity or simply because he felt that old familiar yen to see what was over the next hill, he either bummed rides or took a bus.

"Does Zane know you're here?" Landry finally asked.

Jess shook his head. "Not yet," he admitted.

"I shouldn't have to remind you," Landry ventured darkly, and at some length, "that Nash is happy living with Zane and Brylee."

"So I hear."

"Reminder number two," Landry pressed. "Those papers you signed last year, relinquishing custody of the boy, were binding. You can't just change your mind, swoop in here and carry the kid off to wherever it is you're headed."

"Check," Jess said, with weary resignation. He studied Landry pensively for a few moments, then went on. "Would you mind sitting down? I'm getting a kink in my neck looking up at you."

Landry sat. "What. Are. You. Doing. Here?" he asked, parceling out the words one by one.

Jess shook his head, the familiar easy smile back on his lips, resting there, placid and singularly annoying. His hair was getting thinner, Landry observed, but there were no discernible cuts or bruises on him, so it was probably safe to assume he was telling it straight about paying off his gambling buddies, if nothing else. To Jess, lies and the truth were not polar opposites—they were options, tools to adjust his own flexible reality. In fact, it was a pretty good bet that he'd been twisting things around to suit himself for so long that he no longer knew the difference. If he ever had.

"Maybe," Jess said, "I'm here to try and mend a few fences, with you and your brother. No need of it with Nash—he understands me. Accepts me as I am."

Landry leaned back in his chair, folded his arms. "Nash is a kid," he said flatly. "Maybe he still thinks you give a damn for anybody but yourself. Thing is, he's smart, so he'll probably grow out of it."

Jess sighed deeply. "I know I made a few mistakes—"

"A few mistakes?" Landry bit back the other things he could have said, for whatever reason, but he was remembering the hard times just the same, the old days, when he and Zane were kids. He was remembering, in vivid detail, how his mom could never afford to wear clothes that didn't come from a thrift store or a yard sale or a charity box in some church— and how many times she'd had to scrounge behind the cushions of a ratty couch in a rented trailer or a run-down motel "suite," trying to come up with enough change for him and Zane to pay for lunch at school. Maddie Rose had known without being told that her sons, right from kindergarten on, would have gone hungry before they'd accepted a state-sponsored meal.

They'd done just that, a number of times.

Landry could still feel that grinding ache in his

belly, on occasion, along with the secret shame of doing without. Even now, with more money than he knew what to do with, he never took a plate of food for granted.

"Okay," Jess conceded, after clamping his jaws together for a while, "I made a *lot* of mistakes. But here's something to think about, Mr. Gentleman Rancher—it might just be that you need to forgive me even more than I need to *be* forgiven, because holding on to all those grudges is eating you up inside. Even I can see that. What it all boils down to is this. You'll never be genuinely happy until you let go of all that resentment and move on."

"Tell that to Zane," Landry retorted, feeling his neck and ears go crimson. "*He's* about as happy as a man can be, now that he and Brylee are married and about to start a family, and he probably wouldn't spit on you if you were on fire."

Jess let out a long, low whistle of exclamation. "Harsh," he said.

Landry said nothing, because, secretly, he agreed. He *had* spoken harshly, and he *did* wonder if despising his father all these years hadn't messed up his life in some pretty significant ways. He considered his workaholic career strategy, back in Chicago, and then there was the way he'd never been able to connect with Susan—

"Inside, boy, you're still an angry kid, wanting the world to make things up to you," Jess went on, with the utter confidence of somebody who'd never felt the need to stay faithful to his wife and stick around to help her raise their children. Maybe he figured he was on some kind of psychological roll here—Dr. Phil with a little more hair and a gambling habit. "As for Zane, he might have it together now, but he was wild for a long time. And he's got one bad marriage behind him, just like you do—Tiffany, I think her name was. Pretty little thing, with curves in all the right places, but about as deep as a mud puddle after a weeklong heat wave."

"Is this going somewhere?" Landry asked. "Or is it just your normal self-aggrandizing song and dance?"

Jess favored him with another benevolent look, this one bordering on saintliness. "My point," he said, "is that somewhere along the line, Zane must have decided blaming me wasn't worth the energy it took. That—and the fact that he's found the right woman in this Brylee gal—is why he's happy and you're not quite there."

Who says I'm not happy? Landry thought peevishly.

Maybe he didn't ask the question out loud because he wasn't ready to hear the answer.

Jess was quiet, too, letting all that pontificating sink in, Landry supposed.

Finally, when he couldn't sit still for another second, Landry shoved back his chair, stood and stalked over to the Crock-Pot. He took two bowls from a cupboard, two spoons from a drawer.

Then, using a ladle, he plopped some of Highbridge's stew into one of the bowls, jammed in a spoon and set the food down in front of his father with enough force to send some of the thick broth spilling over the side to stain the tablecloth. After that, he filled the second bowl for himself.

The two men ate in silence for a while. Then Jess pushed his bowl away, sighed and said, "That's good grub, but I can't eat like I used to." He chuckled dryly. "Can't do a *lot* of things like I used to."

Landry hoped his old man wasn't planning to elaborate on that statement. He still had an appetite, and he wanted to keep it until he'd stowed away some more of Highbridge's specialty.

Instead, Jess shifted on his chair, extracted a beat-up wallet from his hip pocket and opened it to pull out a photograph, carefully trimmed to fit in one of the little plastic sleeves.

"If anybody had good cause to carry a grudge," he said sadly, "it was this woman."

Landry glanced at the picture, blinked and then squinted, not quite believing his eyes.

"Your mother," Jess added unnecessarily.

Yep, the worn image, probably a product of one of those cheap instant cameras, showed Maddie Rose sitting up in a hospital bed, wearing a robe, the paisley turban on her head there to hide the loss of her once-abundant hair. She was impossibly thin, her formerly vibrant skin had turned a muddy shade of gray and the shadows under her eyes were as purple as fresh bruises. Her cheeks were sunken and gaunt, her arms sprouting needles and tubes. And in spite of all that, she was smiling.

To make the scene all the more unreal, there was Jess Sutton, right beside her, perched on the edge of her mattress, with one arm wrapped firmly around Maddie Rose's sparrow-delicate shoulders. She was resting her head on his shoulder, as naturally as if he'd never abandoned her to scramble for a living and raise two obstinate, hyperactive boys on her own.

"I was there at the hospital with her, when she passed away," Jess said, his voice convincingly hoarse, his eyes misted over as he gazed into the distance. "I told Maddie Rose I was sorry for all the things I did, and even more for everything I *didn't* do. You know what she said?"

Landry didn't—couldn't—reply. His throat was too constricted, and he had to deal with the scalding sensation behind his eyes.

"Maddie Rose said—" Jess had to stop, clear his throat, start over. "She said she'd always believed that most folks did the best they knew how, with what resources they had, and that I was no exception. She wouldn't have taken me back, or anything like that, even if she'd lived, but your mother was willing to make peace with the past and let all the bad memories go."

Landry couldn't refute any of what Jess said—not after he'd looked at that picture and seen the beatific expression on his dying mother's face—but he wasn't about to brush aside all the things he'd seen Maddie Rose grapple with over the years, either. He sure as hell wasn't.

So he got up and left the kitchen without another word.

Back in his room, Landry swapped the sweatpants for jeans and a shirt, pulled on socks and boots and headed for the barn.

There was nothing to do but ride—ride until he could think straight again.

CHAPTER THIRTEEN

BY THE TIME the Sunday sun finally sank behind the western horizon, leaving a soft lavender twilight behind to darken slowly into a star-spangled country night, Ria felt good, bordering on terrific.

No trace of the hangover from hell lingered and, sore as her thigh muscles were from that morning's unavoidable horseback ride, undertaken at Landry's insistence, she'd had a productive day, tending to chores, chatting with Quinn, who worked tirelessly beside her the whole time.

Last night's brief but profound sense of clarity was back, too—a quiet, joyous secret for the time being, something to ponder in her heart as well as her mind, too sacred to share just yet. Better to wait and see if the transformation was a lasting one—if it was, she might or might not talk about it.

Deep down, Ria still wasn't convinced that the experience had been anything more than a fluke or—and this seemed likely, sensible woman that she was—simply her brain's biochemical attempt to counteract all that alcohol with a flood of feel-good hormones. Still, she could hope the new state of mind would continue and, darn it, she was *happy*.

For once, she meant to take each moment as it came, counting her blessings instead of examining and reexamining the past, trying to work out the whys and the wherefores. Nor, she promised herself, would she stray into the future—*here be dragons*—figuratively peering into some crystal ball for clues.

So it was that Ria hummed while she made dinner, enjoyed every bite and puttered about the house, tidying a stack of magazines here, dusting there, while Quinn worked in the kitchen, clearing the table and loading the dishwasher.

That was their agreement: one of them would cook; the other would clean up afterward. They'd trade off, they'd decided, so neither of them had to do the same tasks over and over again.

Later, still in a state of quiet bliss, Ria sat on the porch steps for nearly an hour, content to watch the stars pop out of a black sky like little silver surprises, and to breathe in the combined scents of flowers blooming all around her. Eventually, though, the mosquitoes drove her inside again, and she made her way to the kitchen, planning to brew a cup of herbal tea and call it a night.

Quinn sat at the computer, her shoulders slightly hunched, and it took Ria a moment to translate the girl's body language.

"Is something wrong?" Ria asked, concerned but still in a very Zen mood. Methodically, she selected a tea bag—raspberry lemon—from the appropriate canister, then opened the cupboard door to choose a mug, all while she waited for Quinn to answer.

"Kind of," Ria's only niece said, after much delay, her voice barely above a whisper.

Ria frowned, forgot the tea-making process for a moment and turned to look over at Quinn. "What do you mean, 'kind of'?"

Back stiff, shoulders rigid, Quinn seemed to be trying to block Ria's view of the monitor, and with a slight and suspiciously furtive movement of her right hand, she worked the mouse, causing the screen to flicker and then go dark.

Ria didn't move—somehow, crossing the room and standing next to Quinn would be an intrusion, it seemed to her, a violation of the child's personal space.

It *was* strange, however—a buzz of tension charged the atmosphere, and, now that she'd shut off the computer, an obvious if subtle effort to hide something she'd seen on the monitor screen, she seemed frozen in place.

Even Bones, previously sleeping off his supper on his bed, which lay near Quinn's feet, suddenly opened his eyes, lifted his head and perked up his ears.

Still, Quinn sat unmoving, keeping her back to Ria. The nape of her neck, visible where her hair parted to fall forward, over her shoulders, went pink. She'd been so different earlier, when she and

Ria were still working outside, moving sprinklers around the front yard, and chattered a mile a minute all through supper.

Whatever she'd seen on the computer had changed all that.

Ria spent a few moments speculating on the possibilities—an online newspaper blurb about Meredith— *Portland Businesswoman Indicted?* A snarky email from one of the other girls who'd attended Clare's slumber party? A posting on a lost-pet website, pleading for the return of a dog matching Bones's description? *What?*

Finally, Ria simply said the girl's name.

At last, Quinn turned around in the swivel chair, reluctance etched into every line of her, to look directly at Ria. The child's happy glow, present since her return from the party at Whisper Creek, glowing brighter and brighter as the day went on. The time outside had been good for her, hours spent breathing fresh air, soaking up sunshine and getting a little exercise. The animated shine of healthy activity had faded from her eyes, and she looked impossibly tried, emotionally drained.

Before, Ria had been more curious than worried. Now she was becoming more and more alarmed, waiting for Quinn to speak.

When she finally did, tears were brimming in her eyes. "Somebody is trying to make you look bad," she said, chin and voice wobbling while she struggled visibly to regain her composure. "There are some *really* awful people in this world!"

In a way, Ria was relieved. When it came to calamities, there were far worse things than petty smear campaigns—if that was what Quinn was telling her.

"Quinn," she said, crossing the room at last, "I need to know what's going on." She gestured toward the blank monitor. "Show me."

Glumly, her niece turned around to face the nearly obsolete desktop again, made a few deft moves and brought the screen back to life.

Since she had a clear conscience, the image that met Ria's eyes in the immediate aftermath of millions of pixels scrambling to reassemble themselves and create a whole, jolted her like a zap from a stun gun.

There she was, her last-night self, ridiculously drunk, right there in the Boot Scoot Tavern for all to see, barely able to remain upright, judging by the way she hung off Landry like a kudzu vine. She'd wrapped both arms around his neck, her head tilted back so she could look up at him with a bleary expression that came dangerously close to stupefied adoration. At the same time, she strongly resembled a critter stranded, frozen, in the middle of a dark road, blinded by oncoming headlights.

Even as she told herself it was no big deal—everybody made a fool of themselves at *some* point and, besides, places like the Boot Scoot were ground zero for the unwary—Ria felt a little sick. She drew in a quick, shallow breath and put a hand to her mouth. Having made a mutual agreement, no words required, she and Quinn changed places, Ria sinking into the chair, Quinn standing behind her.

"Is that really you?" Quinn asked, very softly after an interval marked only by the steady *tick-tick-tick* of the old-fashioned kitchen clock on the wall directly above Ria's desk.

Ria didn't answer right away, considering the question a rhetorical one, since there was no mistaking her identity in that picture. And she was busy checking out the string of comments posted underneath the image.

The first one was snide—and anonymous, of course, as chickenshit potshots usually were. "I guess we can all stop hoping for a hot date with a certain very sexy cowboy, girls. He's obviously getting plenty of action."

The following posts were of *some* consolation, but still humiliating to read.

"You ought to be ashamed of yourself, whoever you are, spying on people like that!" J.B. of Parable had scolded the instigator. "How petty and mean-spirited can you get?"

"This is definitely dirty pool!" accused K.C., also of Parable. "Sleazy stuff, no matter how you spin it. And what did Ria Manning ever do to you anyhow?"

"Some people," added another woman, a resident of Three Trees, "have too much free time on their

hands, going around taking pictures on the sly. Why
don't you get a life?"

Opal Beaumont didn't even try to hide her identity—everybody in the county knew her, because she
was married to a popular pastor and because she was
a force to be reckoned with in her own right. "Just
when I think I've seen it all, when it comes to just
how low some folks will stoop, out of pea-green envy
and spite, I run across something like this. Ria is a
decent, hardworking woman, and you, Mr. or Ms.
Anonymous, are a low-down coward in clear need
of repentance. P.S., church services start at 9:15 and
11:00, every Sunday."

Ria had to smile, albeit wanly, at Opal's pitch for
religious intervention.

After Opal, Cleo—Zane and Brylee Sutton's out-
spoken housekeeper—put in her two bits. "Amen,
my sister! I know Ria and she's no drunk. Shame
on you, whoever you may be, trying to make a good
woman out to be a hussy when she certainly ain't
anything of the kind!"

With a ragged laugh, Ria closed her eyes, propped
her elbows on either side of the keyboard and began
rubbing the skin over her temples with the fingertips
of both hands, hoping to avert the headache that was
circling, drawing ever nearer, like a hawk about to
swoop down on its prey.

"There are more," Quinn said, gently massaging
the rock-hard muscles in Ria's neck and shoulders
now. She made an effort, bless her, at bucking up,

trying to find the bright side. "But the pictures aren't so bad, really, now that I think about it, and anyway, you can see how the whole thing backfired. Whoever took those pictures will be lucky if they aren't tracked down and lynched!"

Of *course* there were more pictures, but Ria didn't need to see them. The effect would be the same—she'd feel more embarrassment, more regret, more anger at being singled out and deliberately humiliated by some stranger. And she already had all the embarrassment, regret and anger she could handle.

She opened her eyes, sat up straight and drew in a resolute breath. She'd just have to take responsibility—she *had* behaved badly, after all—find ways to brazen this thing through until another small scandal took its place. She would hold her head high and endure the inquisitive glances and small barbs that were bound to come her way in the near future.

What else could she do, besides making sure she never made the same mistake again?

A light rap at the back door startled Ria out of her musings, and it must have jolted Quinn, too. She stopped massaging her aunt's aching shoulders and stepped back, looking toward the door as though she expected a band of Puritans were just the other side, carrying torches and demanding that the scarlet woman be handed over. Ria got up, not afraid, but grateful for the distraction from her much-publicized fall from grace, and went to the door, peering through the glass in the oval window to see who was there.

She recognized Zane Sutton, near neighbor and husband of her good friend, Brylee, standing there on the porch, looking apologetic and mildly anxious, both at once.

Ria turned the lock, twisted the knob and pulled, then unlatched the hook that fastened the screen door beyond.

"Zane," she said, troubled because she knew he wouldn't have come over, especially at night, and without calling first, if he didn't have a good reason for being there. "What is it?"

Zane, the movie star turned devoted husband and respected rancher, looked chagrined, though he attempted a reassuring grin. He acknowledged Quinn with a glance and a slight nod before turning his attention back to Ria. "This is kind of awkward," he said, "but I'm looking for Landry. He got riled and took off on horseback a few hours ago, according to Highbridge, and, well, he ought to be back by now." He paused, cleared his throat and went on. "I was hoping he might be here, but it looks like I was mistaken."

Ria shook her head, trying to swallow the lump that had suddenly formed in her throat, making it impossible to answer. *Had* there been an accident? Was Landry lying somewhere out there in the gathering darkness, hurt or even—

No. *No.*

But, just for a millisecond, she was back in Portland, standing in her front doorway, one beautiful spring day, stricken by a terrible premonition as she watched the district fire chief and the chaplain getting out of a car on the quiet street, their faces grim as they prepared themselves to tell a wife that her husband was dead.

Ria reined in her imagination, fixed her attention on the here and now to such an extent that she felt hyperalert.

"We haven't seen Landry—Mr. Sutton, I mean— since this morning," Quinn put in, cautiously helpful. "Are you going to call the police?"

Zane managed a flicker of a grin then, shook his head once. "Best not be too hasty when it comes to mustering the troops," he said. His gaze shifted back to Ria. "Apparently, Landry had a run-in with somebody earlier in the evening, and he's got a quick temper. He can handle a horse as well as anybody, though, and if he runs into trouble, he'll take care of it." Zane stopped and sighed, and Ria wondered if he believed what he was saying, or if he simply regretted worrying her and wanted to backtrack a little. "Knowing Landry, he's fine, holed up somewhere out there, thinking things through. He'll come back when he's ready."

Ria opened her mouth, closed it again.

For all Zane's reassurances, she had to fight an almost primitive urge to put on her boots and a warm jacket, grab a flashlight, go out and personally search every inch of every acre of Hangman's Bend Ranch until she found Landry.

Well practiced at fretting over various worst-case scenarios, her brain wanted to *obsess*—even panic.

What if—what if—what if—? The half-formed question echoed in her head, but it would not come out of her mouth. Which was probably a good thing.

She remembered to breathe. Did so.

Zane tilted his head slightly to one side, looked closely at Ria's face. "You're all right, aren't you?" he asked quietly.

Ria managed a nod.

Once again, Quinn spoke up. "If Landry shows up, should we say you're looking for him?" she asked. She might have been worried, like Ria, but her eyes were wide with awe, just the same, as she took in the masculine perfection that was Zane Sutton. She'd probably never met a famous person before, and she was very young, so a little ogling was normal.

"I guess it would be okay to tell him I stopped by," Zane said, with a hoarse chuckle and a move toward the door behind him. "It'll probably make him mad, since he's bound to resent my interference, like always, but that's my problem, not yours."

Still strangely mute, Ria followed Zane out onto the porch, saw his gelding, Blackjack, waiting patiently in the bright glow of the motion light affixed to the roof.

It was already dark—and he'd come on horseback? While that explained why she and Quinn hadn't heard the distinctive roar of a truck engine, it worried her, too. Whatever he'd said about Landry being able to take care of himself, Zane was prepared to search for his brother in places where a vehicle couldn't go.

The pit of Ria's stomach tightened hard, as though some invisible fist had closed around it. Finally, she found her voice, though, and when she heard it, as if from a short distance, a place outside the confines of skin and skull, she barely recognized it as her own. "You'll keep looking for him, though?"

Zane, who had been holding his hat in one hand while he was inside the house, put it back on his head with a decisive motion of his right arm. Then he nodded. "Till hell freezes over, if necessary," he replied.

And then he walked away.

"Maybe we should join the search, too," Quinn said eagerly when Ria went back into the house.

Since she'd had the same thought—without the "we" part, of course, because she'd never considered taking Quinn along, not even for a nanosecond—Ria chose her words carefully.

"That wouldn't be a good idea," she finally responded, her tone both firm and gentle. "For one thing, we don't have horses, and for another, we'd be more hindrance than help, particularly if we wound up getting lost ourselves and thus compounding the problem."

"We could take the car," Quinn suggested.

Ria had to shoot that idea down, too, of course, but she felt bad about doing it. Quinn was so earnest, so ready to jump in and do what she could to help, and those were qualities that ought to be encouraged, at least under ordinary circumstances.

"I'm afraid that wouldn't work, either," she explained patiently. "If Landry's truck wouldn't take him where he wanted to go—hence, the horse—and Zane is out *looking* for him, also on horseback, there's no reason to think a compact car is up to the challenge."

Quinn watched Ria closely, neither agreeing nor disagreeing. "Do you think he's all right? Landry, I mean?"

"He's a grown man, honey," she reminded the girl gently, aware that she was whistling in the dark, just as Zane might have been doing earlier. "He's strong and he's smart and he knows the terrain. He'll be fine."

Quinn seemed at least partially convinced.

Now, Ria thought, if she could only convince *herself*.

Quinn bit her lower lip. "About that internet thing—"

"That," Ria said, meaning it, "is not important." She smiled. "Why don't you turn in early tonight, sweetheart? You must have been up late last night, and you worked very hard today."

At first, the girl looked as though she might resist the idea, but, finally, she nodded in acquiescence. "I'll take Bones outside to do his thing first," she said. At the door, the little dog at her heels, she turned to look back at Ria. "What about you? Are you going to go to bed early, too?"

Ria hesitated, then, too tired to dodge the truth, she shook her head. "Not for a while yet," she said, smiling very slightly. "I never got around to having that cup of tea I promised myself, remember?"

Quinn probably wasn't appeased, but she sighed, nodded again, went outside with Bones.

They both returned a few minutes later. Quinn's voice was soft, even fragile, as she asked, "If—if something happens—you'll wake me up, won't you?"

"Nothing's going to happen, Quinn. I'm sure Landry is fine." Even if he wasn't, Ria reflected, trying not to let her lingering concerns show in her face, she probably wouldn't know about it before morning, at the earliest.

"But if something does—?" Quinn swallowed. "I'd hate to wake up in the morning, thinking everything was okay, and then find out—well—that it *isn't*."

"I'll let you know, I promise," Ria said, very quietly.

Quinn mulled that over, then yawned. "Okay," she agreed, with the resilience of youth. Bones following behind her, a one-dog parade, Quinn stopped by the bathroom to wash her face and brush her teeth, paused in the doorway to offer a good-night and shut herself and her faithful companion away in the spare room.

Ria knew she should take her own advice, go to bed, try to get some sleep.

She *also* knew she wouldn't so much as close her eyes.

So she did night things, like shutting off most of the lights and making sure the doors were locked, brewed the long-delayed cup of tea and sat down in her rocking chair to keep her quiet vigil.

NO DOUBT DRAWN by Landry's small bonfire, the blaze encircled by sooty stones that had probably been right there on that spot, a sandy cove in an arm of the Big Sky River, for a hundred years, minimum, Zane rode in sometime around midnight.

He dismounted, leaving his horse next to Landry's, above a fairly steep bank, where there was grass to graze on and a trickle of creek water meandering through. For a few minutes, Zane prowled around at the edge of the firelight, probably working the kinks out of his leg muscles.

Typically, he said nothing. He was just *there,* which, with Zane, was a statement in itself. He'd always lived by the philosophy that what a man did said more about him than words ever could, no matter how eloquent those words might be.

For Zane, home was Brylee, not any particular house, and he'd left her, in the middle of the night no less, to saddle up a horse and come looking for his brother. That conveyed a message that moved

Landry, deep inside, and made the backs of his eyes prickle: Zane cared about him.

But he wasn't a man to make small talk.

And that was fine with Landry, seated on a flat rock near the fire, silent as a totem pole or a cigar-store Indian, because he wasn't much in the mood for palavering, either.

Better to keep his mouth shut and be thought a fool, as the old saying went, than to speak up and remove all doubt.

After a while, Zane ambled over to Landry's fire and sat himself down on a log. He considered the low-burning blaze for a long time before he spoke, and when he did, his tone was tinged with frustration as well as concern.

"Aren't you too old to be running away from home, little brother?"

A muscle bunched in Landry's jaw, and he prodded the shrinking flames with a stick, stirring the embers, watching as sparks flew up in a small flurry, like so many fireflies, some winking out on the bank, some floating as far as the river, reflecting the stars, whispering ancient mysteries to itself as it passed.

While Landry's considerable pride would have had him deny that he was running from anybody or anything, he knew the lie would stick in his throat like a thistle ball if he tried to utter it, and Zane would have seen right through him anyhow.

The brothers' shared DNA and common history made it hard for either of them to hoodwink the other, no doubt about it, and that was exasperating, for Landry *and* Zane. They were so alike physically, in fact, that folks had taken them for twins when they were younger—a misconception they'd actively encouraged, and they were *still* mistaken for each other once in a while.

Back when Zane was still making movies, Landry had often been approached by complete strangers, on the street, in restaurants, even at the gym, wanting his autograph or to take a "quick" picture with him. When explaining proved to be useless—or worse, a major disappointment to some hapless fan of Zane's—Landry had stopped resisting, signed his brother's name to table napkins, the backs of receipts and envelopes and flyers, anything that happened to be at hand, and smiled big for the camera.

The process always took longer than it should have, maybe because it often meant posing for group shots, then with each individual member of the family or crew of friends, *then* with passersby who'd seen what was going on, recognized "Zane" and decided they needed pictures, too.

Looking back, Landry chuckled gruffly at the recollection, shook his head.

"I came out here to think," he said, when he'd left Zane's smart-ass question about running away dangle long enough.

"Imagine that," Zane remarked easily. "You, thinking, I mean."

Landry didn't rise to the bait. He'd been the one

to set up this camp, such as it was, and that made it his turf, at least for the time being, though it was hard to say whether the spot was on his part of the ranch or on Zane's. The bottom line was, he hadn't issued any invitations.

Zane remained unruffled by Landry's silence, as always. He just sat there, watching the fire, which was dwindling again, for lack of fuel, and kept his own counsel for a long time.

Then, just when Landry was ready to extinguish the blaze by kicking plenty of sandy dirt over it, get back on his horse and go home, leaving Zane to sit there like a sphinx all night if he wanted to, Landry heard himself break the silence, a thing he had not intended to do.

"Dad's back," he told Zane.

"I know," Zane answered easily, leaning forward to rest his forearms on his thighs, fingers interlaced, hands suspended between his knees.

Still another silence descended, broken only by the crackle of the fire, the chirp and click of insects and the comfortable sounds of two good horses, close by, content to nibble grass and wait patiently for whatever came next.

"He was with Mom," Landry finally ground out. "When she died, I mean."

"Unlike you and me," Zane said quietly.

"Unlike you and me," Landry confirmed. He'd been in the middle of final exams when the end came for Maddie Rose, and Zane had probably been competing in some tin-buckle rodeo at the back end of nowhere.

They both ruminated for a while.

"Is that what's been bothering you all this time?" Zane asked presently. "That neither of us knew how sick Mom was, or could have scraped together enough cash to go to her and say goodbye if we had?"

"Hell, yes, it bothers me," Landry said, testy now.

"You think I felt any different?" Zane replied evenly.

Landry swore under his breath. "How is it that we never talked about what happened?" he rasped. "It was as if we'd had some kind of falling-out—but damned if I can recall one."

Zane sighed, took off his hat, held it while he scratched the back of his head with the same hand. "If I had to hazard a guess at what went wrong between you and me," he answered, at some length, "I'd say it was because we each decided we knew what the other thought without bothering to ask if we had it right."

"Here's what I thought," Landry said, pacing because he couldn't stand still for another second, let alone sit. "I *thought* you were too damn busy chasing buckles and women to care if Mom was sick or well. If you had, you'd have bothered to check on her once in a while."

"I called Mom every other week," Zane said mildly. He didn't sound defensive, just tired. "She always told me she was doing just fine, and she sounded good, so I had no reason to think otherwise."

Landry scowled. Back then, finishing school and working as many shifts at the coffee place as he could, scrambling for every dollar he earned, never quite making ends meet, he'd been preoccupied 24/7. Since he couldn't afford a cell phone and he downright refused to call Maddie Rose collect, he'd written his mother letters instead. Always short ones—he was *busy,* after all—always a series of disjointed phrases, rather than full sentences, jotted down over a period of several days, like next week's grocery list.

Being the person she was, Maddie Rose had never complained. Instead, she'd penned long, chatty letters, whether it was her turn to write or not, reminding him to eat right and get some rest, not to work so hard, telling him funny stories about the other waitresses, the customers, how the ladies' bowling league was faring at the time and, without fail, stressing how proud she was of both him and Zane, how much she loved them. In all that time, the woman had never once admitted to any health issues more serious than bunions, or, once in a while, after a long shift, she might say her back was "a little sore."

"She didn't want us to know she was sick," he finally said.

"So it would seem," Zane said, standing up, stretching and giving a yawn.

"But it was just fine with Mom if *Jess Sutton* knew," Landry muttered, furious and confused and

with a jagged tear running right through the middle
of his heart.

It was nothing new, that rip; he'd just learned to
ignore it most of the time.

Zane rested a hand on Landry's shoulder, lightly
and briefly. "I don't reckon our mama had much
choice in the matter," he allowed, his voice quiet.
"Jess tracked her down somehow—he was always
good at that, remember—probably planning on hit-
ting her up for whatever was left of that week's tip
money or her Christmas fund before taking off again.
Instead, he found her in a hospital, getting ready to
die. And for once in his worthless life, the son of a
bitch actually stepped up, like a man, and played the
loving husband. I think that was probably what Mom
wanted more than anything else in the world—to
see him one last time, I mean, and make some kind
of peace."

"It doesn't piss you off, that Mom didn't tell us
she was *dying?*"

"No," Zane said, there beside that river, with the
moon a mere sketch of itself and the stars provid-
ing the only light. "It breaks my heart. But she did
what she thought was right, Landry, however mis-
guided that choice might look in retrospect. The
point is, it was *her* choice to make. Mom gave us
all she could—raised us to be tough, to roll with
the punches, work hard and make our own way in
the world. She *loved* us, little brother, and she made
sure we knew it, every day of our lives. We'll prob-

ably never have a clue how hard it all was for her, either one of us. So if the lady wanted to die on her own terms, well, for my money, she had sure as hell earned the right."

This was a long speech for Zane, the classic man of few words.

Landry took it all in, chewed on it as he and Zane headed up the bank toward the waiting horses.

When they'd both mounted up, and reined the geldings in the direction of home, a breeze swept through, rustling the leaves of the cottonwood trees and the pines alongside the trail.

They'd covered a fair amount of ground when Zane cleared his throat, adjusted his hat and said, "It's probably going to stick under your hide, what I'm about to tell you, but here it is. I stopped by Ria's place earlier, looking for you. I told her you'd been gone from home long enough to worry Highbridge, said you were probably fine and she shouldn't worry. She pretended to believe me, but I got the impression she was pretty worried anyhow."

Landry nodded and adjusted his own hat—it was catchy, that gesture, like when somebody yawned and got everybody else yawning, too. "I'll stop by and see if she's still up," he said.

"She's still up," Zane assured him, with a sidelong glance and quirk of a grin.

"In the future," Landry went on, in measured tones, "I'd appreciate it if you minded your own business, big brother. I figure you meant well, but the fact is, Ria and I still have a lot to work through, and getting her all stirred up because I was late for supper won't make things any easier."

Zane nudged his horse from a walk to a trot, and even in the dark, with his hat shadowing his features, Landry saw the flash of his brother's grin.

"Duly noted," Zane said.

"You know about the internet thing?" Landry ventured, keeping up. "The pictures of Ria and me at the Boot Scoot last night, I mean?"

"Everybody does," Zane answered. Though not surprising, this reply was hardly a salve to Landry's spirits. "It's just another shit storm, though, and it'll blow over in time, like they all do."

"Easy for you to say," Landry grumbled. When Zane got home, Brylee would be waiting, warm and willing, in their bed. *He,* on the other hand, could look forward to another confrontation with his fuss-budget butler, if not more lectures from dear old Dad.

They'd reached the logical place to part ways by then, Zane heading one way, Landry another, and they both stopped their horses, sat facing each other.

Zane laughed a little over Landry's comment. "I speak from experience," he said. "Brylee and I traveled many a rocky road before we finally faced the fact that we were in love and ought to do something about it."

"Ria's still wearing her dead husband's wedding band," Landry admitted.

"Then I guess you'd better get down to business,"

Zane replied affably, "and love that ring right off her finger so there'll be room for yours."

Love the ring off Ria's finger?

Landry was stumped by the concept at first, and by the time he had a retort ready—he'd been about to spout the old bromide about how you can lead a horse to water, but you can't make him drink—Zane had already ridden off into the night, making his exit with a Zorro-like flair.

Grandstander, Landry thought uncharitably, but something had eased inside him, since Zane had caught up to him an hour or so before, and they'd swapped opinions. A few knots had been untied, a few barriers undermined, if not completely torn down.

He might be up to his ass in alligators, Landry reasoned, what with his dad underfoot for who knew how long, and the other development, that Ria had evidently been declared the official online poster child for at least one twelve-step group, if not more. *And* she wouldn't take off that damn ring.

But he just might have his brother back. His sidekick and partner in crime.

Landry swallowed a celebratory whoop, even as his eyes stung something fierce, and rode on, taking an overland shortcut that brought him to Ria's place within minutes.

There was a light shining in her kitchen window, he saw, with nervous relief. Maybe Zane had been right, and Ria *was* waiting up for him.

Landry dismounted, left his horse untethered outside the picket fence, found the side gate, opened it and crossed Ria's lawn to climb the steps of the back porch. There, he lifted his hand to knock, then paused to draw a deep breath and give himself one more chance to change his mind and get the hell out of there.

He came down on the side of staying.

Eventually, he *would* love Ria out of that wedding band, and every stitch she might happen to be wearing at the time, too.

It might not happen tonight, or next week, or next month.

But it would happen, if only because he'd finally made up his mind about a number of things and, like Zane, he was not only too cussed stubborn to give up, but he didn't know how to quit, either. Much of the credit for that trait, which could be a blessing or a curse, depending, went to Maddie Rose Sutton.

"Thanks, Mom," Landry said softly.

And then he raised his hand again, smiled to himself and knocked, quietly but with purpose.

CHAPTER FOURTEEN

THE SOUND OF a knock at her back door startled Ria a little, even though, on some level, she'd been hoping to hear it.

She got out of her rocking chair, flipped on the porch light just in case her caller wasn't the one she was expecting and felt a rush of—well, *something*—when she saw that she hadn't kept her sleepy vigil in vain.

Landry was standing on the doormat, shoulders squared, expression pensive, hat in hand.

The dead bolt clicked loudly as she released it, and the screen door creaked on its hinges. Ria made a distracted mental note to oil them and promptly forgot all about the hinges *and* the oil.

The two of them stared at each other for a long moment, Landry looking just as bewildered as Ria felt.

She stepped back to let him in, averting her eyes while she engaged in a private scuffle with her inner bimbo and the powerful urge to fling herself at Landry, wrap her arms around his neck and her legs around his waist and kiss him all over his face.

But there was a counterurge, too—he'd stressed her out, made her worry and miss most of a night's sleep, so part of her—a *big* part of her—wanted to take another approach altogether, wanted to kick, bite and scratch, calling Landry names—bad ones—the whole while.

"I'm not staying," he said.

"Fine," Ria replied coolly, "because I wasn't planning on *letting* you stay."

The remark sparked one of those crooked half grins, impervious and a tad cocky, that invariably weakened her knees, turned her breathing shallow and made her heart skitter like a flat stone skipping over water.

And eventually sinking.

Still holding his hat, Landry shifted his weight, ever so slightly, from one foot to the other and then back to center.

"Zane figured he'd worried you, stopping by earlier and all," he said. "Now that you know I'm okay, I'll say good-night."

They reached another impasse in the moments after he'd spoken, a strange interlude during which neither of them moved an inch, despite obvious intentions to do otherwise. That invisible current arced between them again, a kind of magnetic field, vibrating, expanding like a new universe taking shape.

Ria found herself thinking Landry might kiss her. She'd slap his face if he tried, she decided.

Or give in to her most primitive instincts and

kiss him right back, and heaven knew where *that* would lead—Quinn was in the house, so a hot time in the old bedroom was out of the question, but there was all that countryside out there, full of soft, secret places to lie down on sweet grass, sheltered by shadows—

Ria derailed her runaway thoughts, not daring to follow that particular train any further than she already had.

Anyway, to kiss or not to kiss turned out to be a moot question in the end, for both of them, because Landry broke the stalemate by giving a half nod, putting his hat back on and turning to walk away.

Ria was relieved. She was also disappointed.

It was a paradox, one she'd have to obsess about for a while, and that meant, tired as she was, that she'd be awake long after she finally tumbled into bed.

LANDRY DIDN'T SEE Highbridge again until breakfast, and by then he was over most of his irritation at being tracked down like a stray calf the night before—an episode that would never have happened if the butler wasn't such an incorrigible meddler.

Highbridge, for his part, was exceptionally quiet, even a little subdued, it seemed to Landry. Apparently, no sermon on decent conduct was forthcoming, for the moment anyway, and that was an almighty relief all by itself.

"Will you be wanting eggs this morning, sir?"

Highbridge asked, in a moderate tone that reminded
Landry of a mediator filling a breach, holding peaceful space between opposing forces teetering on the
verge of all-out war. His gaze never quite connected
with Landry's, though.

Resigned, Landry muttered a "yes" to the egg
offer, pulled back a chair and sat down at the table,
noting that there was only one place setting—his
own.

Where was Jess? Sleeping in? On a hunger strike?

No, Landry decided, Pops was probably at Zane
and Brylee's place, since he'd already struck out here,
angling for a little traveling money.

"Your father left a note," Highbridge said presently, over the sizzling sounds of bacon and the thunk
of the toaster. Highbridge brought a cup of coffee to
Landry, along with a folded sheet of paper, and he set
them both down in front of Landry's plate—coffee
at ten o'clock, paper at two.

Landry felt something crawl down his spine, like
a bug under his skin, and then scurry back up it
again.

He took two slow, deliberate swallows of coffee,
pausing to savor each one of them, delaying as long
as he could, before finally unfolding the note.

He hadn't expected a flowery apology or a po-
etic discourse on the wonders of forgiveness, but the
single word Jess had written did come as a surprise.

Goodbye.

Landry sat in silence for a while, trying to put

names to all the conflicting things he was feeling just then, and not getting very far with the effort.

"He left?" he finally asked when Highbridge set a platter of bacon, eggs and fried potatoes before him.

At last, Highbridge met Landry's eyes. "Yes, sir," he said.

"To go where?" Landry inquired, somewhat tersely.

Highbridge offered up his version of a shrug. "He didn't say. Mr. Sutton asked me for a small loan and a ride to the interstate highway, and I obliged on both counts." He paused then, pursing his lips and raising his eyebrows slightly, as though preparing to be called a sucker and subsequently defend his actions. When the accusation didn't come, he went on. "It happened last night, while you were—out. In your absence, I would normally have consulted Zane, but, of course, that wasn't possible."

"Of course it wasn't," Landry drawled, the response mildly spoken but edged with sarcasm. "Because you'd already sent Zane out chasing after me."

Highbridge's gaunt cheeks reddened ever so slightly. Was it possible he regretted butting in, even just a little?

Probably not. After all, he was always right, wasn't he?

"Shall I make more toast, sir?" Highbridge asked, his eyes playing the avoidance game again, darting from here to there but never coming in for a landing.

"This'll be plenty, thanks," Landry said dismissively.

And then he concentrated on eating his breakfast, leaving Highbridge to do his own thing, undisturbed.

There were other things to think about.

For one, the annual rodeo, over in Parable, was under a week away now, and although Landry hadn't been broadcasting the fact, he'd be competing in the saddle-bronc event. He'd paid his entry fee well in advance, and never considered backing down, even after getting that faceful of dirt—make that *three* facefuls—the day old Pure Misery kept throwing him in Walker Parrish's corral. Other broncs, on other days, had done pretty much the same thing.

Still, Landry meant to go over to Walker's ranch as soon as he'd finished eating and get in some more practice if he could.

With luck, he might fare better than he had done those other times, when he'd climbed back into the saddle, over and over again, and gotten his ass handed to him for his trouble.

Landry turned the rodeo cowboy concept over in his mind a couple of times, making an admittedly optimistic effort—okay, an *impossible* effort—*not* to think about Ria for a while, since he did more than enough of that already. In the long—or not so long—run, it was a loser's game, of course, like deciding not to ponder pink elephants, but he needed a break from the stress and agitation the woman churned up in him, and he'd take what relief he could get.

Jess's speedy departure and one-word note had certainly captured his attention, not that there was likely to be any respite anywhere along that mental trail, either.

But there was a cryptic element to the fare-thee-well missive, a troubling sense of hidden meanings, as if "goodbye" might be code for something much more complicated.

Landry sighed and went on eating. And thinking.

It wasn't surprising that his father had lit out so fast, or that he'd "borrowed" money from High-bridge—these things were typical of Jess Sutton, as much a part of his makeup as muscle and bone. The pigeons changed—this time, the role had fallen to Highbridge—but the basic M.O. was always the same: set up the mark with a sob story and a truck-load of sloppy sincerity, empty flattery and horse-shit remorse, get what he wanted and disappear as quickly as possible.

Nothing new there. The familiar pattern held.

At the brass-tacks level, it was the note that nagged at the edges of Landry's mind.

The thing was, Jess *never said* "Goodbye." He just packed up and split, usually when nobody was around to catch him sneaking off, and then he'd stay good and gone until he was flat broke or close to it, and feeling sentimental.

If confronted on his way out the door, the old man might have managed a jovial "So long, now" or a perky "See you soon," but "Goodbye," in its cur-rent context, at least, had a ring of finality to it that didn't mesh with Jess Sutton's style. Sure enough, he could be counted on to duck out at some point—that was about the *only* thing Jess could be counted on for—but if he could avoid it, he didn't burn his bridges behind him—he liked to keep his options open for next time.

Spinning his brain gears and getting nowhere in the process, Landry finally decided he was making a big deal over nothing—most likely, Jess's perplexing "Goodbye" meant just that: goodbye, adios, adieu, until we meet again.

Landry was faced with a choice—he could sit and brood over something that was probably meaningless or he could get outside, tie into the day and make it count for something.

And riding broncs was as good a way to do that as any.

So Landry did his barn chores, then saddled a fresh horse, leaving the gelding he'd ridden the night before to take his rest in the comfort of his stall, and started across Hangman's Bend Ranch, following the creek from his section of the property to the base of the trail winding through Zane's share.

Though his intentions were set, Landry wasn't in any particular hurry, so he made a point of stopping off by the other place. He spotted Brylee first, a vision in shorts, a cotton top and a floppy hat, working in her vegetable garden. Cleo was in the backyard, hanging white sheets on the clothesline.

Seeing Landry, Brylee smiled and beckoned to him.

Cleo glanced his way, too, but instead of smiling,

she scoured him with a quick, disapproving scowl, picked up the laundry basket at her feet and stomped back into the house like a one-woman march on Washington.

Grinning a little, Landry rode over to the edge of the tall chicken-wire fence that enclosed the sizable garden patch, inclined his head slightly in the direction Cleo had gone. "I see my reputation precedes me," he said dryly.

Brylee pulled a face, a kind of comical wince, made her way over to the fence, tilted her head back and looked up at him through the hexagons of wire. The floppy brim of her straw hat did nothing to hide the snap of annoyance in her eyes and the set of her chin.

She wasn't smiling anymore.

"What were you thinking, Landry Sutton?" she demanded, quietly but fiercely. "Taking Ria to the Boot Scoot Tavern, of all places? Were you *trying* to set her up to look like a fool, plying her with liquor—?"

Landry broke the flow of Brylee's diatribe with a raspy chuckle. "You sound like Highbridge," he said. "And neither one of you seems to need a pulpit to stand behind while you call down the fire of righteousness and burn me for a hopeless sinner."

Brylee glared. "We're not afraid to cry foul, if that's what you mean."

Landry went on as if she hadn't said that last thing. "Anyway, you've been known to frequent the Boot Scoot yourself, Mrs. Sutton—in fact, that's where I met you for the first time, remember? You showed up for a date with Zane in a sexy red dress, a pair of I-mean-business high heels and an attitude, if I recall the scene correctly."

His brother's wife blushed at the reminder, but her feet were firmly planted and her fists were bunched atop her hipbones, so it was a safe bet she wasn't ready to back down. "That was different, and you know it!" she sputtered.

"Was it?" Landry asked lightly.

Brylee blushed even harder. "Okay, maybe it wasn't," she answered, softening around the edges a little but clearly begrudging him even that one very small concession.

Then, "But it turned out all right, didn't it?"

Brylee was referring, of course, to the fact that she and Zane had fallen in love, despite their habit of butting heads hard enough to strike sparks, and they'd wound up married, even crazier about each other than before and committed, for the duration.

"Maybe things will turn out all right this time, too," Landry suggested. "Did you ever consider that, Mrs. Sutton?"

"No," Brylee said briskly, "I did not. You *have* seen that mess on the internet, haven't you?"

"I have," Landry confirmed.

The signs were there by now: Brylee's temper was beginning to subside. Being a class act and a real lady made it hard for her to maintain a fit of peevishness for long, Landry figured, and, sure enough, that radiant smile finally broke through, bright as a stream of sunshine shafting through stacks of gray clouds.

"Honestly, Landry," she went on, with a great sigh and a sister-in-law's abiding affection, "sometimes I could just *shake* you."

He grinned down at her. "That's been tried," he said. "Didn't change a thing." He stood up in the stirrups, looked around. "Is my brother at home, by any chance?"

Brylee shook her head, pretty much back to normal now. "Zane's over at Walker and Casey's," she replied. "They just took delivery on a bunch of new bucking horses, prime stock for next week's rodeo, and a lot of the ranch hands are busy on the range, inoculating calves and the like, so Walker needed some extra help in the corrals."

Landry nodded, feeling oddly validated. He'd been headed for Walker's place anyhow, and now he could make himself useful when he got there, instead of just asking for the favor of a chance to break his damn fool neck. He'd lend a hand wherever it was needed, then offer to try out one or two of the fresh broncs when the other work was done.

Walker was always looking for volunteer bronco-busters; today, he'd want to weed the duds out of the herd, the ones that would make reliable saddle horses but weren't cussed enough for rodeo, then identify the best buckers, the ones with go-to-hell wired right into their DNA and a marked determination to launch any cowboy who tried to ride them into outer space.

It was all part of a stock contractor's job—especially a successful one, like Parrish.

When Landry got to Timber Creek, he found the main corral churning with dust kicked up by a couple of dozen or so pissed-off horses. Walker, mounted on a fine buckskin gelding, greeted him with a grin and waved him over to where the action was.

"You're a sight for sore eyes!" Parrish yelled, over the din of whinnying cayuses and the handful of mounted cowboys cussing as they tried to herd some of the ill-tempered critters into smaller corrals adjoining the big one, others into holding pens. Like the ranch workers, the boss of the operation was coated in dirt from the crown of his battered hat to the soles of his well-worn boots, not being one to supervise from a distance. "Provided you're here to help sort out this bunch of knot-head hay burners, that is!"

Landry grinned and replied with a salute, confirmation enough that he was there to do whatever needed doing.

Walker offered a few loud instructions, and Landry and his horse waded into the fray.

The work was hot, dangerous and dirty—the incoming horses were as good as wild, carefully bred to be ornery, and today, they definitely lived up to their billing.

Landry rode, switched mounts when his own got tired and rode some more.

After a couple of hours, he and Zane and Walker and the others finally got the last of the four-legged devils into corrals and holding pens, a few to this one, a few to that.

By then, Landry was tired, saddle-sore and wearing at least three layers of dirt. His beard was coming in, a bristly stubble that made his face itch. And for all of it, issues with Jess, his half-finished house, a glaring metaphor for his life, and the sheer frustration of loving a woman who was determined to cling to the memory of a dead man, he was happy. Happier than he'd ever been in any boardroom, clean and combed and freshly shaven, clad in a tailored suit to boot.

"I guess you'd like to try out one or two of these maniac broncs," Walker said to Landry, when the dust was beginning to settle a bit and the ruckus was dying down.

Zane, nearby and still in the saddle, overheard Walker's words and darted a glance Landry's way, followed by a hard frown.

"You guessed right," Landry told Walker, undaunted.

Walker looked him over with amused respect. "You're a sucker for punishment, Sutton," he drawled, eyes twinkling, one side of his mouth cocked up in a semblance of a grin. "That's what makes you a cowboy, I reckon. You're as reckless a fool as the rest of us."

Zane rode closer, his gaze fixed on Landry's face

and not likely to come *un*fixed anytime soon. "What the hell do you think you're—"

Landry was off his horse and on his way to the one empty corral before Zane could finish the sentence.

He was quick, though, and he caught up, swinging down from the saddle and standing directly in front of Landry, solid as a brick wall. He was holding Blackjack's reins in one leather-gloved hand, reaching out to take those of Landry's horse with the other.

"You might want to get out of my way, big brother," Landry said.

Zane didn't budge. "Landry," he grated out, keeping his voice down since he had business with his brother at the moment and nobody else. "Maybe you don't remember the last time you tried to ride a bronc and damn near got killed?"

The words got Landry's back up, all right. Zane had never had any trouble riling him.

"I remember," he said, through his teeth. "I got thrown. So what?"

"So maybe you ought to lay off busting broncs for a while," Zane shot back.

"Are *you* planning to lay off the bronc-busting, Zane?" Landry asked, his voice deceptively mild. "Seems to me I saw *your* name on the rodeo roster last time I looked."

"I've had a lot of experience," Zane argued. That much was true; before stumbling into the movie business, Zane Sutton had faithfully followed the rodeo circuit, getting his share of bruises, bloody noses and broken bones along the way, but making a name for himself, too.

Landry rolled his shoulders, loosening up and dead sure there was no sense in refuting the irrefutable. Zane knew his rodeo, all right, and he was way ahead of Landry when it came to buckles and prize money—but then, this competition wasn't about following in his big brother's boot-prints. It was about meeting a challenge Landry had set for himself and himself alone. It was about being scared as hell, pinning a number on his shirt the day of his event, lowering himself into the chute and riding in spite of the fear any sensible man would have, faced with fifteen hundred pounds of badass horse.

"And there's only one way to *get* experience, now, isn't there?" he asked.

A vein pulsed at Zane's left temple, and he clenched his teeth for a moment, gathering his temporarily scattered forces before leaning in and snapping, "Damn it, Landry, this is crazy—like it or not, you're still a greenhorn—and besides that, *you have nothing to prove*—not to me or anybody else!"

"You're wrong there, big brother," Landry answered calmly. "I *do* have something to prove—to myself."

With that, he turned his back on Zane and walked away, leaving his horse for his brother to take care

of and climbing the corral fence to wait for the
first ride.

Zane still didn't back down, being cut from the
same cloth as Landry. Instead of standing down,
he turned the two horses over to a ranch hand and
stalked after Landry, scrambling up the rails in the
fence to perch beside him.

"Don't do this," he said. He'd probably meant the
words as a command, but they came out sounding
more like a plea. "If you get hurt—"

"If I get hurt," Landry replied reasonably, "I get
hurt, Same as you, same as anybody."

"But—" Zane started out, before losing his momentum and beginning again. "Why, Landry?"

By then, Walker was leading a fractious, balking
bronc, one of the new bunch, their way.

"Because I need to know I can do it," Landry said,
without looking at Zane. "It's that simple."

Zane swore under his breath, and it was colorful.

Simultaneously, Walker rode up alongside the
fence with the bronc, expertly releasing the slipknot
in the lead rope when Landry swung out onto the
animal's heaving, dusty back.

For a nanosecond, nothing happened. And then
all hell broke loose, a fitting description, since that
critter bucked as if it was possessed by the devil. It
swiveled and lunged, pitched forward, then reared
back, evidently trying to shake Landry's skele-
ton apart and leave the bones on the ground in a
bloody heap.

It was terrifying. It was *great*.

Landry gave a shout of laughter and held on for dear life.

ON MONDAY MORNING, while Ria and her niece and the dog were on their way to the bank in Three Trees, in Ria's unprepossessing compact car, planning to deposit the take from Saturday's farmers' market, Quinn's cell phone rang.

Ria knew instantly, by the girl's tense expression, that the caller was Meredith.

"Okay," Quinn said, after a wary "hello" and some listening. "Okay, yeah—I understand. Right. Well, I'm sure we can figure something out—sure, I'm fine—"

Ria did her best to concentrate on the road, not Quinn's end of the conversation, which was patently none of her business, but she couldn't help what she felt—a sense of impending change, *irrevocable* change. Something was coming, she knew that for certain, something colossal and possibly awful.

Quinn went on talking. Listened. Talked again.

Meredith's voice was mere static, her words indiscernible from where Ria sat.

Finally, Quinn said goodbye and ended the call.

They were on the outskirts of Three Trees by then.

"What?" Ria asked, unable to contain her trepidation *or* her curiosity.

"Meredith's coming to Three Trees," Quinn said, sounding and looking like a person in a trance.

"Why?" Ria said, though she was all too sure she already knew the answer.

Meredith was coming to collect her daughter, drag her back to Portland or force her to go to camp, and there wasn't a single thing Ria could do about it.

Thoughtfully, Quinn tucked her phone back inside the special pocket in her purse. "She said she needed to get away from things for a while," the girl replied. "So she booked a room at some bed-and-breakfast place. She's driving, and she'll be here in a couple of days."

"That's all she said?" Ria was reeling. Meredith was coming *here,* to Three Trees, Montana? It was still too incredible to fully comprehend.

"She didn't say anything about making me go to camp, at least," Quinn said, obviously as stunned as Ria was. "Or making me go with her when she leaves." A sigh, too deep and too heavy to come from a seventeen-year-old. "All she really said was that she needed some time to think—lots of it—and a place fifty miles from nowhere might be just the place to do that."

Ria was glad to see the bank just ahead, because her palms were damp, and therefore slippery on the steering wheel, and her knees had dissolved, broken themselves down to the particle level.

At the moment, not hysterical but shaken, just the same, and seated behind the wheel of a moving vehicle, she represented a danger to herself and others, and even though there was hardly any traffic, the only responsible thing to do was get off the street.

Operating on automatic pilot, Ria pulled into the parking lot at the bank, chose a slot near the entrance, in the shade of a well-established maple tree, and zipped into it to brake, shift into Park and shut off the engine. Then she sat there, numb, confounded and just a smidgen pissed off at the prospect of her half sister about to land, practically without warning, square in the middle of her life. Knowing Meredith, she'd arrive with all the subtle grace of a storm trooper, after which things would start blowing up on all sides like a scene from one of the *Die Hard* movies.

It was crazy.

Meredith, who probably didn't own a pair of jeans, beating a retreat to Cowboy Town, of all places? Meredith, who wore white—*off*-white when she felt adventurous—mincing around in rural Montana, land of mud and manure and unpaved roads, perennially dusty?

She was obsessing, Ria knew that, and it had to stop, this instant. Ria Manning would not allow herself another meltdown, especially in front of her niece.

"I'll go inside and make the deposit," Quinn volunteered. "You just sit here and breathe, okay?"

"Okay," Ria agreed, unclamping her back molars and sucking in some air.

Her silent mantra was *everything will be all right.*

Quinn pushed open her car door, zippered deposit bag in hand, and headed off on her mission, leaving Ria and Bones, who was ensconced in the backseat, to—what?

Oh, yeah. She remembered now.

They were supposed to *breathe*.

CHAPTER FIFTEEN

TRUE TO FORM, Meredith rolled up in front of Ria's modest house two days later, driving her pearl-white Jaguar and looking beautiful, in her patently Nordic ice-princess way. She gave the horn a merry toot and waved through the spotless windshield.

Ria and Quinn were busy weeding flower beds in different parts of the yard when zero hour finally came, both of them on their knees, both of them grass-stained, sweaty and grubby with garden dirt and, up until now, perfectly content and present to what they were doing.

Ria got to her feet, rummaging for a smile as she did so, silently reprimanding herself for not being the least bit glad to see her only sister, her one remaining blood relative besides Quinn. Hadn't she offered to help Meredith in any way she could, after learning of her business problems? Why was she so resistant to the idea now?

Quinn, meanwhile, called Bones to her side, as urgently as if he'd been about to dash out into heavy traffic, rose to her feet, and, when the dog reached her, she quickly scooped him up into her arms. Held him protectively.

Meredith swung gracefully out of the Jag, clad in her usual pristine white. At least she wasn't wearing a tailored suit and high heels, Ria thought stupidly—or chain mail and other battle gear.

Predictably, Ria's sister had chosen an cotton-eyelet sundress that set off her artificial tan, completing the look with matching sandals. There wasn't a wrinkle or a smudge anywhere on her person—the woman might have been magically teleported straight to this little farm in Montana from a dressing room at Nordstrom or Neiman Marcus, instead of driving for hours and hours and then *more* hours.

How did she do that? Ria wondered, as she had so many times before.

Meredith, for her part, didn't move for a long time—she seemed poised to jump back into her car and speed out of there, if it came to that. Maybe she expected a grizzly to come bounding out of nowhere, growling and slavering, intent on gobbling her up like a character in an old-time fairy tale of the un-varnished variety, such was her aversion to wide-open spaces. Meredith preferred skyscrapers, paved streets and plenty of concrete sidewalks.

Ria finally shook off these thoughts, scraped up a smile and started toward her sister, flanked by a singularly unenthusiastic Quinn. The dog, who had recently developed a penchant for finding icky things on the ground and rolling in them, gave off a distinctly unpleasant scent, though he showed the good sense not to bark the way he did when the mail carrier or the UPS man pulled in.

Maybe, Ria thought, Bones was scared to let out a peep. Smart dog.

Meredith, meanwhile, eyed both Ria and Quinn with an attempt at smiling aplomb and a quick step backward. If she'd been wearing a sandwich board, the words scrawled on it, in big letters, would almost certainly have read *Please do not hug*.

"Isn't anyone glad to see me?" Meredith trilled, clearly uncomfortable and doing her damnedest to look otherwise.

"That depends," Quinn replied cautiously, and with a slight edge to her voice. "I'm not going to camp, and you're not going to put Bones in some shelter, either. Once I'm sure we're on the same page, I might be a *little* glad to see you."

Meredith flinched and kept her mouth shut, stuck for an answer, it seemed.

Ria moved closer to Quinn, slipped a reassuring arm around the girl's shoulders, which were trembling a little. "Take it easy, sweetheart," she said quietly.

Meredith's smile clung, brittle, to her perfectly outlined, rose-colored lips, and she flung manicured hands out from her sides, doing her imitation of good-natured frustration. "You can keep the dog," she said, in sweet-and-sour tones, still maintaining her careful distance. "And, in any case, it's too late to start camp. They're well into the summer program and it's very comprehensive, so they're not admitting anyone else."

The implication was plain enough: *you blew it, kid. You're missing out on some* really *great stuff.*

"Meredith," Ria ventured politely, "why don't we go inside? There's iced tea, and it's much cooler in the house—"

Meredith cut Ria off with a glance sharp enough to slice overripe tomatoes paper-thin. "I wouldn't want to inconvenience you," she said coolly, with a shake of her head. "I've taken adjoining rooms at what passes for a hotel in the fair city of Three Trees, and *my daughter* and I will be staying there for the time being. *We* need privacy if we're going to save our relationship, and there are other decisions to make, as well."

Decisions that don't, of course, concern you, *Ria Manning.*

Ria didn't react, not visibly, anyway. She should be used to this by now, she reasoned silently, since she'd always been the outsider. But she *wasn't* used to it—she felt like a social climber, a party crasher, not a member of the Whittingford family.

Oh, no, never that.

Quinn, looking on, went rigid, holding poor Bones in such a viselike grip that he gave a little yelp of protest and scrabbled at the girl's chest with his front paws, wanting to be put down.

Reluctantly, her throat working visibly, Quinn

loosened her hold on the dog and then, with the greatest reluctance, set him gently at her feet.

"I told you," Quinn said, when she found her voice again, "*I'm not leaving Bones.*"

This, Ria knew, was a bluff, and a bold one. Quinn was under eighteen, which meant Meredith was still running the show. And she had the full weight of the law behind her.

Ria ached—for the frightened girl, for the helpless little dog, for her half sister, who couldn't seem to get the hang of being a mother.

Meredith gave a sharp little huff of exasperation in response to Quinn's brave statement. "All right, all right, you can keep the dog," she said, unable to hide her distaste but, remarkably, willing to make a concession. Meredith didn't make concessions.

Bones immediately trotted over to sniff at Meredith's gleaming coral toenails, and she gasped in alarm, her expression pained as she met Quinn's gaze again. "This *creature* had better behave himself, though," she added, with a kind of tremulous bravado, "because I had to put down a *big* damage deposit before the hotel would agree that we could bring him inside." The pitch of Meredith's voice rose slightly and she did another slight jig as Bones took an interest in her ankles and commenced to sniff those instead of her toenails. "H-honestly," she declared, elegantly fretful, "I thought these country towns were supposed to be oh so *tolerant* of livestock, and that hotel has the nerve to tout itself as 'pet friendly' on its website, then turns around and *demands* a ridiculous sum for doing the customer a 'favor.'"

Quinn and Ria exchanged a look of grim amusement. Bones was *livestock?*

Quinn decided to round up the herd, gave a low whistle and smiled very slightly as Bones came right back to her. He was officially her dog now, since he was duly licensed, and Quinn took good care of him. He'd even been to the vet for an exam and the necessary shots, and when it came to training, he was a quick study.

Ria glanced at her niece, saw that she was biting her lower lip, engaged in some inner struggle as she looked warily at Meredith—but there was hope there, too, a fragile yearning to make lasting peace with the woman who had, after all, given birth to her.

Quinn might be nearly grown, but she still wanted, still needed, a mother.

And it did appear that Meredith was really trying to bridge the gap between herself and her daughter; she was willing to give a bit of ground for once, an astounding thing. Moreover, her overture had included Bones, and that was even *more* astounding. Anybody who knew Meredith, at all, would have bet she'd dig in her heels for sure when it came to accepting the dog.

"Is this for real?" Quinn asked, and it was clear that she desperately wanted a yes, but, nobody's fool, she was plagued by lingering doubts. Little wonder, given her and Meredith's history of casual estrangement. "Because if this is some kind of trick, *Mom,* and your *actual* plan is to ditch Bones at the first opportunity, I will *never* forgive you. Never, ever, *ever.* I swear we'll hit the road again if you try anything, Bones and me both, and that'll be the end of it—no second chances."

The kid drove a hard bargain, Ria thought fitfully. How would this all turn out?

She felt a shudder go through her, even though the early afternoon was warm and sunny. No doubt about it, Quinn meant what she said, and Ria could only offer a silent prayer that Meredith understood just how much was at stake here.

To everyone's surprise—probably even her own—Meredith's pale blue eyes suddenly filled with tears. "Do you have *any idea,* Quinn Whittingford, how many dreadful, horrible, *unspeakable* things can—and *do*—happen to teenage runaways—girls *and* boys, every minute of every day?"

"I watch the ID network," Quinn replied nonchalantly, with a curt little nod. "So yeah, I guess I have a pretty good idea. But I'll still take the chance, if that's what I have to do."

While Meredith was still recovering from *that* statement, not even bothering to swipe at the tears that were washing away her mascara and slipping down her cheeks in small black runnels that zigzagged like little rivers to drop off her chin and stain her formerly impeccable white dress, Quinn stood stock-still, silently unrelenting.

"If we're going to make this work," Meredith finally blurted out, between soft, shoulder-quaking sobs, "*I'll* have to be the mother, Quinn. I promise things will be different—we'll talk things through, and you'll have your say in every decision that concerns you—but if you think I'm going to let you raise *yourself,* while I conveniently look the other way, you are so, completely, *spectacularly* wrong!"

Ria was downright proud of her half sister in that moment—Meredith was willing to lighten up, but she wasn't about to abdicate her role as a parent, either.

You go, girl, Ria thought.

Meredith reached into the car for her designer handbag, opened it and plucked out a clump of tissue, dabbing at her eyes, swiping at her wet cheeks, rubbing away the last of her foundation and blusher. Then, having regained a semblance of dignity, she straightened her spine, looked directly at Quinn and said, "You have my word—whatever happens after our peace talks, whether you decide to stay here with Ria or go back to Portland with me, the dog stays. I'll—I'll just have to get used to him. Somehow."

Quinn, it seemed, was finally convinced. "I'll get my things," she said.

Then she and Bones crossed the lawn, bounded up the porch steps and vanished into the house.

Meredith and Ria just stood there, enveloped in

awkward silence, Meredith with her eyes fixed on the far horizon, Ria looking straight at her half sister. It was a one-sided stare-down, and winning by default was still a victory.

Finally, Ria folded her arms, tilted her head to one side and asked, "What happened, Meredith? What's changed?"

At last, Meredith returned Ria's gaze. "I've lost so much," she said, her voice small again, void of its usual crisp disdain for the inconvenient daughter of Daddy and the showgirl. "The company's going under—there's no way around it—and most of the little money I have left will be gone by the time this is all over." Pain shadowed her eyes, but a faint glint of determination remained, Ria was glad to see. "I can't lose my daughter, too."

Ria swallowed the lump that rose in her throat, looked away, looked back. "I understand," she said quietly. "And, for what it's worth, Meredith, I'm not your enemy."

Meredith's shoulders slumped slightly, and she sighed so deeply that Ria's heart ached in sympathy. "I know," she replied. "You were there for Quinn when it counted, and I'll always be grateful to you for that."

Ria waited a few moments before pushing the envelope just a little further. "So maybe—someday—we could talk to each other without winding up in a shouting match or a catfight?"

Meredith smiled, thinly, weakly—but she smiled.

"That would be good," she replied, after a few moments of hesitation. "When—when we're ready—"

Translation: *if* we're ready, ever.

Since she was starting to feel as though she might cry herself, Ria made her excuses and went into the house to see if Quinn needed help. She'd accumulated more than her backpack could hold, over these few days—Bones's bed, the big bag of kibble and all the other canine gear, chew toys and a leash and special shampoo.

Meredith waited in the car.

Half an hour later, Quinn and Bones were on their way, the giant swirl of dust trailing behind Meredith's Jaguar swallowing them up.

Feeling strangely, poignantly hollow, Ria slowly went into the house, and instantly, confronted by the emptiness of the place, that hollow inside her was swamped, overflowing, with loneliness. She leaned back against the closed door for a while, closing her eyes, willing herself to be strong, keep it together.

Quinn was *Meredith's* child, after all, not her own. The girl belonged with her mother, if that was at all possible, and with some rough going ahead, Meredith needed Quinn, too, though whether she'd ever admit as much or not was anybody's guess. People had only so much change in them, Ria reminded herself, some more than others.

Meredith might backslide, or she might continue to make progress. There was no way to know.

When she'd recovered a little, Ria went into the

bathroom, splashed her face with cold water at the sink, dried her skin with a hand towel and marched herself back outside.

She still had flowers to weed, soil to hoe, hoses and sprinklers to drag from here to there and back again. Later, she promised herself, she'd take a luxuriously long shower, with no worries that she might run out of hot water because Quinn had already used most of it up. Then she'd have an early supper— something light and quick, like a green salad—and, finally, she'd cap off the evening by balancing her books and paying a few bills.

She would get through this latest transition just fine, she assured herself, the same way she'd gotten through everything else.

She'd get used to living alone again, too. After all, it wasn't as if she had a choice in the matter, and heaven knew she'd had plenty of practice at flying solo.

Same song, second verse.

On Saturday morning, Ria woke up at the usual time, i.e., the butt crack of dawn, even though she knew there would be no farmers' market today, no flowers to cut and arrange in buckets of water for transport, no finicky old truck to load or start up with the turn of a key, a few hard pumps to the gas pedal and a fervent prayer or two.

The annual Parable County Rodeo had officially opened the night before, kicked off with the usual fireworks and marching bands and a whole lot of community spirit—not that Ria had been there to participate.

Oh, no. She was in survival mode and, for her, that meant staying close to home, working until she was ready to drop and not thinking about Landry Sutton, or Quinn, or even Bones, if she could possibly help it.

Mostly, she couldn't avoid the memories; they tended to sneak up on her at unguarded moments.

She considered the rodeo. By today, the event of the year would be in full swing, complete with crowds, a carnival of impressive scale, for such a small community, with all kinds of rides and games, lots of deep-fried everything readily available and vendors from far and wide, selling all manner of goods, from boots to dinner plates, low-end jewelry to solid gold and silver belt buckles, hand-painted vests and handbags—name it—all with a Western theme.

Ria wanted no part of the hoopla, or so she told herself. By 10:00 a.m., however, she'd run out of chores to do, and she was restless.

Surfing the internet was out, since she was still a little paranoid about accidentally running across more unflattering pictures of herself, and even knowing that the to-do had already dwindled to nearly nothing didn't help.

"What I need," she said aloud, standing in the middle of her kitchen with a cup of herbal tea cooling in her hand, "is a dog. Or a cat. Or both."

She sighed. And now she'd been reduced to talking to herself—out loud no less. What was next?

As it turned out, *Highbridge* was next. He drove up in his Bentley, honked his horn to bring Ria outside and made her laugh for the first time in days.

When the most dignified man she'd ever known climbed out of that august car of his to smile at Ria, she saw that he was wearing a ten-gallon hat, denim pants, a plaid shirt with a Western-cut yolk and mother-of-pearl snaps, even a bandanna around his neck. And there were honest-to-God boots on his feet.

Ria stared at him in delighted wonder, temporarily speechless as he affected a loose-hipped amble and came toward her.

"Howdy, ma'am," he said, in a very bad American accent, pausing at the bottom of the porch steps.

Previously, Ria couldn't even have *imagined* Highbridge's dour self in such a getup—she'd never known him to wear anything but his staid butler's garb, and sometimes suspected that he even *slept* in a starched shirt, long tails and spats. Now, seeing her usually taciturn friend dressed like an extra in a pretalkie film featuring Tom Mix or some other old-timer, was absolutely mind-blowing.

"Is it Halloween?" she teased. "Or did you lose a bet?"

He chuckled. "Neither," he said. "I'm on my way to the rodeo, over in Parable. You see, my illustrious employer is competing in an event—saddle-bronc riding, I believe—and I thought it only proper to show support." He paused, and his mouth took on a wry twist, quickly gone. "*Or* rush him to the nearest hospital, if that proves necessary."

Ria's eyes widened. The news shouldn't have surprised her, but it did. She hadn't seen Landry since the night he'd stopped by to inform her that he was still alive, so the rodeo thing had gotten by her.

She'd been so wrapped up in not obsessing about him, or about Quinn and Bones—and doing it anyway—that she could barely think straight.

On top of that, the mother-daughter peace treaty being hammered out in a Three Trees hotel room—*another* thing to obsess about not obsessing about—seemed to be taking forever.

"Landry *can't* be entered in the rodeo," she finally blustered. "That's too dangerous—he might—"

Ria ran out of steam then, though only briefly, because she was already shoveling metaphorical coal like crazy.

"He sure enough is, though," Highbridge replied, in another bad attempt at cowboy-speak. "If his score is high enough—and assuming he doesn't get himself crippled or killed, of course—he'll be riding again tomorrow."

"No," Ria insisted. As if she had any say in the matter.

Highbridge smiled. "I thought you might like to accompany me," he said, in his own very British accent. "To the rodeo, I mean."

"Just let me get my purse and lock the house," Ria replied hastily. On one level, she knew she wouldn't be able to stop Landry from competing in one of the most dangerous sports going, but on another, she was determined to try.

When she and Highbridge finally arrived at the Parable County Fairgrounds, some forty-five minutes later, Ria could barely sit still.

The moment the car came to a stop, she bolted, ran ahead to the ticket booth, leaving Highbridge behind without so much as a "so long." She waited impatiently in line, paid the price of admission with a bill still damp from being clutched in her palm. A man stamped the back of her hand, and she dashed for the arena.

When she got there, the bleachers were jammed with fans from near and far, and the aisles were hopelessly crowded. She stopped, gasping for breath, wondering what, if anything, she could do.

And then the announcer proclaimed over the loudspeakers that the next event would be saddle-bronc riding.

It was an omen, Ria decided. She'd arrived just in time to—what? See Landry break his fool neck? Throw her arms around him and beg him not to ride? She still didn't know.

But instead of finding a seat in the stands, as any sensible person would have done, any sensible person who wasn't wildly in love with a crazy man, that was, Ria ran, pushing her way through cowboys and stock-tenders toward the no-woman's land behind the chutes.

In the process, she literally collided with Zane Sutton. He gripped her by the shoulders to keep her from falling and gave her a quizzical grin. "You're not supposed to be back here," he said. "It's not safe."

Ria was way past the point of caring whether she was safe or not. "Where's Landry?" she asked, twisting in Zane's gentle but very firm grasp.

Zane inclined his head in the direction of the catwalk, just behind the chutes. "He's up next," he replied, letting her go at last.

She whipped her head around instantly, looking for Landry.

And there he was, standing on the ground beside the steps leading up onto the steel scaffolding where cowboys waited their turn to ride, calmly adjusting his hat and watching as the first competitor in the lineup got ready for his chance to risk life and limb.

Ria rushed toward Landry, but there were a lot of cowboys milling around in between, and by the time she reached the place he'd been standing, he'd climbed onto the catwalk and lowered himself into the chute and onto the back of twelve to fifteen hundred pounds of hatred on the hoof. The gate was being hauled open.

Everything seemed to be happening in slow motion, and all Ria could hear, besides a faint thudding sound, was the rush of blood in her ears. Somehow she got to the fence, squeezed in and watched as the ride began.

This, too, unfolded with maddening slowness—it seemed to Ria that each second was a freeze-frame, part of a slide show.

For her, that was the longest eight seconds in history.

Landry leaped off the horse when the buzzer sounded, piercing the swath of silence that had surrounded Ria until that moment. Crossing the arena, he finally spotted her. A cocky grin slanted his mouth.

He paused to grab his hat, paid no attention to the tallying of his score on the big digital reader board affixed to a beam above the announcer's booth.

It was a time out of time, it seemed to Ria. She existed. Landry existed. Everything and every*body* else was gone.

Like a figure in a misty dream, Ria raised her left hand so Landry could see it. Then she slid Frank's wedding band off her finger and tucked it into her jeans pocket.

Seeing this, Landry narrowed his eyes briefly, as though not quite believing what they were telling him. Then a smile broke across his face, and he bounded toward her, scrambling over the fence.

And that strange sense of inhabiting a separate world, a magical place with a population of two, didn't let up.

He stood in front of Ria, looking down at her, his

hands resting on either side of her waist. Neither of them heard his score when it was announced, as it must have been, and neither of them cared.

Finally, Landry took Ria's hand and shouldered through the gathering, pulling her after him, his strides so long that she had to hurry to keep up with him.

On the way out, Ria caught sight of Highbridge, seated halfway up in the bleachers. He took off his huge hat and nodded to her, his mouth twitching slightly with his rendition of a grin.

Obviously, he knew precisely what was going on, but Ria didn't have the chance—or the inclination—to stop and explain. What could she say? *Thanks for the ride into town, but I won't be needing one for the return trip?* Her cheeks burned.

She and Landry reached the smaller lot behind the arena, where cowboys and other participants parked. There were trucks and horse trailers everywhere, but only a few people.

"Landry," she gasped, "*slow down.*"

"*Hell,* no," Landry replied. Reaching his truck, he opened the passenger-side door, picked Ria up bodily and practically flung her into the seat.

She was still catching her breath when he climbed into the rig on the other side, reaching past the steering wheel and the gearshift to take her left hand in his, run the pad of his thumb over the bare skin where the ring had been.

"You're sure?" he asked, his voice gruff, his eyes watchful.

Ria drew a deep breath, let it out slowly. "I'm sure," she replied.

The ride back to Three Trees was a blur, just as the rodeo had been.

Ria's heart thudded in her throat the whole way, but this time it wasn't because she was afraid. Oh, no. This was pure anticipation.

When Landry drove right past Ria's driveway, she was a little confused.

Then, minutes later, his mailbox came into view. He slowed down just enough to keep all four truck wheels on the ground as he made the turn, and sped up again as soon as it was behind them. He stopped the rig within a few feet of his odd but impressive house—part framework, part rustic mansion—shut off the engine, took off his hat and thrust a hand through his hair.

When Landry looked her way, she saw the whole vast expanse of the big sky right there in his eyes. "I love you, Ria," he said. "I know it's crazy, and it's too soon, and all the rest of it, but it's true just the same. Nothing in my life has ever been truer."

Ria couldn't speak, she was so stricken with love for this man.

He put his work-roughened hands on either side of her face, leaned toward her and touched his mouth to hers. Since neither of them had thought to unfasten their seat belts, the position was an awkward one, but that didn't matter.

Landry kissed Ria, a mere brush of their lips at first, soon transforming into something much deeper, something demanding and totally, completely *right*. By the time the kiss ended, Ria had gone blissfully weak.

Taking his time now, Landry got out of the truck, came around to her side, lifted her off the seat and carried her toward the house, then inside.

She didn't notice a single detail about the place, not then. It could have been a castle, or a cave in the side of a mountain.

Ria was aware of only two things: the hard, hot substance of Landry Sutton and the fire he'd ignited inside her.

CHAPTER SIXTEEN

RIA WAS DAZED, stupidly happy, when Landry kissed her again, this time in the privacy of his bedroom. It was a lingering kiss, a demand, an exploration, a conquering and a surrender—all of that, and more.

But it ended too soon. Ria looked up into Landry's handsome face, confounded.

He ran his fingers over her hair, then kissed her briefly on the forehead.

Her blank expression must have amused him, because he chuckled. "Woman," he said, in a sexy rasp, "I just came from a rodeo. What dirt I didn't eat is ground into my hide, under a couple of layers of dried sweat—in other words, I need a shower before the next event."

A tingle of anticipatory relief teased Ria in some very sensitive parts of her anatomy.

"I'll be waiting," she said, unbuttoning her jeans.

Landry uttered a single exuberant swearword and fled.

The moment she was alone, Ria slipped out of her shoes, then pulled her T-shirt off over her head and tossed it aside. Next, she unzipped her jeans, shed them without hesitation and flung them after the T-shirt. She was down to her bra and panties now, but she kept them on—she wanted *Landry* to peel them away, to bare her breasts and the tangle of curls at the juncture of her thighs with those strong, skilled hands and—

Stop thinking, Ria ordered herself. *Stop now.*

Her imagination was in overdrive for sure, and if she wasn't careful, she'd have a spontaneous orgasm, all by herself. That, like the bra and panties, was *Landry's* department.

And pleasing him in return would be hers.

Through the closed door to the master bath, Ria heard the shower spray turn on. Her heart beat in time with the pounding rhythm of the water, and little pulses throbbed in the usual—and *un*usual—places, all over her body.

Hurry, Ria urged Landry silently, but, at the same time, she was deliciously certain that he wasn't a hasty man, not when it came to lovemaking. The few incendiary, soul-consuming kisses they'd shared had been previews of coming attractions, she reflected, smiling at the unintended pun. The main feature was still ahead, and that, too, would probably turn out to be a prelude to something even greater.

This thing Ria felt for Landry was a mystery, a phenomenon of nature, a thing of liquid fire, molten lava stirring in the darkest depths of a volcano long disguised as a peaceful mountain. She'd never experienced anything like it, never even *imagined* it was possible.

Looking back over the past year, she realized there had been tremors from the day she first encountered Landry Sutton, at a party Zane and Brylee had given, an outdoor shindig with live music and catered food, and half the county in attendance.

Zane had been the one to introduce them, and Landry's smile had immediately knocked Ria back on her figurative heels. His attention was strangely *nourishing,* she'd thought, a little panicked, as inexorably persuasive as spring sunshine blanketing a field, penetrating far beneath the surface, awakening seeds from their long winter's sleep, tugging at them until they cracked open, sprouted and finally broke ground, there to grow and blossom and bloom in the light.

The very impact of the man's personality, his mere presence in the world she'd thought she knew, had been seismic for Ria and, therefore, terrifying. Vulnerability had definitely *not* been an option back then—and it was pretty scary in the here and now.

Ria had been wide open to everything as a child, a quiet little ghost haunting a family she never quite belonged to, forever on the outside, looking in. Sure, she'd known that her mother loved her; it was just that the poor woman was perennially distracted, focused on pleasing her husband, constantly bailing water in an effort to keep her leaky marriage afloat.

Ria's father would watch his younger daughter sometimes, frowning slightly, as though he thought she looked familiar but couldn't quite place her. According to Meredith, then a fractious adolescent with issues of her own, "Daddy" had been gravely disappointed when he found himself with another girl-child, instead of the son and heir he'd hoped for.

Through all this, Ria didn't feel sorry for herself, nor was she particularly depressed—she was just, well, *resigned.* As childhoods went, Ria had soon realized, hers had been better than most.

So, throughout the growing-up years, she coped. She got good grades in school, played on the soccer team, participated in student government. While she didn't run with the popular crowd, she had plenty of friends. In high school, Ria dated regularly but remained carefully detached—she was no prude, but when whatever guy she happened to be seeing at the time began to say things like "if you loved me, you'd…" she was out of there.

Romantic love? Please. Ria had long since decided that, if such a thing existed at all, it was reserved for a very fortunate few.

Later on, in college, she'd dated older guys, men, not boys, blue-collar types who had served in the armed forces or attended the proverbial school of hard knocks before going for their degrees. She'd had sex with a few of them, and found it pleasant but not particularly memorable. Deep down, she'd gone right on guarding her heart, keeping her distance, playing it safe.

Soon enough, Ria had finished school and gone to work full-time for her father's company, Whittingford International, as she was expected to do. She had her own tiny apartment, an old car and a lot of lonely evenings to fill.

So Ria had joined a gym, stopping by on her way home from the office four nights a week to get a little exercise.

There, she'd met Frank.

He was cute, and muscular, he made her laugh, and though he was clearly attracted to Ria, he didn't come on too strong. One crisp Saturday morning in the fall, having just showered after a missed workout, Ria ran into Frank in the corridor between the men's and women's locker rooms. Frank had asked if she'd like to have coffee with him, and she'd said yes, and that was the beginning. By Christmas, Ria not only believed in love—she was *in* it, head over heels.

The wedding, big, beautiful and wildly expensive, took place the following spring. Ria was completely happy, and everything seemed possible. Frank made good money as a firefighter—they could manage fairly well on his income if they were careful—and they began to talk about starting a family. Ria looked forward to getting pregnant, and took an indefinite leave of absence from her job, wanting to make sure she could handle staying at home.

It was almost embarrassing, how much Ria liked being a housewife—her friends were getting advanced degrees, scrambling up academic or corporate ladders, while she was more than content with her domestic-goddess role. By then, she and Frank were serious about getting pregnant.

Maybe they were *too* serious, because month after month, Ria's period arrived right on schedule. Slowly—so slowly that neither of them really noticed—things began to change. They didn't make love as often, or laugh as much. And, while they didn't have any knock-down, drag-out fights, they began to bicker occasionally.

And then came the betrayals—the first was Frank's. He had that one-night stand while he was out of town, taking special classes. It was harder to place blame for the second, much worse betrayal— her husband's sudden, tragic death. Frank hadn't planned on dying any more than Ria had planned on losing him, but there it was. He was gone, killed on the job.

After that, Ria had simply shut down. She didn't live; she survived. She might have stayed on that track forever, too, if she hadn't come across the farm, listed on an internet real-estate site, and, on a whim she still couldn't explain, even to herself, bought the place. Moved there, ignoring the shocked protests of her friends.

Three Trees, Montana? Was she kidding?

It was no joke; Ria threw herself into making her new life work.

Almost immediately, Murphy's Law being operational, a potential complication arose when she met Landry Sutton at a barbecue at Zane and Brylee's place. Until then, no man since Frank had made her feel *anything*, good, bad or indifferent.

But there were things about Landry that set off warning signals in Ria's mind and heart the moment Zane introduced them. Landry's slightly crooked grin had rocked Ria to the core, and his husky "hello" made her breath run quick and shallow.

Here was a man who knew what he wanted and invariably got it, she'd thought, unnerved by her own reactions to him. According to Brylee, Zane's younger brother was divorced and available.

According to *Ria,* the man was just plain dangerous—too good-looking and too engaging to be anything but the love-'em-and-leave-'em type. No doubt, in addition to at least one discarded wife, Landry had left a long trail of brokenhearted women behind him.

Ria had expected him to make polite excuses and move on to charm someone new, but he lingered, easily drew her into conversation. The way he'd looked at her, the way he'd smiled, had made her dizzy.

In self-defense, Ria had decided then and there not only to dislike Landry Sutton thoroughly, but to steer clear of him as much as possible. And she'd followed through on the plan—until he'd hauled off and kissed her, in a field of daisies and zinnias, the day after the buffalo raid.

Now, only a few days later, here she was, standing in Landry's bedroom, wearing nothing but a bra and panties and a rash of goose bumps, waiting—no, *eager*—to surrender.

Where on earth was her *sensible* self, the Ria who had borne up under heartbreak for so long, and forged a new path for herself in a new place? She had no clue.

To keep her brain from doing any more time traveling, either to the past *or* the future, Ria shifted mental gears and looked around the large but sparely furnished room, noting the bare walls, painted a muted shade of sage-green, more a hint than an actual color. She examined the beamed ceiling, noted the tall windows that made up the far wall, took in the enormous stone fireplace. Finally, having drawn the inspection out as long as she could without rooting through bureau drawers or peeking into the closet, Ria allowed herself to focus on the bed.

It was quite plain, Landry's bed, given the grandeur of the room itself. King-sized, she estimated, with a simple brass headboard, thick pillows without shams and a sturdy-looking patchwork quilt in place of a spread.

Ria heard the shower water stop, braced herself and waited for the bathroom door to open. There was a click, and she turned to see Landry, naked except for a towel slung around his lean waist, his skin tanned and beaded with sparkling droplets of water. His eyes widened slightly when he looked at her, saw that she'd stripped to her panties and a bra. He smiled, almost imperceptibly, and let his gaze drift the length of her, at his leisure.

Ria stifled an involuntary whimper as her nipples hardened under the thin lace of her bra. The sensation trailed down her body right along with Landry's slow, *slow* glance, leaving her moist beneath her panties, with that familiar feeling of expansion, of getting ready to take him inside her.

Landry approached, stood directly in front of Ria, and despite the light of passion in his eyes, his expression was solemn.

"We need to get one thing clear, before this goes any further," he told Ria, his voice low and husky and very earnest. "This isn't a fling, or a one-night stand. It isn't the start of an affair. It's the beginning of forever, and if forever isn't what you have in mind, then we need to stop, right now."

Stop? *Now?* Ria was astounded. *Stop*—when the very air around them quivered with this strange energy of passion and need? Was the man from another planet?

And what about this *forever* thing?

Okay, Landry *had* said he loved her, out there in the truck, and she not only believed him, but she loved him back with an intensity that frightened her. But what red-blooded man talked about "forever" when he and the woman he was with hadn't even been to a movie together, for pity's sake, let alone swapped promises or made love?

Ria tried to speak, but not a sound came out. No matter—she wouldn't have known what to say anyhow, baffled as she was, and bereft. Landry had made her want him—and he'd done it on purpose. Now, all of a sudden, he was suggesting that they *stop?*

Reading her face, Landry cupped a hand under Ria's chin, his lips on the verge of another smile, his eyes searching hers. "It's forever or nothing," he ground out. "Which one do you want?"

Ria swallowed. She couldn't deal with *nothing,* now that she'd fallen so hard for this man, struggled so to let go of her past, finally found forgiveness and peace within herself—*and* made what was probably the most daring decision of her life: to take a chance, put all her chips on the table and allow herself to love again.

All or nothing, that was the choice Landry offered.

"I'll take forever," Ria said.

"That's good," Landry replied, his voice gruff and yet incredibly tender. He reached behind Ria and unfastened her bra, pulled it down over her shoulders and then off and admired her bare breasts until she needed his touch so badly that she gave a small, crooning moan.

With a throaty chuckle, Landry cupped her bounty in his hands, running the sides of his thumbs slowly, lightly, across her nipples.

Ria was so aroused that she would have begged the man to take her, hard and fast, standing up, right there in the middle of the room, but she knew he wouldn't do that—knew for certain that he was going to make her wait and wait—so she simply let go and gave herself up to the exquisite, almost unbearable pleasure of his fingers, then his mouth.

Oh, dear God, his mouth.

Landry bent his head, clasped his hands together at the small of her back and suckled at Ria's nipples till they throbbed with wanting, teased them with feathery passes of his tongue. The implicit promise in these attentions made Ria lean back in his embrace, offering herself to him, made her bury frantic hands in his hair and utter his name, over and over again, in ragged, soblike pleas.

She didn't just *want* Landry to take her; she *needed* taking. Needed it the way she needed her next breath, her next heartbeat.

But Landry had other ideas.

He went down on her instead, kneeling before her, dragging her panties down over her thighs and off and then burrowing in, taking her full into his mouth as she gave a low, shuddering cry of welcome.

As he continued to ply her that way, to tease and murmur, Ria threw back her head in total surrender, let out another cry of pleasure, this one almost a howl. She felt boneless, liquefied, and she knew she would have sunk all the way to the floor if Landry hadn't held her firmly with those strong hands of his, keeping her upright.

That first climax, when Landry finally allowed Ria to go over the edge, was shattering, a many-splendored thing, light catching on light, fire meeting fire, and it seemed to have no beginning and no

end—peaking, subsiding, peaking again, each pin-
nacle more intense, each descent curving right back
up, and up, and up, eternal as the tide.

Ria was well past any capacity for restraint by
the time the ecstasy reached its highest pitch again,
in a long, sweeping crescendo that made her entire body convulse as she pressed herself against
Landry's mouth, and he feasted on her until she was
exhausted, until she couldn't give any more. He made
her offer up everything, and the final triumph wrung
a string of primitive sounds from her very depths,
low, hoarse shouts, broken groans, desperate little
whimpers.

And then the cries solidified, and formed themselves into words.

"I—love—you—" Ria gasped. *"So—so much—"*

Ria was still quivering with tiny aftershocks when
Landry rose to his feet and, just when her knees
would have buckled, caught her and swept her up in
his arms, all in a single graceful motion.

He carried her to the bed, pulled back the covers
and laid her down on cool, crisp sheets.

"You were saying—?" Landry teased, stretching
out beside Ria, parting her legs with a gentle press
of his hand, sliding down and down to kiss the tender insides of her thighs.

Ria was just beginning to settle back into herself,
almost coherent. "I was about to say—" But she'd
forgotten what she'd been about to say, in the heat
of the ongoing seduction. She began to writhe as

Landry parted her. "Oh, God, Landry—not again—what are you—?"

He flicked at her with just the tip of his tongue.

"Go on," he urged, in a mischievous growl, as Ria gave a lusty shout and arched her back, raising herself high for him. As easily as that, as quickly as that, Landry Sutton had rocketed her from nestling comfortably into a satisfied stupor to full-spectrum, raging arousal. How was that possible?

Go on, he'd said. As though they were having a casual conversation—as though he hadn't turned her into a volcano—one about to erupt—here in his deceptively unassuming bedroom.

Ria was wild, tossing, flailing in ecstasy, about to lose herself again, but she managed to gasp a response. "*Damn* you, Landry—I said—I love—you—"

She repeated the *I love you* over and over, faster and faster, more and more desperately.

Landry nibbled at her, and chuckled when she finally broke off the fevered declaration to give a long, purrlike moan. It was the cry of a tigress.

"I happen to feel the same way about you," he rumbled, nuzzling her again, lifting her boneless legs, draping one over his right shoulder and one over his left. "Hold on tight, darlin'," he warned, "because I'm about to make you love me a whole lot more."

A tremor of sheer need flared up in Ria when she felt his mouth on her again, now teasing, now greedy, and she rocked her head from side to side on the pillow, delirious, as he drove her steadily, inexorably skyward again. He held her high off the mattress, the palms of his hands strong under her buttocks, savoring her like a thirsty man scooping up water from a stream. This time, though, Landry didn't torment her with little delays.

No, this time he enjoyed her in earnest, stayed with her when she began to buck like a wild mare, throwing her head back on the pillow and finally, completely, letting herself go. Landry didn't let up when she began her quivering descent, either, but led her slowly, so slowly, back from the far side of the stars, back into his arms, back into his bed.

Ria had never felt the way she did now—emptied out and, at the same time, gloriously filled—totally female, saturated with light, gloriously and fiercely loved. Wanted. She lay still and replete as Landry shifted, reached for something on the nightstand. He was putting on a condom, she thought dreamily.

Finally, it was *his* turn to soar heavenward and burst apart in fragments of light, like fireworks splashing across a night sky, while she moved beneath him, around him, running her hands gently up and down his back, crooning to him as the pressure built, urging him to let go.

Except it didn't turn out like that, exactly. The instant Landry drove inside her, Ria was electrified again, her back arching so she could take him in deeper, her gentle caresses turning rapidly to clutching, raking the flesh on his back with her nails.

She sobbed his name as yet another climax seized her, shook her with the force of an earthquake and then, instead of letting her drift blissfully earthward, hurled her higher instead. And still higher.

Landry took his time, his strokes long and deep and slow.

Ria watched him from beneath her lashes as she met with another release and then another, helpless against the ever-mounting pleasure, the merciless, pounding pleasure—how much longer could she endure it?

Finally, Landry stiffened, uttering a long groan, the cry of something wild and purely male, taking its mate but also letting itself be taken. The powerful muscles in his neck and chest and shoulders tightened visibly as Landry shoved his hands down hard into the mattress, thrust his head back and rasped out Ria's name again and again, with each flex of his magnificent body. Even when he climaxed, it happened in surges, a thrust, another thrust, a sigh that seemed torn from him.

When it was finally over, both lovers sank like stones into the sweet oblivion of sleep, completely spent.

Ria awakened a long time later, after sunset, surfacing by degrees, only to find herself being ministered to by Landry and soon in the middle of a soft, slow and utterly scrumptious orgasm. She whimpered and buckled, but the release was leisurely, rather than fierce, like before. Her eyelids were too heavy to lift to look at him and, besides, the orgasm went on and on, muted and sweet, and all she could do was ride the undulating wave of it, let it carry her wherever it would.

Landry was watching her face when she finally floated in for a landing, sighed contentedly and opened her eyes. Propped up on his left elbow, he smiled down at her, looking sleepy and rumpled in the dim light from the bathroom and obviously very pleased with himself. His free hand, she realized, was between her legs, at least one finger was inside her and the heel of his palm rested over the damp, still-throbbing nubbin of flesh he'd been caressing.

"I still want forever," he told her.

He didn't pull his hand away, and Ria didn't want him to. She gave another sigh—he was arousing her again—and slipped her arms around his neck, giving a little gasp of joyful despair when the tip of his finger found her G-spot and plied it expertly. "How can you be so sure of that, Landry Sutton?" she asked, though she barely had the breath to speak. "That you want forever, I mean."

"I'm sure," he said, with amused conviction. A mischievous light flickered in his eyes and Ria gasped again as he continued to work her with his finger. "It might have taken me longer to decide if the sex hadn't been so damn good."

Ria laughed, a soft, strangled sound, stroked Landry's hair and the hard length of his jaw, marveling at the miracle of this man's love for her, and hers for him. "I kind of enjoyed that myself," she answered. "The sex, that is." A croon escaped her, and, once again, her back arched. The man knew his way around a woman's body, she thought, as he made slow circles inside her, and she got wetter and wetter, aching for him.

His efforts were exquisitely focused, though, and, as always, unhurried.

X marks the spot.

"Yeah," Landry drawled. "I noticed."

Already half out of her mind again, Ria balled up one fist and pretended to slug him in the shoulder. He chuckled.

She couldn't help crying out once more, softly, as he deftly raised the pitch of her pleasure, making her reverberate like a tuning fork. "How—how did this happen?" she whimpered, rolling her head from side to side, scrambling to part her legs farther, grant him even more access.

Landry's grin broadened, warming her like sudden light. "The usual way," he answered, with that damnable ease of his. And where was all that self-control coming from? Ria knew he wanted her; his erection was huge, and it burned against the outside of her thigh, but his every move, his every word, was easy, almost languid. "You took your clothes off," he reminded her, "and I did the same. It was all pretty straightforward after that."

Ria laughed again, but her eyes filled with tears— happy ones, and tender. "That isn't what I meant,"

she scolded softly. "And you know it. I'm asking—
h-how did we—*oh, God, don't stop*—fall in love—
so quickly?" She gasped, swallowed, closed her
eyes, about to be swept away but determined to finish saying what she wanted to say. "Not that long
ago—oooooooooh—a few days, a week at most—
yes, yes, please, Landry, yes—we didn't even *like*
each other—"

Landry considered her words solemnly, but with
that same twinkle in his eyes, and the conquering
went on, uninterrupted. "I figure we were striking
sparks from the beginning," he said, after a few moments. "We've known each other almost a year, remember."

"But—" Another raspy cry, and then Ria's hips
flew, as surely as if they'd sprouted wings.

Landry's palm moved against her, gently and so
very slowly, while his finger did its work, and she
had to close her eyes and concentrate on the rising tumult inside her, and then outside, too, until all
there was of the universe was Landry, his touch, his
murmured words and the wonderful, terrible wanting he roused in her.

Ria wailed softly as that wanting got still more
wonderful, still more terrible.

Even then, Landry showed her no quarter. He
kissed her eyelids, one and then the other, and then
he began making his way down over the warm curve
of her right breast. Her nipples strained, ready-
ing themselves for his mouth and tongue, and she

moaned the only word she had the strength to utter, *"Yesssss,"* stretching that single syllable as far as it would go.

"Hold that thought," Landry murmured, reaching her waiting nipple, circling it with the tip of his tongue, then sucking it gently, rhythmically.

He was methodical, slowing his pace, then increasing it.

Each time Ria neared the release she craved, he somehow kept her from tumbling over the precipice.

Dazed, wild, exasperated, she found the breath to plead just once more. "Landry," she sobbed. "Don't make me wait—I need you—*now.*"

He released her nipple just long enough to run a fiery trail of kisses over to its waiting counterpart. "You're insatiable," he said.

"I'm *desperate,*" she countered.

He chuckled again, laved her nipple until it was so hard it ached and finally took it into his mouth—and Ria, knowing that he'd just given her his answer, that there would be no rushing, stopped resisting, stopped begging and simply let herself feel the lovely things Landry was doing to her.

When they were finally joined, body to body, soul to soul, it was as if two galaxies had collided, exploded into fragments, then sparks.

And it rained fire for a long, long time.

LANDRY SLEPT HEAVILY that night, the sleep of satisfied exhaustion, and if he dreamed, he had no recollection of it the next morning, when the first rays of sunlight teased his eyes open.

Beside him, Ria slumbered on, her arms flung back over her head in abandon, her fingers still curled loosely around the brass rails in the headboard, long after she'd gripped them in the frenzy of the most recent orgasm—somewhere in the wee hours—an apocalyptic event that had finally used both of them up.

Now the top sheet was all that was left of the covers, and it wasn't covering much more than Ria's belly button and part of her right thigh. Her breasts, full and warm, the nipples tightening under a soft breeze flowing in through a nearby window, were mighty tempting.

Landry might have given in, if Ria hadn't opened her eyes, narrowed them to slits and warned, *"Don't you dare,* Landry Sutton." She hopped out of bed, searched the floor for her clothes, found the T-shirt and pulled it on with a resolute yank of both hands. "I'm chapped all over, and I'm sore, and if I have even one more climax, I think it will kill me!"

"Death by orgasm," Landry mused, lying back on his pillow, cupping his hands at the back of his head. "Now, *that* would be a fine way to go."

Ria tried hard to look stern, but in the end, she had to laugh. "Where," she demanded, "are the rest of my clothes?"

"Believe me," Landry answered, "I wasn't keeping track of them."

Ria dropped to her hands and knees—a position that tested Landry's powers of restraint even more than watching her nipples harden while she slept, just begging to be tasted—and peered under the bed.

At least, that was what he *thought* she was doing.

From that angle, he couldn't tell.

Unhurried, Landry began to plan for the next round.

Meanwhile, Ria finally straightened, her hair attractively mussed, clutching the formerly lost garments in one hand. "How am I going to get out of here without Highbridge seeing me?" she asked in a loud whisper.

"He'll be in the kitchen," Landry told her mildly. "And that's a ways from here, so there's no need to whisper like that."

Ria blushed, remained on the floor while she squirmed awkwardly into her panties and jeans, and somehow managed to put her bra back on without lifting her T-shirt so he could get one more look at those delectable breasts of hers.

Damn the luck.

"You are entirely too calm about this!" Ria accused, getting to her feet and flinging her arms out for emphasis. She narrowed her eyes again. "Are you smirking?"

"Yep." Landry grinned up at her. "Seems to me you're riled enough for the both of us," he pointed out. "Anyhow, we're adults, Ria, not kids. And unless something's changed since last night, we're in love." He waited, holding his breath, because he suddenly wasn't sure how she'd answer.

"Nothing's changed," she admitted glumly, and at nerve-racking length. "I'm still crazy about you, heaven help me."

Thank God, he thought.

He went back to enjoying Ria's agitation, the flash in her eyes, the apricot-pink glow in her cheeks, the way her perfect chest rose and fell with her breath. It was almost as good as having sex with her. Almost.

"Well, then," he said reasonably, "I guess there's no point in trying to sneak around, is there? Besides, I'd be willing to bet my half of this ranch that Highbridge already knows what we've been up to anyway."

Ria's cheeks got even pinker, a glorious sight. "Oh, great," she muttered. "You said he was way off in the kitchen, out of earshot—"

"It's a big house," Landry observed lightly. "But Highbridge isn't deaf—and he definitely isn't stupid."

Ria went rigid, her breasts still tantalizing even in a bra.

Oh, those breasts.

"What's *that* supposed to mean?" Ria snapped.

Landry sat up slowly, just in case he needed to fend off an onslaught of fists and fingernails, and feigned bewilderment. "A couple of times," he reminded her, "you got pretty carried away." A pause followed, expertly timed, if Landry did say so himself, to bring Ria from a simmer to a boil. He rolled his shoulders in a shruglike motion and assumed a pensive expression. "Maybe he thought there was a she-wolf around someplace, howling at the moon."

Ria yanked one of the pillows from behind Landry and started battering him with it, employing a two-handed swing.

He laughed, and of course, that only riled her more.

Just when Landry was about to take Ria down again, and make good use of all that feistiness, a light knock sounded at the bedroom door.

"Highbridge," Landry told Ria in a stage whisper. "Shall I tell him to come in?"

She glared, silently daring him to push her just one more inch, but when Highbridge spoke from the hallway, she bolted and fled to the bathroom.

"Breakfast for two, sir?" the butler inquired mildly, matter-of-fact.

Landry was grinning so hard he thought his face might split.

The vibes coming at him through the closed door of the bathroom were almost tangible.

He raised his voice a little, to make sure Ria heard his reply. "That'll be just right, Highbridge," he answered cordially. "We'll be out in fifteen minutes or so."

A pause. "Very good, sir," Highbridge replied.

And then he walked away, footsteps slowly fading.

Still holed up in the bathroom, Ria gave a stifled squeal. She *had* heard the exchange with High-bridge, then.

Excellent.

Humming under his breath, Landry got out of bed, opened a few drawers in the bureau and found himself clean jeans and a blue T-shirt, an old favorite washed and worn often enough to be comfortable against the stinging scratches running the length of his back. He got dressed, crossed to the bathroom door, rapped briskly. "Ria," he said smoothly, "if you don't come out of there, I'll come in after you, and if that happens, I guarantee you, we'll be *very* late for breakfast."

BREAKFAST WAS THE tenth circle of hell for Ria, she was so mortified, but she was also hungry, so she ate, sitting there at Landry's kitchen table in yesterday's clothes, all too obviously fresh from his bed. Her face was as red as if she'd been sunburned, and she worked hard to dodge Highbridge's glances, praying he wouldn't force a conversation.

Landry, the arrogant bastard, sat calmly across from her, reading a newspaper and sipping coffee as though this were any ordinary day.

Ria kicked him, under the table.

He merely grinned at her for a moment, then went right on reading about beef prices and wheat tariffs and the political scandal of the day.

Highbridge refilled her coffee cup, gracious enough, now that he'd registered the full extent of her embarrassment, to pretend she was invisible, like an imaginary friend attending an equally imaginary tea party.

Finally, after clearing his throat, the butler excused himself and left the room, elegant coattails rippling in his wake. Gone were the Stetson, the jeans he'd referred to as "dungarees," the shirt with snaps and the boots.

Maybe she'd dreamed the whole thing, Ria mused.

And maybe she was still on the wrong side of the looking glass. *We're all mad here.*

CHAPTER SEVENTEEN

"WHAT ARE WE going to do now?" she demanded, whispering again.

Landry lowered the newspaper and studied her casually. "Apply for a marriage license," he said, as though the answer should have been obvious. "And get hitched as soon as we can."

Something in Ria started to slide again, scrabbled for traction. "Is this that forever thing again?" she grumped.

He smiled, imperturbable. No matter how hard she worked at getting under his hide, Landry Sutton remained calm. It was exasperating.

"Yep," he replied affably. "It's the forever thing."

"What if we just—well—got engaged? Informally, of course. We could have a long courtship, like Zane and Brylee did, take time to get to know each other better—"

"Bad idea," Landry interrupted.

Ria's heart was starting to race. "*Why* is it a bad idea?"

"Because you're probably pregnant," he said, his tone reasonable, matter-of-fact.

Ria gasped and pressed both hands to her abdomen, as though expecting to feel the kick of tiny feet. "We used condoms," she reminded him tersely, but her voice was as weak as her ability to resist Landry Sutton, in or out of bed.

"Until I ran out of them," Landry clarified.

"You ran out of condoms?" Ria demanded. *"When?"*

"Is that important?"

Was he kidding?

"Oh, my God," Ria breathed. She could have strangled Landry in that moment, but at the very same time, she felt something else entirely—a sort of dizzying, exultant hope that somehow they *had* conceived a baby. A child, *Landry's* child, would be the fulfillment of one of Ria's most cherished dreams for her life, worth any risk, any scandal.

Landry arched his eyebrows slightly, folded the newspaper carefully and set it aside. "Are you planning on holding out for a big wedding?" he asked, with a thoughtful frown. "Because that could be awkward."

Ria imagined herself sweeping down the aisle of a church, a bride in full regalia, with a belly the size of a prize pumpkin at the county fair.

The image, however comical, wasn't what caused her to shake her head and say, "No. No big wedding."

She'd had one of those when she married Frank.

This time around, Ria wanted a different kind of ceremony, a different kind of *marriage*.

Later, looking back, Ria would conclude that that was the moment, the turn in the road, when she'd finally and fully forgiven Frank, and let him go for good.

Landry didn't comment; he merely stood and began clearing the table.

Ria was grudgingly surprised. He could be such a—such a *man*. Now he was carrying dishes to the sink. Would he *ever* stop surprising her? She hoped not.

"So we're just going to *get married*—just like that?" she asked.

Landry rinsed one of the plates under the faucet and set it in the dishwasher before he countered, with a twinkle, "How else would you be able to face Highbridge at breakfast every morning?"

"Who says I'll *be* here every morning?"

"I do," Landry answered easily.

"And what you say goes?" Ria challenged, only too aware that the heat in her blood wasn't just anger, but rising passion. Damn Landry Sutton, if he'd taken her to bed right then, she'd have gone willingly, chafed skin, aching thighs and all.

"I didn't say that," Landry replied.

"Then what *are* you saying?"

Landry leaned back against the counter, folded his arms and regarded her as if she were a column of numbers to be added up. "I guess I'm saying that I'm a little old-fashioned in some ways, and you might as well know it. I want you in my bed, no doubt about that, morning, noon or night. I'll protect you, I'll provide for you and I'll never cheat on you, Ria."

Tears stung Ria's eyes. "You promise? Because that would be the one thing I couldn't—"

"I know," he answered, and it was clear from his tone that he *did* know. She hadn't told him about Frank's one-night stand, had she?

"*How* do you know?" she asked, barely breathing the words.

Landry sighed. "I think it was something I saw in your eyes the other night, when you asked me if I'd been faithful to Susan. I didn't think about it much at the time—we were both tied up in knots, if you recall—but after a day or two, I figured out that you must have been hurt that way yourself, and you were scared as hell it might happen again."

Ria rose from her chair, crossed to Landry, slipped her arms around his waist. "You're an amazing man," she said, with a moist smile, rising on impulse to kiss the cleft in his chin. "And a perceptive one, for all your bullheaded arrogance."

Landry chuckled, kissed her lightly, briefly, on the mouth. "I was right?"

"Aren't you always?" Ria teased, resting her cheek against his shoulder. Sighing slightly. "Would you hold me for a while, please?"

Landry's arms tightened around her. "Anytime," he said, with a low chuckle. "Of course, there's a certain risk involved."

She tilted her head back, looked up at Landry, playing the game. "And that would be—?"

He made a growling sound. "That would be," he said, "the very strong possibility that we'll wind up right back in bed."

Ria widened her eyes. "It's broad daylight."

Landry grinned, bent his head, nibbled at her right earlobe. "That doesn't bother me, lady," he informed her. "If I didn't think Highbridge might walk in at any moment, I'd take you right here, right now—after making you crazy first, of course."

"Of course," Ria echoed slyly, grinding against him a little, against the rock-hard heat of him, pressed against her upper abdomen. She touched him boldly, closed her fingers around him, delighted in the way he groaned and closed his eyes for a moment.

Ria nibbled at the side of Landry's neck, un-snapped a couple of his shirt buttons.

He moaned her name.

She ran her palm along the length of him, felt him throb behind the denim of his jeans. "If you can't stand the heat, Mr. Sutton," she murmured, loving the way the pulse at the base of his throat leaped when she brushed her lips over the skin there, "then maybe we'd better get you out of the kitchen."

Landry groaned again, but the sound was part chuckle. "Speaking of heat…" he muttered. Then, with a raspy gasp, he added, "Woman, you are kill-ing me."

A loud crash and a resounding "Bloody hell!"

from Highbridge—probably a warning of his imminent arrival, just in case what *was* going on in the kitchen was what was going on in the kitchen—sent Landry and Ria scrambling for cover. The back door being the nearest exit, they bolted through it, laughing like a couple of kids who'd just swiped the cookie jar.

"Take me back to my place," Ria said, climbing into Landry's truck without waiting for him to agree.

He got in, pushed the ignition button. "What the hell is going on here?" he asked, pretending to be confused.

"The better question," Ria informed him, "would be what the hell is *coming off there?* You're in for it, Landry Sutton."

He laughed again. "You promise?" he asked.

"You can take it to the bank," Ria replied.

Less than ten minutes later, they were inside the cottage. The place was deliciously cool and quiet. They headed straight for the shower, stripping off their clothes as they went, leaving the garments strewn behind them. Under the spray, they kissed, lathered each other, kissed again.

Ria felt strong and powerful, like an Amazonian queen. When Landry pulled her toward him, though, already focused on her breasts, she shook her head, closed one hand around his erection.

This time, there was no denim to get in the way.

He gave a ragged groan, and Ria let her fingers

and palm glide along the length of him, slowly at first, then more and more rapidly.

"We did this your way last night, cowboy," she told Landry. "Today, we're doing it mine."

Ria brought her man to the edge, but she didn't allow him to go over it. Instead, she shut off the water, handed Landry a towel, wrapped another around herself, though she was anything but cold, and headed for the bedroom.

Landry followed, still bewildered, still huge and hard.

In the middle of the room, Ria dropped her towel, and fire leaped in Landry's blue eyes, but he just stood where he was, still wet from the shower, like a man in a trance.

She prowled as she crossed the small distance between them, ran her hands lightly from the sides of his waist to his thighs.

And then she was kneeling.

Landry uttered a sharp, husky gasp when she took him into her mouth.

Her name became his litany, and with deliberate slowness, Ria proceeded to drive Landry Sutton crazy, nibble by nibble, tease by tease, caress by caress. She made him wait—then moan—and then wait some more. She was enjoying every moment, every nuance of what she was doing to him and the way he was responding.

Finally, Landry gave a low shout, and his fingers, burrowing gently, feverishly, in her hair while she ravished him, suddenly locked around her head. "If you—don't stop—*right now*—"

Ria didn't stop.

He cried out again, in surrender and in useless protest. Then his powerful body flexed violently— once, twice, a third time—and Ria flexed with him, followed his every move, fierce joy coursing through her all the while.

When it was finally over, Landry was a little unsteady on his feet, but he still had the strength to draw Ria up from her knees. They both went sprawling onto the bed, Landry breathing hard, Ria whispering to him, caressing him as he made the slow descent to earth.

After a few minutes, Landry fell into a light sleep, and Ria's heart swelled with the poignancy of all she felt for him—he was impossibly strong, damnably sure of himself and yet willing to be vulnerable.

She lay there for a while, snuggled against him, then got up, padded into the bathroom, washed her face and brushed her teeth. Next, she followed the path of discarded clothes until she found her jeans.

Frank's ring was still in the pocket; she took it out, studied it for a moment, then closed her fingers around it again. She found a small box, saved from the Christmas before because it was too nice to throw away, placed the framed picture of Frank inside and then the wedding band.

Moving on to the living room, and the coat closet beside the front door, she stood on tiptoe to slide the box onto the high shelf. She'd gathered the photo albums, too, and stowed them alongside the box before she realized Landry was there.

He stood in the doorway, wearing his jeans and nothing else, his hair rumpled, his eyes peaceful, though she could see desire stirring in their blue depths.

Ria smiled, dusted her hands together, closed the closet door and went to him, again crossing a divide—the one between before and forever.

There would be no going back.

EPILOGUE

THREE DAYS LATER, Ria and Landry were married by
the Reverend Walter Beaumont, in his small church
in Parable. Zane was Landry's best man, but young
Nash stood up with them, too, looking proud in his
one and only suit.

Quinn served as maid of honor, while Meredith
sat among the other guests, looking not quite so icy
these days. To Quinn's delight, she'd agreed to move
into the cottage, since Ria had already joined Landry
on the ranch, just as he'd predicted she would.

"We'll stay until Quinn finishes high school,"
Meredith had told Ria the day before, when they
were seated side by side on the steps leading to the
front porch, Bones dashing happily around the familiar yard. "She loves it here, and I need a quiet
place to reinvent myself, so it works for both of us."

Ria had hugged her sister then, on impulse, and,
though Meredith hadn't exactly hugged her back,
she didn't pull away, either.

It was a beginning, to be followed, most likely, by
a lot of other beginnings, but that was okay with Ria.

Now, as Mrs. Beaumont struck a resounding

chord on the church organ, everyone turned in the pews, smiling at the bride—Walker and Casey and their two older children were there, as were Slade and Joslyn Barlow, Hutch and Kendra Carmody and Boone and Tara Taylor. Brylee sat with the sheriff and his wife, glowing with a secret of her own, Cleo stationed protectively at her other side. The announcement hadn't been made yet, but both Ria and Landry, given a variety of clues, had guessed what was going on. Zane and Brylee were expecting a baby.

Highbridge, ready to give the bride away, stood tall beside Ria, beaming and proud. Ria, clad in the pale blue silk dress Quinn and Meredith had helped her choose, felt beautiful.

She turned and winked at the butler. Her dress was gorgeous, all right, but she wasn't sure which of them was better dressed, because Highbridge had on the spiffy tuxedo he'd once worn, he claimed, to serve afternoon tea at Buckingham Palace. The queen herself had accepted two delicate watercress sandwiches from his tray, the story went, and he'd retired the outfit when the day was over, for the sake of posterity.

It touched Ria's heart that he'd taken the prized suit out of mothballs in honor of the occasion, airing it on the clothesline and brushing it thoroughly that morning.

"Shall we?" Highbridge asked, with a slight grin. "We've already missed the first cue."

Ria nodded. "We shall," she replied as the organ music began again, from the top.

She kept her eyes on Landry, standing up there at the altar, and walked resolutely toward him, without a doubt in her mind—or her heart.

He watched her approach with an expression of mingled delight and impatience.

As Ria and Highbridge passed the front row of pews, she caught a glimpse of Zane, Nash and Landry's father, seated by himself, his thinning hair slicked down, a carnation tucked into the buttonhole of his suit jacket.

"I thought the old ticker was about to give out on me for sure, when I left here a few days back," he'd told his son and future daughter-in-law the evening before, when he'd suddenly arrived at their door, suitcase in hand. "Got as far as Boise and checked into a motel to wait for the end. Nothing happened right away, so I decided I'd like to hear *one* of my boys' voices just once more, so I called the boy on the phone. He told me the two of you were fixing to get hitched, and I plumb forgot about going to meet my Maker, packed up and headed straight for the highway and stuck out my thumb."

Ria had been amused by the story, and very touched by the effort Jess Sutton had made to get back to Three Trees in time for the ceremony.

At first anyway, Landry hadn't said much.

Ria and Highbridge had exchanged glances, made an unspoken agreement to give father and son some

space and left the kitchen, Highbridge retiring to
his quarters, Ria making for the master bedroom,
where she perused the stack of design magazines
she'd bought in town that day.

Now that they were getting married, Landry had
declared, it was time to call in the builders, turn the
place into a real home. He'd buy more buffalo, too,
and maybe some cattle in the bargain, get a real herd
started. The house was to be Ria's project; the livestock would be Landry's.

The magazines did not provide much distraction,
however, and Ria finally set them aside. She reached
for the small blue velvet box resting on Landry's
dresser, opened it to admire the simple but elegant
pendant inside, a silver horse's head on a gossamer
chain. Landry had given Ria the necklace earlier that
day, eyes twinkling as he asked her to "go steady"
with him—for the rest of time.

When Landry had joined her in bed, it was very
late, and he'd said nothing about his talk with his
father.

Ria hadn't asked any questions—it was a given
that a breach as deep and wide as the one between
Jess Sutton and his sons could not be spanned in
a single conversation—she'd simply put her arms
around her man, nestled in close and said, "I love
you."

Landry had made love to her then, slow, sweet,
almost reverent love.

The memory thrilled through Ria even now, in

the generous light of a July afternoon, as she and Highbridge took the last few steps toward the man she loved, and would continue to love, today, tomorrow and always.

Landry took her hand when she reached his side, squeezed gently, held on.

"Dearly beloved," the minister began ebulliently, "we are gathered here—"

Ria listened to the time-honored words of the marriage ceremony, holding each vow and promise Landry made in her heart, tucking them away to be treasured all the days of her life. She offered the corresponding replies in a soft, clear and very certain voice—she'd never been as sure of anything as she was of her love for the man beside her, of his for her.

Wide golden bands were exchanged, Ria's inset with diamond baguettes, Landry's plain and sturdy, both rings symbolizing a love as sweeping and eternal as the big Montana sky.

Finally, Reverend Beaumont pronounced Landry and Ria husband and wife.

"You may kiss the bride," he announced, in his wonderful, booming voice, beaming at Landry.

"My pleasure," Landry replied gruffly, turning to Ria, cupping her face in his hands. His eyes shone and the expression she had come to cherish was there, the baffled joy of a man who had just made some marvelous, unexpected discovery.

He bent his head to touch his lips to hers, just briefly, and then kissed her in earnest.

Some of the wedding guests applauded, while others laughed with delight, and still others snapped pictures. All the while, sunshine streamed through the stained-glass windows high above the altar, falling over the bride and groom like a benediction, splashing them with bright golds and crimsons, deep greens and blues, vivid purples and pearly shades of white, the patterns ever-changing, like those inside a kaleidoscope.

Looking ahead, Ria knew their life together, hers and Landry's, would be like that, a shining, beautiful thing, often surprising, always growing. There would be a few shadows, too, of course—that was the natural order of things—but with Landry at her side, Ria could face anything.

The organist sounded a triumphant chord.

Mr. and Mrs. Landry Sutton hurried down the aisle, hand in hand, just beginning their long journey to forever.

* * * * *

Be sure to watch for Linda's next novel,
THE MARRIAGE PACT,
the first in a brand new Western Wyoming-set trilogy,
coming in June from Harlequin HQN.

Love has a dangerous side in these compelling classics from *New York Times* bestselling author

JAYNE ANN KRENTZ

WRITING AS STEPHANIE JAMES

Stormy Challenge

While Leya Brandon thinks her heart isn't at risk, she clearly underestimates Court Tremayne's all-consuming desire to win her for his own. Little does she know that Court has no intention of stopping his pursuit…not until he leaves her hungering for the fulfillment only he can give.

Reckless Passion

With his carefully groomed Southern manners, Yale Ransom might have stepped straight out of *Gone with the Wind*. But stockbroker Dara Bancroft senses a passion beneath the glossy surface of her prospective client, and recklessly she offers him an unspoken challenge, never expecting that their conversation could explode into desire she's never felt before. But she pushes him too far, and now Yale wants to make her pay…straight from the heart.

"Krentz's storytelling shines with authenticity and dramatic intensity."
—*Publishers Weekly*

Available now!

Be sure to connect with us at:

Harlequin.com/Newsletters
Facebook.com/HarlequinBooks
Twitter.com/HarlequinBooks

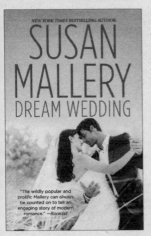

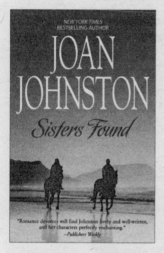

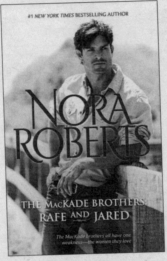

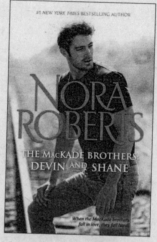

LINDA LAEL MILLER

77787	A LAWMAN'S CHRISTMAS: A McKETTRICKS OF TEXAS NOVEL	___$7.99 U.S.	___$9.99 CAN.
77774	BIG SKY WEDDING	___$7.99 U.S.	___$8.99 CAN.
77765	BIG SKY SUMMER	___$7.99 U.S.	___$9.99 CAN.
77722	A WANTED MAN: A STONE CREEK NOVEL		
77721	THE MAN FROM STONE CREEK	___$7.99 U.S.	___$9.99 CAN.
77720	BIG SKY RIVER	___$7.99 U.S.	___$9.99 CAN.
77681	McKETTRICK'S HEART	___$7.99 U.S.	___$9.99 CAN.
77677	McKETTRICK'S PRIDE	___$7.99 U.S.	___$9.99 CAN.
77643	BIG SKY COUNTRY	___$7.99 U.S.	___$9.99 CAN.
77642	McKETTRICK'S LUCK	___$7.99 U.S.	___$9.99 CAN.
77580	CREED'S HONOR	___$7.99 U.S.	___$9.99 CAN.
77561	MONTANA CREEDS: LOGAN	___$7.99 U.S.	___$9.99 CAN.
77555	A CREED IN STONE CREEK	___$7.99 U.S.	___$9.99 CAN.
77502	THE CHRISTMAS BRIDES	___$7.99 U.S.	___$9.99 CAN.
77492	McKETTRICK'S CHOICE	___$7.99 U.S.	___$9.99 CAN.
77446	McKETTRICKS OF TEXAS: AUSTIN	___$7.99 U.S.	___$9.99 CAN.
77441	McKETTRICKS OF TEXAS: GARRETT	___$7.99 U.S.	___$9.99 CAN.
77436	McKETTRICKS OF TEXAS: TATE	___$7.99 U.S.	___$9.99 CAN.
77364	MONTANA CREEDS: TYLER	___$7.99 U.S.	___$7.99 CAN.
77200	DEADLY GAMBLE	___$7.99 U.S.	___$9.50 CAN.

(limited quantities available)

TOTAL AMOUNT	$_____
POSTAGE & HANDLING	$_____
($1.00 FOR 1 BOOK, 50¢ for each additional)	
APPLICABLE TAXES*	$_____
TOTAL PAYABLE	$_____

(check or money order—please do not send cash)

To order, complete this form and send it, along with a check or money order for the total above, payable to HQN Books, to: **In the U.S.:** 3010 Walden Avenue, P.O. Box 9077, Buffalo, NY 14269-9077; **In Canada:** P.O. Box 636, Fort Erie, Ontario, L2A 5X3.

Name: _____

Address: _____ City: _____

State/Prov.: _____ Zip/Postal Code: _____

Account Number (if applicable): _____

075 CSAS

*New York residents remit applicable sales taxes.
*Canadian residents remit applicable GST and provincial taxes.

HARLEQUIN® HQN™
™ www.Harlequin.com

PHLLM0114BL

REQUEST YOUR FREE BOOKS!

2 FREE NOVELS
FROM THE ROMANCE COLLECTION
PLUS 2 FREE GIFTS!

YES! Please send me 2 FREE novels from the Romance Collection and my 2 FREE gifts (gifts are worth about $10). After receiving them, if I don't wish to receive any more books, I can return the shipping statement marked "cancel." If I don't cancel, I will receive 4 brand-new novels every month and be billed just $6.24 per book in the U.S. or $6.74 per book in Canada. That's a savings of at least 22% off the cover price. It's quite a bargain! Shipping and handling is just 50¢ per book in the U.S. and 75¢ per book in Canada.* I understand that accepting the 2 free books and gifts places me under no obligation to buy anything. I can always return a shipment and cancel at any time. Even if I never buy another book, the two free books and gifts are mine to keep forever.

194/394 MDN F4XY

Name   (PLEASE PRINT)

Address   Apt. #

City   State/Prov.   Zip/Postal Code

Signature (if under 18, a parent or guardian must sign)

Mail to the Harlequin® Reader Service:
IN U.S.A.: P.O. Box 1867, Buffalo, NY 14240-1867
IN CANADA: P.O. Box 609, Fort Erie, Ontario L2A 5X3

Want to try two free books from another line?
Call 1-800-873-8635 or visit www.ReaderService.com.

* Terms and prices subject to change without notice. Prices do not include applicable taxes. Sales tax applicable in N.Y. Canadian residents will be charged applicable taxes. Offer not valid in Quebec. This offer is limited to one order per household. Not valid for current subscribers to the Romance Collection or the Romance/Suspense Collection. All orders subject to credit approval. Credit or debit balances in a customer's account(s) may be offset by any other outstanding balance owed by or to the customer. Please allow 4 to 6 weeks for delivery. Offer available while quantities last.

Your Privacy—The Harlequin® Reader Service is committed to protecting your privacy. Our Privacy Policy is available online at www.ReaderService.com or upon request from the Harlequin Reader Service.

We make a portion of our mailing list available to reputable third parties that offer products we believe may interest you. If you prefer that we not exchange your name with third parties, or if you wish to clarify or modify your communication preferences, please visit us at www.ReaderService.com/consumerchoice or write to us at Harlequin Reader Service Preference Service, P.O. Box 9062, Buffalo, NY 14269. Include your complete name and address.